2/10

STEALTH

BOOKS BY STUART WOODS

FICTION

Stealth* • Contraband* • Wild Card* • A Delicate Touch*
Desperate Measures* • Turbulence*
Shoot First* • Unbound* • Quick & Dirty* • Indecent Exposure*
Fast & Loose* • Below the Belt* • Sex, Lies & Serious Money*
Dishonorable Intentions* • Family Jewels* • Scandalous Behavior*
Foreign Affairs* • Naked Greed* • Hot Pursuit* • Insatiable Appetites*
Paris Match* • Cut and Thrust* • Carnal Curiosity*
Standup Guy* • Doing Hard Time* • Unintended Consequences*
Collateral Damage* • Severe Clear* • Unnatural Acts* • D.C. Dead*
Son of Stone* • Bel-Air Dead* • Strategic Moves* • Santa Fe Edge†
Lucid Intervals* • Kisser* • Hothouse Orchid‡
Loitering with Intent* • Mounting Fears§ • Hot Mahogany*
Santa Fe Dead† • Beverly Hills Dead • Shoot Him If He Runs*
Fresh Disasters* • Short Straw† • Dark Harbor* • Iron Orchid‡
Two-Dollar Bill* • The Prince of Beverly Hills • Reckless Abandon*
Capital Crimes§ • Dirty Work* • Blood Orchid‡ • The Short Forever*
Orchid Blues‡ • Cold Paradise* • L.A. Dead* • The Run§
Worst Fears Realized* • Orchid Beach‡ • Swimming to Catalina*
Dead in the Water* • Dirt* • Choke • Imperfect Strangers
Heat • Dead Eyes • L.A. Times • Santa Fe Rules†
New York Dead* • Palindrome • Grass Roots§ • White Cargo
Deep Lie§ • Under the Lake • Run Before the Wind§ • Chiefs§

COAUTHORED BOOKS

Skin Game** (with Parnell Hall)
The Money Shot** (with Parnell Hall) • Barely Legal†† (with Parnell Hall)
Smooth Operator** (with Parnell Hall)

TRAVEL

A Romantic's Guide to the Country Inns of Britain and Ireland (1979)

MEMOIR

Blue Water, Green Skipper

*A Stone Barrington Novel
†An Ed Eagle Novel
‡A Holly Barker Novel
§A Will Lee Novel
**A Teddy Fay Novel
††A Herbie Fisher Novel

STEALTH

STUART WOODS

G. P. Putnam's Sons

New York

PUTNAM
— EST. 1838 —

G. P. PUTNAM'S SONS
Publishers Since 1838
An imprint of Penguin Random House LLC
penguinrandomhouse.com

ISBN 9780593083161

Printed in the United States of America
1   3   5   7   9   10   8   6   4   2

This is a work of fiction. Names, characters, places, and incidents either are the product of the author's imagination or are used fictitiously, and any resemblance to actual persons, living or dead, businesses, companies, events, or locales is entirely coincidental.

1

_S_tone Barrington woke earlier than he should have and was, for a moment, disoriented. Sunlight was streaming through a two-inch gap in the drawn curtains of the room, and he never slept with curtains drawn. Except in England.

He sat up in bed. He was, indeed, in England, in the house called Windward Hall that he had owned for some years. He had landed in the early evening in the Strategic Services Gulfstream 600, on which he had caught a ride from Teterboro, New Jersey. The company jet was in England or Europe on almost a weekly basis, and the private runway on his land was long enough to accommodate it for landing and takeoff. It was a convenient way to commute between his New York residence and his house in England.

He looked at the bedside clock: a little after six AM. He fell back onto his pillow, tried for another hour of sleep, and failed. He had come alone to England, so there were no opportunities of an erotic nature to keep him occupied until the kitchen was open for business—and he was hungry. He got out of bed, flung open the curtains in the room, and then got back into bed with yesterday's crossword puzzle, which he had not finished.

He regretted not inviting a companion on this trip, but his mind turned to the beautiful woman whose country house was just across the Beaulieu River from his. At that moment, his cell phone rang. "Hello?"

"Good morning," she said with a husky voice. "I hope I didn't wake you."

"Good morning, Felicity. I wish you were here to wake me properly."

"I'm nearly there, darling," she replied, chuckling, "just across the river."

"Then come and have breakfast with me."

"I'd like to have *you* for breakfast, but I have to be in London at nine-thirty for an important meeting at the Foreign Office." Felicity was the director of MI-6, the British foreign intelligence service, which came under the purview of the foreign minister.

"What a pity," Stone said.

"Not to worry. I'll be down tomorrow afternoon for the weekend. Why don't you host a dinner party?"

"Well, I didn't bring any guests with me, so I guess it will just have to be the two of us."

"Tell you what," she said. "I will assemble the guests for a table of, say, eight?"

"What a good idea. You're better acquainted with the locals than I."

"Consider it done. I'll bring the place cards with me, so don't bother about that. Shall we say seven for eight?" In British parlance, this meant dinner at eight, and show up at seven, if you'd like a drink first.

"Perfect. I'll get the cook to work on a menu and I'll unearth some good bottles from the cellar."

"I will look forward to it," she said.

"And bring your toothbrush. We'll make a weekend of it."

"What a good idea!" She made a kissing noise and hung up.

Stone went back to his crossword, a happier man.

The following evening, in his Royal Yacht Squadron mess kit—essentially, a tuxedo with a short, naval-style jacket and the appropriate insignia—Stone inspected the beautifully set table in the small dining room, then went to the library, where drinks would be served. It was about three minutes past seven when he heard the doorbell, and a couple of minutes later, Dame Felicity Devonshire entered the library, followed by three couples. One he recognized as Felicity's boss, the foreign minister, Sir Oswald Towne, and his wife, Lady Towne; another was a younger man in a proper naval mess kit, sporting quite a lot of braid, and his apparent wife; the third couple looked familiar.

"Stone," Felicity said, "of course you know Sir Oswald and Lady Towne—Ozzie and Deirdre." They all shook hands. "And this is Admiral Sir Timothy Barnes, and Lady Barnes, Tim and Kate." More handshaking. "Tim is the First Sea Lord," Felicity added. Hands were shaken.

Stone knew that that post was the Royal Navy equivalent of the American chief of naval operations.

"And," Felicity said, "I don't know if you've met the newly elected commodore of the Royal Yacht Squadron, Derek Drummond, and his wife, Hildy." Drummond was also dressed in a Squadron mess kit, which should have been a clue.

"Congratulations on your election," Stone said, shaking their hands.

"Thank you, Stone. It's good to see an American member here," the commodore replied.

"It's good to be here," Stone said.

Geoffrey, the butler, served champagne and cocktails, and there was chat among the guests and their hosts.

"Do you have a place in the neighborhood?" Stone asked Tim Barnes.

"No, I had to come down from London for the launching of a new submarine. Ozzie and Deirdre were staying with Felicity, and she asked us to join them, so my barge brought us from Portsmouth to her dock on the Beaulieu."

"What does an admiral's barge consist of these days?" Stone asked.

"A very comfortable Nelson motorboat of forty feet. It's suitable for a weekend place."

Felicity joined them. "Tim has also just come from a visit to our Station Two, in the Scottish Highlands. He was kind enough to give me a lift back in a naval aircraft."

"Why does MI-6 have a station so far north?" Stone asked.

"Station Two is our training facility for new recruits to the service," she said. "I drove up there last week for my own inspection, but I was called back to London and had to leave my car there and fly back."

"Is this the Aston Martin DB11?"

"It is, and I miss it already."

"How will you get it back from Scotland?"

"A good question. Would you like to drive it back?"

"That's a very tempting thought," Stone said. "I've never driven that car."

The foreign minister joined them in time to hear that exchange. "You look like a fit fellow," he said to Stone. "You might enjoy a taste of the training up there."

"Good idea," Tim said. "The place is run by an old chum of mine, a colonel in the Royal Marines. I'd be happy to give him a call and tell him not to be too hard on you."

"Is this a sort of boot camp, then?" Stone asked, intrigued.

"The first two weeks are very much a boot camp," Tim replied. "Lots of hikes and runs, weapons training, hand-to-hand fighting, that sort of thing. The next two months are all the secret stuff: codes, tradecraft, communications. All the James Bond stuff."

"They're in the first week of training now," Felicity said. "You could join them for the second week, then drive the car back." She turned to the FM. "Stone is a consultant to our colleagues at Langley, so he's a family member, in a way. He's also been of help to us on occasion."

"Then I don't see why he shouldn't have a bit of fun at our expense," the FM said. "Send me an authorization to sign—and, of course, a release for his signature, absolving us from any liability for serious injury or an early death."

"You make it sound like such fun," Stone said, "but . . ."

"Nonsense," the FM chortled, clapping him on the back. "It's all decided and authorized."

They were called in to dinner, and Stone put the thought of a Highlands vacation out of his mind. He noticed that Felicity had left the table to use her phone for a few minutes, but that often happened.

She returned to the table. "Good news," she said. "We're flying some equipment and a few people up to Station Two tomorrow, and the aircraft will pick you up at your airstrip at seven o'clock tomorrow morning."

Stone choked on his wine.

"I envy you the experience," the FM said. "Just the sort of romp I'd have enjoyed in my youth."

"I'm not all that young," Stone said, and everyone laughed heartily.

2

Stone woke up with a warm hand cradling his genitals. He checked the narrow opening in the curtains: still dark outside.

"Ah, you're awake," Felicity said, climbing on top of him.

"What time is it?"

"Five AM," she said. "You've time for love, breakfast, and packing. We're starting with love."

They spent a half hour on love, then Stone dove into a shower. When he came out, Felicity was dressed.

"I'll call Stan to help you with the boat," he said.

"Not to worry. My car is picking me up here in about three-quarters of an hour."

"Call down for breakfast," he said. "Just press the button marked Kitchen. I'll have the usual. You have whatever you like." He grabbed a large leather duffel, and began stuffing things into it.

"Oh," Felicity said, "just pack what you'll need for the return drive; Station Two will provide you with everything else." She picked up the phone and ordered breakfast.

....

At seven AM Stone stood at the hangar on his airstrip and watched the airplane turn final. To his surprise, it was a Dakota, the British name for the American DC-3 or C-47. It touched down lightly, ran down half the runway, then turned 180 degrees and stopped where he stood. He walked toward the airplane, the propeller whipping his clothes around him. The rear door opened, and a man in fatigues, what the Brits call "battle dress," clapped his hands together and held them out to receive Stone's duffel. Stone climbed the ladder and was directed forward past other luggage, each with a green canvas object secured to it. There were no proper seats, so he set himself down on a sort of canvas bench that was affixed to the airplane's bare metal. There was no insulation.

He got into his seat harness up front, just aft of the cockpit, which gave him a good view of the pilot and his controls. The rear door was closed, the ladder stowed, and the pilot advanced the throttles slightly, applied right brake, and spun the airplane around. He then shoved the throttles all the way forward, and the airplane left the ground in what seemed to Stone an amazingly short time.

He was handed a set of ear protectors, like a headset without the wiring, and he gratefully put them on. There was no point in trying to speak to his companions because the engine noise was too great, and they were wearing the same earmuffs he wore.

The man next to him handed him a copy of the *New York Times*—yesterday's international edition, as it happened—and in the next hour and a half he read every word of it. They were somewhere over the Midlands, at eight thousand feet, on top of a cloud layer. He started on the crossword, which was challenging enough to engage him for another hour and a half.

The airplane began a descent, and suddenly, all the passengers were on their feet, strapping on backpacks. A sergeant handed Stone one and helped him get into it. He got close to Stone's ear and lifted a muff. "Ever jumped before?" he yelled.

Stone shook his head. "What are you talking about?" he shouted back, but the man couldn't hear him. Stone could hear him shouting, though. The man took a length of nylon line from behind Stone's shoulder and clipped one end of it to a steel cable running the length of the cabin. "Static line," he shouted. "Count to ten. If your chute doesn't open by the time you're finished, pull this." He held up a triangular piece of tubing, took Stone's arm and moved it out and up from his body. "Rip cord," he said.

"Wait a minute!" Stone shouted, but the group of men had started shuffling aft, and the sergeant grabbed Stone's arm and marched him along, snatching the muffs from his ears. There was a red light over the open rear door, and as he watched it went out, and a green light came on. People began to jump out of the airplane. As Stone approached the open door he craned his neck to get a look outside, and as he did the sergeant pushed him through the door. "Noooooooo!" Stone yelled as he fell into the daylight. Immediately, he felt a hard jerk, and he looked up to see his parachute billowing.

Suddenly, it was quiet as the airplane flew away. There was no wind, and Stone could hear a dog barking somewhere on the ground. The parachutes of those who had jumped before him were stretched out in a line. Looking down, from what he estimated was a thousand feet or so, he saw a mostly bare, green landscape, with a tree here and there.

He knew from old movies that he could pull on the straps holding him to alter his direction, but he seemed aligned with everyone else, so he didn't see any point in experimenting. He began to think about how he was going to handle the landing. The others had their feet together, so he kept his that way.

As he neared the ground he seemed to be going faster and faster as it rose to meet him, then his feet struck the ground and he fell, rolling over. The chute settled over him, blocking his view of everything.

"Get out of there!" someone shouted and pulled at the nylon. Stone got to his feet and figured out how to release the harness, then he was standing and, amazingly, alive. A man was gathering up his parachute.

Another man tugged at his sleeve and pointed up. Stone looked to see several chutes floating down. "That's your luggage," the man said. Stone was surprised that he wasn't shouting, but speaking fairly normally. "It will be taken by truck to your quarters."

"How do I get there?" Stone asked.

"You run," the man said. "Follow the others, and don't get lost or you might never be seen again." He pointed Stone in the right direction and gave him a shove. Stone was wearing a pair of high-topped, thick-soled walking shoes that he used on pavement, and they worked fairly well. He began jogging along, unbuttoning his jacket as he warmed up.

A half hour later the group pulled up at a gate in a high chain-link fence with coils of razor wire at the top. Stone wondered if that was meant to keep people out or, perhaps, in. He was pleased to see that he wasn't breathing any harder than the other men in the party. They were herded through the gate and into a Quonset hut, with its semicircular roofline. There were folding chairs inside the hut; people were getting out of their warmer clothing and mopping their brows. Stone followed the line, just as he had done since they jumped, making him the last to sit down.

A man wearing a military sweater with epaulets came into the hut and walked to the front of the room. "Listen up," he said. "I am Captain Moffat. You no longer have names; you are designated"—he pointed at Stone, then down the line—"Alpha, Beta, Charlie, Delta, Echo, Foxtrot, Golf, Hotel. While you are at Station Two you will not tell anyone your former name, nor anything about yourself. Does anyone not understand that?" He waited for a moment and was met by silence. "Your luggage has been placed in your quarters, and your designation will be on the door. Clothing conforming to your height, weight, and measurements will also have been placed in your quarters. Wear only what you are issued."

He switched on a light, illuminating a screen on which there was a drawing. "This is a map of Station Two: memorize it. If you are slow and stupid, you will be given a map. Would anyone like a map?" No one spoke.

Stone started memorizing the map, which wasn't complicated: headquarters, living quarters, dining hall, gymnasium and workout facilities, supply, clinic, armory, motor pool.

"The weapons carried by staff and guards are loaded with live ammunition. Try very hard not to give anyone a reason to shoot at you. Now, get up and follow the sergeant to the dining hall. Eat. Go to your quarters and remain there until you are awakened at dawn. Upon your awakening, at six AM, you have thirty minutes to shower, dress, and get to the dining hall. You will have thirty minutes to eat. After that, it gets easier: all you have to do is exactly what you are told. Get out."

They got out.

3

---

tone slept soundly, dreamlessly, until a loud bell rang for about thirty seconds. By the time it had stopped he was half dressed. He carried his overcoat, gloves, and a knitted cap as he went to the dining room. Once there he was handed a tray containing a plate of fried eggs, boiled potatoes, and buttered toast, along with a glass of orange juice and a mug of black coffee.

He found a seat at a table with others, and everyone ate hurriedly and silently. Finally, a man in battle dress with sergeant's stripes stood up and yelled, "Follow me for our morning run."

Everyone got into their outer gear and into line, shuffling toward a door where the sergeant waited. Then they were running, faster than a jog. Stone reckoned they ran a mile, slowing to a five-minute walk at the halfway point, before finishing fast. Then they found themselves at a shooting range, with a row of tables waiting for them. Each table held a semiautomatic pistol and an assault rifle, plus magazines and ammunition for each weapon. The sergeant spent a couple of minutes demonstrating how each weapon was to be loaded, cocked, and placed on safety. Then he ordered them to fire the weapons—first the rifle, then the pistol—on his command from various positions: prone, kneeling, and standing. Another sergeant walked behind them, offering advice. No one said anything to Stone.

After they had fired from each position, their targets were lowered into a pit, where patches were placed over the holes they had made. Stone's sergeant stepped behind him. "Alpha," he said, "you are an excellent shot with the rifle and a poor shot with the pistol. You will need extra pistol training." The sergeant yelled out for another run, and everyone but Stone and one other trainee ran off. The two of them then got another half hour of training with the pistol, and Stone's marksmanship with the handgun improved markedly. He was glad to be firing, instead of running.

"Now," the sergeant said, "follow the corporal for your run."

Stone sighed and did as he was told.

They finished up in a gymnasium with a thickly matted floor, where another sergeant gave them knife training, pointing out that the knives employed were neither rubber nor wood, but steel, and that they should try not to kill each other, as there was a lot of paperwork involved if that should occur.

Then another run, and back to the gym for unarmed defense training. The NYPD police academy had given Stone a grounding in this, and he was told that he excelled. Then a man shouted at him, "Heads up! Knife attack!" Stone looked up to see a middle-aged but fit-looking man walking toward him with a knife. "I don't have a knife," Stone said.

"Never mind," the sergeant said. "All you have to do is stop him from killing you." His assailant was already starting to wave the knife around. Stone managed to avoid a lunge at his throat, but the tip of the blade drew lightly across his neck as it passed, so Stone redoubled his efforts to not be killed. During another pass, he managed to get hold of his assailant's wrist and twisted the knife from his grasp. The man fought back, but Stone managed to get him onto the mat with his arm twisted behind him.

"Alpha," the sergeant said, pulling him to his feet by his collar. "See the soldier at the end—the one with the medical kit—for treatment."

The bleeding had been stopped in short order, a topical antibiotic was applied, and his slight wound was bandaged. "He missed your jugular by a quarter of an inch," the medic said.

They had a lunch of beef sandwiches and beer, then started training again. By the time Stone reached his quarters late in the day, all he could do was throw himself onto his bed and sleep, fully clothed, until the dinner bell rang. Then he pulled himself together, got a quick shower, and made it to the dining hall before the spaghetti and meatballs ran out.

The rest of the week was filled with more training, physical and mental, combative at times. By the end of six days, Stone felt the way he wished he'd felt upon his arrival.

On the morning after his last day of training, Stone was packing his things and getting into civilian clothes when the sergeant came into his room and tossed him some keys. "Alpha, yours is the Aston Martin, I believe."

"Right, Sergeant." Stone put the keys into his pocket.

"Why don't we give you a bit of a time trial?" he said.

"In the car, I hope?"

"Don't worry, mate, you've had your last run." He took a map from his pocket and explained the route, which was mostly a perimeter road around the camp. "Leave your gear here. We'll pick it up later." The sergeant led the way out of the building to a parking lot Stone had not seen before. The Aston was waiting for him, looking as if it had just been hosed down. He got in and started the engine while the sergeant walked to the road and beckoned for him to follow. Stone drove up to him and waited for instructions.

"Got your route memorized?"

"Yes, Sergeant."

"Try and get it done in under three minutes. I'll be here." He held up a stopwatch. "Ready, set, go!"

Stone already had the car in gear and accelerated like a rocket up the road. He tracked the turns, hitting every apex, and reckoned he was halfway around the perimeter when he saw a landmark, a bridge over a roaring river, with a turn just before it. He shifted down for the turn, then accelerated, then something went wrong: there was a noise, the car drifted right and struck the embankment beside the river, then it left the ground, still turning. The car struck the river upside down.

It took Stone, hanging by his seat belt, a moment to reorient. It wasn't hard, because the top of his head was wet, and water was pouring in from the broken passenger window. "I've got to get out of here," he said aloud to himself, but his brain wasn't fully working yet, and it took a face full of water to get him moving. He tried and tried to escape the cabin, but nothing electrical was working, and the car's roof had been smashed down on him. And the windows were too small for him to get through. He was having to hold his breath and grab more air in the moments the car was rocked by the current.

Stone began to flag, and there was no one to help.

4

Upside down and still not entirely conscious, Stone felt that the water creeping up from his scalp would be over his nose very soon. As if to confirm his judgment, he began to drink through his nose, but he couldn't keep up.

He blew the air out of his nose. Then he shut off that passageway internally, but his mouth was next and that wouldn't do. He took hold of the seat belt, tight across his chest, and began following it with his hand to its end on his left side. He found it and felt for the release button, which, under load, did not cooperate. He mustered all the strength he could into his thumb and forefinger and tried again. This time the button began to move and, finally, to his great relief, released the metal hook.

His relief was premature, though, because his face was now underwater, and he was still upside down. He pressed against the steering wheel with both hands and found his feet trapped in the footwell of the car. No good. He tried shifting his ass into the passenger seat, and that freed his legs, and he managed to get his head above water and suck in a few deep breaths.

The water was still rising, though, and he realized that he had to get out of the car. He drew his knees up to his chest and tried to kick out the windscreen, and for his trouble, his left ankle sent a stab of pain all the way to his brain. He tried to kick again, using only his right foot, and failed. He tried opening both doors, but they were jammed. Then he noticed that there were lights burning on the dashboard, indicating that the car still had battery power. He groped for the electric window switch on the passenger side. To his amazement, the window began to retract. Water poured through the window, and then it stopped retracting.

He got another gulp of air, then tried the driver's-side window switch. This time the window slid all the way down, but the flow of water into the car increased to a torrent. He held on to his final breath and tried to wait patiently for the car to fill up. It took longer than he had hoped, but when it was full, the pressure of the incoming water equalized, and he was able to get his legs through the open window. That was as far as he could go, because his feet now rested against a large rock.

In desperation, he tried again to kick out the windscreen and failed again. Air began to leak from his nose, and he knew he was done.

Then there was a loud noise—metal against metal, he thought—followed by whining and scraping sounds and the movement of the car. The water now reversed itself and began to flow out the windows, but it was too late for him. He slipped into unconsciousness. There was no tunnel and no light at the end of it; instead, a kind of peace as he gave way to inevitability.

He woke up again, freezing and coughing up water. He lay on a roadway—no, a bridge—next to a large military vehicle, the front bumper of which contained a winch and a cable; beyond that lay the crumpled car. Oh, Christ, he said to himself, I've totaled Felicity's Aston Martin. Then he fainted.

....

He woke again—this time from a sleep. He was in a hospital bed, partially cranked to a sitting position. A nurse, he thought, there has to be a beautiful nurse in this place. Instead, an angry face filled his vision. It rested atop a Royal Marines uniform, which wore a colonel's insignia of rank: a crown and two pips.

The face screamed at him, "What the fuck do you think you are doing, Barrington?"

Stone did not like people screaming into his face. He groped for the bed control, found it, and moved the frame until it was fully upright, all the time pushing the angry face away from him. "I'm recuperating!" he shouted back. "And I don't need you yelling at me!"

"Do you know what rank you are shouting at?" the colonel demanded.

"Certainly," Stone shouted again, "and I outrank you! I'm a civilian!"

The colonel, taken aback, took a step away. "Calm yourself," he ordered, "and tell me what happened to Dame Felicity's car."

"I believe it found itself upside down in a river," Stone replied, more calmly now. With his new perspective he pointed at a white lump at the foot of his bed. "What is that?" he asked.

"It's a boot," someone to his left said. This one wore a white coat over his uniform, but Stone couldn't see the insignia.

"I've got a broken foot?"

"No, you've got a badly sprained ankle," the man replied. "That's the worst you can claim. You have to stay off it for a while, and the boot will help remind you of that."

"Take it off," Stone said sullenly.

"No," the doctor replied, then turned on his heel and marched away.

Then a beautiful nurse appeared. "The doctor is right, you know," she said, suppressing a laugh. "He's a pain in the arse, but he is right. You're on crutches for the duration."

"The duration of what?" Stone asked.

"Your pain and inability to walk without crutches. At least a week, maybe a month."

The colonel, whom Stone had been ignoring, stepped back into the picture. "As to rank," he said, "you are a trainee in my company, and as such, you will take orders from me and do it respectfully."

"Colonel," Stone replied, as gently as he could. "I graduated from your torture chamber this morning—or was it yesterday? That fact puts me outside your command and back into the rank of citizen, though not of this country."

"Good God!" the colonel thundered. "If you weren't a cripple, I'd drag you down to the gym and thrash you to within an inch of your life!"

"Threats are unbecoming in an officer of your rank," Stone replied evenly.

The nurse covered her mouth with a hand, stifling another laugh.

"You will report to me instantly when you are ambulatory," the colonel said, seething.

"I will not report to you in any circumstance," Stone said, "ambulatory or not."

The colonel executed a quick about-face and marched out of the ward.

A ward was what he was in, Stone reflected. There were a

half dozen beds, with only one other occupied, by a marine with a leg in a cast, elevated. "That's givin' it to the old bastard," the man said to Stone, admiringly.

"Thank you, sir," Stone said, then turned back to the nurse. "Now you," he said. "May I ask your name?"

"I am Rose McGill," she replied.

"And I am Stone Barrington."

"I'm aware of that," she said, pointing at his chart.

"Tell me, Ms. McGill . . ."

"Lieutenant McGill," she replied.

"Of course. Is there a decent restaurant in the vicinity of this facility?"

"There is, a very good one, just down the road a mile or so."

"Would you do me the honor of dining there with me this evening?" Stone asked.

"My, you are recovering, aren't you."

"I certainly am."

"Love to," she said.

5

They sat before a cheerful fire in the cozy dining room of the local inn, Stone with his game ankle resting on a third chair at their table.

"That's right," Lieutenant McGill said, "keep it elevated." A glass of single malt scotch whisky sat before each of them. The Scottish proprietor would not admit to ever having heard of bourbon whiskey.

"May I call you Rose?" he asked.

"Of course, Mr. Barrington, as long as we're not on the ward."

"Good, and I'm Stone."

"Stone you shall be."

Stone took a breath to speak, but she held up a restraining hand. "Before you start interrogating me, I have questions for you," she said.

"Fire away," Stone replied.

"There are all sorts of rumors about you and why you were training here."

"Yes?"

"Yes. Who are you, and why were you training here?"

"Do we have enough whisky, or should we order more? This is going to take a while."

"More, please."

Stone crooked a finger at the proprietor and signaled for more whisky. "Now," he said, after the man had complied, "I am Stone Barrington, as it says on my chart. I am an American . . ."

"Well, there's a shock," she said mockingly.

". . . from New York City, on the northeastern seaboard of our Atlantic coastline."

She made a motion for him to continue.

"I am an attorney at law, by profession. Although, after attending university and law school, I became a New York City police officer, serving mostly as a homicide detective for fourteen years, before I was invalided out, after a bullet wound to a knee."

"Oh, that's right," Rose said. "Americans fire guns at each other, don't they?"

"On widely separated occasions," Stone replied. "It was the only time I was ever fired upon."

"I assume, being an American, you drew your own gun and killed your assailant. Isn't that also what Americans do?"

"I did draw my weapon and fire it, but missed. However, my partner, who was a much better shot than I, killed my assailant."

"And what are you doing in the far reaches of the Scottish Highlands?"

"I have an acquaintance who is a high-ranking member of MI-6, and . . ."

"That would be Dame Felicity Devonshire, the director."

"How did you know that?"

"Well, there were, as I said, rumors—that and the fact that you were driving her motorcar when you decided to take a swim. If you weren't friends, you'd have been driving a stolen vehicle and would now be reposing in a dank Scottish gaol, instead of this cozy inn."

"You have superior powers of deduction," Stone said.

"Once again, why were you training here, and for what?"

"I have, from time to time, done business with MI-6. And Dame Felicity, on an occasion when we had both taken strong drink, suggested—no, she *dared* me to do the course. With the reward being that I was allowed to drive the Aston back to civilization. I foolishly agreed. And when I had sobered up, she wouldn't let me off the hook."

"Are you perfectly serious?"

"Perfectly."

"So you came up here and spent a week running about the Highlands, competing with a lot of twenty-two-year-olds?"

"Not quite. It was explained to me that there was a senior level of training available to those who are no longer twenty-two, so I was competing with thirty-five-year-olds, who are mostly in better shape than they have any right to be at their age."

"How'd you do?" she asked.

"Not terribly well," Stone admitted. "Oh, I did all right in the courses—near the top of my class, in fact. I thought I might redeem my physical prowess somewhat by agreeing to a timed drive around their defensive driving course, since I had the Aston Martin DB11 available to me."

"We know how that turned out, don't we?"

"I am reliably informed that, until I misread that turn by the bridge, I was on my way to a record-setting circuit."

"Well, there was that turn, wasn't there?"

"I also have no memory of that turn, or of anything after setting off."

"Now someone will have to buy Dame Felicity a new motorcar. Her insurance company, I expect."

"I fear that insurance companies are far too wily to cover automobile racing—even against the clock—in their policies."

"So you are on the hook for a new Aston Martin?"

"I am, and deservedly so. This afternoon I phoned the London dealership of that marque and ordered her previous DB11 duplicated, for delivery in—well, it was going to be seven months, but when I mentioned her name, that was shortened to two weeks, so she will not long be without transport."

"How much did that cost you?"

"Don't ask."

At that moment their dinner arrived, and they switched from the single malt to a sturdy claret.

They raised their glasses and said "Bon appétit!" together.

"Now," Stone said. "Your turn."

"All right," she said, sampling his Scottish beef and approving. "Born, London, thirty-odd years ago, educated at what you Americans call a 'private' school, then Oxford, followed by medical school, followed by a surgical residency, followed by some years as a general surgeon."

"And why are you here?" he asked.

"I have been on what the medical community here refers to as a *locum*—that is, replacing another physician while he is on leave. I thought this post might be enlightening, and it has been, in fits and starts."

"That is a very short history," Stone said.

"I'm sorry if I bored you."

"Ever married?"

"Briefly, to another medical student. I came away from that feeling that physicians should never marry—not each other, anyway. You?"

"I am a widower. My wife was murdered several years ago by a former lover. I have a son who is now working in Hollywood as a film director and writer."

"I'm sorry for your loss, but it is my gain."

"You know," Stone said when they were finishing dessert, "while I admire your charming little car that we came in, I confess that my temporary disability caused me to be less than comfortable in it. Perhaps it would be a good idea for us to remain overnight upstairs, in what was described to me as their finest bedroom, then hazard the return journey on the morrow."

"Well," she said, "since the morrow is a Sunday, I think that is an entirely sensible suggestion. I accept your kind invitation."

They left their table and, once at the staircase, Stone was able to ascend to the upstairs floor using the banister, followed by Rose carrying his crutches. They entered an impossibly charming bedroom furnished with a large four-poster bed.

"Now," she said, "either you have to sleep with one leg in your trousers, or we must find a way to get them off without causing you undue pain."

"It's good that you are a medic," Stone said.

She met his gaze. "I am a physician, and you will kindly remember that, if you wish to remember this night fondly."

"I am desolated at my faux pas," Stone said. "Dr. McGill."

"In Britain, specialists are not called doctor but are referred to as Mr., Mrs., or Ms.," she replied. And in a trice she employed her medical training to free him from the boot, his trousers, and everything else.

6

They slept late, had a huge breakfast in bed, read the Sunday papers, then returned to the base.

"By the way," Rose said as they alighted in the parking lot, Stone with some difficulty, "it's not my car. It belongs to the base."

He was about to ask how she had traveled to the base when a middle-aged woman appeared at the door of HQ and called out to him.

"Mr. Barrington, the colonel would be grateful for a moment of your time."

"'Grateful'?" Stone muttered. "I expect that is her word, not his."

"He's really not so bad," Rose said. "Go and see him, and behave yourself."

Stone swung along into the building and was ushered into a comfortable office where the colonel sat, gazing at some paperwork. He looked up. "Ah, Mr. Barrington, will you take a seat for a moment?" He indicated the chair on the opposite side of his desk.

Stone sat down and arranged his crutches so that they wouldn't fall onto the floor. "Yes, Colonel?"

"I wish to apologize for my manner in the ward yesterday," he said, sounding sincere.

Stone was taken aback. He had not been expecting conciliation. "Thank you," he managed. "It's possible that I overreacted just a bit."

"Thank you, also. I have had news that caused me to reevaluate your driving skills."

Stone couldn't think of anything to say.

"You see," the colonel said, ignoring Stone's lack of a response, "upon closer examination of the wreckage of the Aston Martin, we have determined that your plunge into the river was caused—not by careless driving, but by a bullet into the right front tire from a rifle."

"Fired by whom?" Stone asked.

"By a man on the riverbank, who had chosen his position poorly and was struck by the car on its way into the river. His body was found a couple hundred meters downstream from where the car came to rest."

"Who was he?"

"His identity remains unknown, as it will probably continue to be, but we have surmised from other evidence that he was all or part of a black parachute operation launched by the Soviets— or, as they like to be called these days, the Russian Federation."

"What is a 'black parachute operation'?"

"It's when someone jumps from an airplane at night, employing a black parachute, so as not to be noticed in the dark."

"And how did you determine this?"

"It is not their first attempt on this installation," the colonel said. "Also, we found his black parachute and backpack, concealed in some brush not far from the river. By the way, since you were not fully conscious at the time of your rescue, you should know that it was made possible because the driver of a heavy lorry with a powerful winch built into its front bumper was a witness to the event and used his winch to extract the car from the river."

Stone thought this over for a moment. "Please thank him for me."

"Of course. Questions?" the colonel asked.

"Just one," Stone replied. "Does this mean that the Ministry of Defence will be paying for Dame Felicity's replacement vehicle?"

"Ah, yes," the colonel said. "I have spoken to the minister, and he has agreed to that. The dealer will be posting your check back to you."

"Oh, good. Please let them know that delivery of the replacement vehicle will take place in less than two weeks, so they shouldn't be slow to issue their own check."

"Noted."

"And will you be offering the Russians their corpse back in return for reimbursement?" Stone asked, trying not to laugh.

"No, we think it is more in our interests for the earth to swallow him up and let the Russians stew about what happened to their man."

"I see."

"It occurs to me that, given your lack of transport, you might wish to take advantage of one of our vehicles going to Glasgow for servicing tomorrow. You can take the overnight train to London from there."

"Thank you, it is rather a long taxi ride to Glasgow, isn't it?"

The colonel rose, walked around his desk, and stood Stone's crutches up for him. Stone got to his good foot and thanked him.

The colonel offered his hand. "Thank you for your enthusiastic acceptance of our rather rude conditions here, and good luck to you."

Stone shook the hand and made his way to the door.

"The car will depart from here at seven AM tomorrow morning, and there will be another passenger, as well. The drive to Glasgow is about four hours; the road is not exactly a motorway."

Stone thanked him again and made his way to his quarters, where he packed his gear, then stretched out on his bed for a nap. Later, he woke up long enough to call his travel agent and book a suite aboard the train from Glasgow to London, then he went back to sleep and stayed that way until the following morning.

Stone was awakened by the bell at six AM. He showered, shaved, and dressed, then he turned his luggage over to a young private and went to the mess hall for breakfast. Rose was nowhere to be seen, and he decided not to wake her so early. Anyway, he didn't know where she was quartered.

He left the building at seven and found a large BMW saloon waiting for him; he also found Rose in the rear seat. "Good morning," he said, giving his crutches to the private and getting into the car. "I didn't know you were coming, and I didn't know where to look for you."

"My locum ended on Saturday," she said, "and I was invited to share your car—or rather, the colonel's BMW."

"I would have thought they would service it here," Stone said.

"They do that with the utility vehicles," she said, "but not with the colonel's car. It goes to an authorized dealer."

They drove away, crossing the bridge where the Aston Martin had met its fate. "Did you hear about the sniper?" he asked Rose.

"The talk around the base is of nothing else," she replied. "Apparently, it's not their first intrusion here. The colonel thinks it's good for morale to kill an intruder now and then. Keeps everybody on their toes."

They drove quickly across the nearly bare Highlands landscape, the monotony occasionally broken by a stand of evergreens, which the Scots called a "plantation." Three hours later the landscape became more welcoming, with the sight of oaks and other deciduous trees, and the appearance of villages and houses. Then, in Glasgow, they were dropped at the main station, and found a porter and their train.

"I've booked a suite," Stone said to her. "Please join me."

"I intend to," she said, "in more ways than one."

A twenty-pound note was of help in arranging for Rose's pre-booked room to be one adjoining his suite, so she could have the smaller accommodation as a dressing room with its own shower.

7

When they were settled into their comfortable sitting room, Stone produced a bottle of Knob Creek from his bag. "Are you feeling adventurous?" he asked, holding it up.

"I expect I will be, after a dose of that," she replied.

Stone poured them each one, and she sampled hers judiciously. "My word," she said. "That is quite drinkable for a foreign spirit."

"Speaking for my country, and the state of Kentucky, I thank you for your broad-mindedness." Shortly, they had another.

The train moved, and Rose said, "I'm feeling a bit peckish. Shall we be among the first for the first seating in the dining car?"

"Of course."

They made their way to the next car and were seated immediately. Industrial Glasgow was passing their window, but soon it gave way to a more rural vista. The sun was already setting.

"It gets dark early at this latitude this time of year," Stone said.

"I expect it's one of the reasons so few people reside in the Scottish Highlands," she replied.

They ordered the lamb and Stone found a decent claret on the wine list. After dinner they took a couple of large cognacs with them back to their suite, and soon they were once again entwined in bed.

"What time do we get to King's Cross Station?" Stone asked, kissing her ear.

"Quite early, so we'll miss rush hour. Still, we have a good seven hours to go."

"Barely enough time for this," Stone said, turning his attention to another area of her physique.

"Take all the time you need," she said.

When they were sated they sat up in bed, tended to their cognac, and watched the Scottish Lowlands fly by their window, under a half-moon.

"When do you have to be back at work?" Stone asked.

"A week from tomorrow," she replied.

"Then why don't you join me for a night at the Connaught, followed by several days at my house on the Beaulieu River, in Hampshire."

"What a nice invitation. Will I have time to restock my wardrobe?"

"Certainly, and you will have room for whatever you want to bring. It's a roomy car."

"Then I accept."

They finished their cognac, then turned again to each other.

At King's Cross they found a taxi and had a fairly quick drive to the Connaught Hotel, in light traffic. Stone gave her the cab to drive her home. "What time will I see you?"

"Oh, by the cocktail hour, I expect."

"I'll let the front desk know you're coming." Stone sent her on her way and checked in. He was relieved that his suite was ready, and he managed a couple more hours of sleep.

Later, Rose was escorted up to the suite by an assistant manager, and her bags were set up on folding racks.

"Where are we dining?" she asked.

"At Harry's Bar," Stone replied. "Do you know it?"

"Only by reputation."

"I predict that you will like it."

"May we have a dance at Annabel's later?"

"I'm very much afraid that Annabel's is now Annabel's in name only, having been closed by its new owners and moved next door. I was a member for a long time, and I was told nothing about all this. I was also told that if I wanted to be a member of the new club I would have to reapply and give references. I asked if I might see the new club before making that decision and was told only members could enter. I decided that I did not wish to belong to a club who would treat an old member in that manner, so I declined to reapply. It's a pity, because I loved the original."

At dinnertime they took the five-minute walk to Harry's Bar and were given a corner table.

"Stone," Rose said, when their drinks arrived, "did you notice, on our drive to Glasgow, that there seemed to be another vehicle following us?"

"I did not. I was wedged into my seat with my foot on the front armrest, so turning around would have been uncomfortable."

"Our driver noticed," she said, "and he eventually put more distance between us."

"What do you think that was about?"

"Word around the base was that there may have been more intruders than the one who shot out your tire."

"Any thoughts on how many?"

"All sorts of thoughts, from a pair to a platoon."

"Then I expect the colonel will hunt them down to a man."

"I hope so. Tell me, is there anything about you that would cause them to set you apart for being dealt with?"

"That's an interesting thought. Are you thinking of my acquaintance with Dame Felicity?"

"Perhaps. I thought it might be that or something else."

"My only dealings with Russians have been, not with the military, but with the criminal element."

"You mean the Russian mafia?"

"Yes. I'm on the board of a hotel group that opened a new one in Paris last year, and in their attempt to buy us out there were attacks on the persons of both me and my French partner. And they were very persistent."

"It seems unlikely that such people would find you at Station Two."

"It does. I suppose, if they were looking for it, the Aston Martin could have caused them to think it would be driven by Dame Felicity."

"I suppose it might have."

"What about you, Rose? Any reason for them to single you out?"

"I think not, and that view is supported by the fact that I was not sought out."

"Perhaps I should take some precautions on our drive south tomorrow," he said.

"What sort of precautions?"

"I also serve on the board of an outfit called Strategic Services, which is a large international security company. I'll have someone from the London office watch our backs tomorrow."

"Oh, good," Rose said. "I feel better already."

"They are very able people," Stone said. "Now, what would you like for dinner?"

8

The following morning, while Rose was in the tub, Stone called Mike Freeman.

"Are you still in England?" Mike asked.

"Yes, at the Connaught. We're driving down to Windward Hall this morning, and we need our backs watched." Stone told him about the incident in the Scottish Highlands.

"How soon are you leaving?"

"In about an hour."

"I'll have a chase vehicle for you by then. It will be a white SUV with darkened windows. And I'll have a couple of men on duty at Windward late this afternoon."

"Thank you, Mike." They both hung up, then Stone called Felicity.

"Ah, there you are," she said archly. "I was thinking you were afraid to speak to me after what you did to my beautiful motorcar."

"You've heard about the sniper and the tire?"

"I have."

"I took that to mean they were after you, not me."

"Oh, really! They wouldn't dare!"

"And your brand-new, duplicate motorcar will be delivered the first of next week, all paid for by the MOD."

"I don't know how you managed to get money out of that lot. I've rarely been able to."

"My native charm, I guess."

"I understand you did quite well on the course—for a senior person."

"I was the oldest in the class."

"Where are you off to now?"

"Down to Windward, then to New York sometime after that."

"I understand you have company."

"Word does get around, doesn't it?"

"You can hide nothing from me," Felicity said. "I should think you would know that by now."

"I know it well, and I would never attempt it."

"Let me know when you're free again."

"Certainly."

Rose came out of the bathroom, and Stone hung up.

"Who was that?"

"We will have a chase car on our way south, and a couple of men watching over the house."

"Very good. When are we leaving?"

"As soon as you're packed," he said, making for the bathroom.

A white Range Rover was parked across the street from the Connaught. The driver's window slid down half a foot and the man at the wheel nodded at Stone. His car arrived and was packed by the bellman, then they were off.

"What sort of car is this?" Rose asked.

"It's a Porsche Cayenne Turbo," Stone replied.

"You should have brought it to Scotland."

"If I had, it would now be on Station Two's rubbish heap."

"A good point, but perhaps they were shooting at the Aston Martin, not you."

"Perhaps I'm overrating my importance."

She looked over her shoulder. "I don't see our protection."

"You're not supposed to, but it's a white SUV with dark windows. So if you see anything like that, don't be alarmed."

They drove southwest, past Southampton and through the village of Beaulieu.

"I know this town," she said. "My father brought me here to the motorcar museum when I was a little girl."

"The museum is still there, if you'd like to pay another visit."

An hour and a half after their departure they drove through the gates of Windward Hall.

"My word!" Rose said, looking at the house. "I wasn't expecting anything so grand."

"In the world of country houses, this is called cozy," Stone replied. "If you want grand, there's an Arrington Hotel next door."

"How many are there?"

"Also Paris, Rome, and Los Angeles." He stopped the car and a couple of staff materialized and took their luggage away.

Before they could get inside, the white Range Rover pulled into the drive and two men got out.

"See anything?" Stone asked.

"Yes, we did," the driver replied. "A black van with a souped-up engine, but we crowded him a little, and he left the motorway an hour back. I expect he was surprised he got rumbled."

"Keep surprising those people," Stone said.

He led Rose into the house and gave her the tour. A table was set for lunch in the library, and they each had a glass of sherry first.

"So, what did our guards say?"

"There was someone behind us, but not anymore. Don't worry, I didn't order them shot. As soon as they knew they were being observed, they broke off the chase."

"I wouldn't have minded if you had ordered them shot," Rose said.

9

After lunch, Stone got a phone call.

"Would you like a couple to join you for dinner this evening?"

"If one of them is you, Felicity."

"One of us is. You know the other, too. See you at six-thirty for drinks?"

"Fine."

"How are we dressing?" she asked.

"Lounge suits for the gentlemen."

"Done."

He hung up and turned to Rose. "Have you ever met Dame Felicity Devonshire?"

"Am I about to?"

"At dinner," Stone said. "She has a house just across the river, and she'll arrive via her motor launch with another guest, whose name has not been vouchsafed to me."

"Fine with me. I saw horses in the meadow. Can they be ridden?"

"They can, if you can." Stone picked up the phone, called the stables, and ordered up mounts.

"Did you bring clothes?" Stone asked.

"I'm ready for anything," she said. "Give me ten minutes."

Stone went to his dressing room and changed, exchanging his invalid's boot for an Ace bandage and a riding boot. Rose returned, togged out in riding trousers, boots, and a Barbour jacket over a turtleneck. "Voilà," she said, curtseying.

They walked out to the stable and found a groom holding the horses. "Yours is the mare," Stone said, "and I usually ride the gelding. Or there's a stallion, if you'd like a few bones broken."

"The mare will be just fine," she said, rubbing the animal's nose and slipping her a carrot from the kitchen. The groom gave her a leg up.

"I'll need a leg up, too, Stan," Stone said. "I've got a wounded ankle." Stan obliged, and they crossed the meadow at a trot, which soon became a canter.

"Are you up for jumping the wall?" Stone called out. "Or shall we use the gate?"

"Just follow me," she replied, taking the wall in stride. Stone followed.

"You're right about the grand house," she said, seeing the Arrington come into view.

"The previous owner was murdered by an old friend," Stone said, "and his widow sold us the house. It was redone by Susan Blackburn, who also redid Windward, under the old owner's watchful eye. I bought the place a few weeks before the work was completed."

Stone looked back and saw the white Range Rover following along the lane across the meadow. "I forgot to tell them we were riding," he said, "but they got the picture."

A little farther along and they came to the hangar and landing strip.

"Your own private airport?" Rose asked.

"It was an RAF base during the last war," Stone replied. "They flew secret missions to France. Sir Charles, the previous owner, kept it in good nick. It's very convenient after a transatlantic flight to land at home."

"What do you do about customs?"

"They drive over from Southampton, for only a slight emolument. So does the fuel truck."

"But there's no airplane in the hangar."

"I flew over on a very nice Gulfstream belonging to Strategic Services. They make the trip two or three times a month for various business purposes. My airplane is smaller, so it's a two-day trip. What with refueling stops and crew rest."

"Sounds like you need a Gulfstream," she said.

"I've toyed with the idea, but it seems far above me. And I enjoy flying my own airplane."

"You couldn't fly a Gulfstream?"

"After a month or six weeks of training," he said, "but it's hard to find the time. Still, if I could bring myself to write the check I could fly as a third pilot and give the crew some rest, just as I do with the current aircraft. I'm part of an investment group that is bringing an initial public offering to the market soon, and if that goes well enough, I might feel comfortable writing it."

They rode down to the Solent, the body of water separating England and the Isle of Wight, crossing neighbors' properties, then back to the house.

"How much time have I got to dress for dinner?" Rose asked.

Stone looked at his watch. "They'll be here in two hours."

"That should be enough," she said, heading off upstairs.

Stone went to his own bath and dressing room. He didn't see Rose again until she walked into the library. It was the first time he had seen her dressed for an occasion that didn't involve taking a hike, a motor trip, or bandaging his ankle, and he was more than impressed. "You do a great deal for a little black dress," he said, kissing her.

"Thank you, kind sir."

"Can I get you a libation?"

"You can get me a good single malt," she said. "I'll watch you drink the bourbon."

He handed her the drink, and they sat down just in time to rise again when Dame Felicity and her companion arrived. Stone introduced the two women; introductions to Felicity's companion were unnecessary, since he was Colonel Fife-Simpson, of Station Two.

10

ife-Simpson looked slightly less military in a well-cut pin-striped suit. "Well, Colonel, I didn't expect to see you again so soon," Stone said.

"Please, it's Roger," he said.

"And we're Stone and Rose."

"Roger is down here at my request," Dame Felicity said. "He's joined us at the Circus." Stone knew that was an old nickname for MI-6, since they had been previously quartered in Cambridge Circus. "He is, as of today, my deputy."

"Congratulations, Roger," Stone said. "Or does a Royal Marine regard that as less than a promotion?"

"It's a promotion any way you slice it," Roger said. "And as if to underline it, I've been promoted to brigadier."

"Twice congratulations, then," Stone said. "The previous owner of this house was a Royal Marine, as were some of his neighbors and one of the house's staff."

"I knew them all," Fife-Simpson replied, "though as a junior officer. I did not know that you had bought Sir Charles's property."

"I was press-ganged into that decision by Felicity," Stone said, raising his glass to her. "To my delight."

"Stone," the brigadier said with a change of tone. "I'm very much afraid that I owe you and Rose an apology."

"Why so?" Stone asked, mystified.

"The people following you from Station Two to Glasgow and, later, in London were mine. I was concerned for the safety of both of you, I assure you. I'm sorry that resulted in you taking on private security."

"Well," Stone said. "You've solved a mystery for me, and I know that it's as much a relief for Rose as for me."

"It certainly is," Rose said.

"May I ask, Roger: Why were you concerned for our safety?"

"I'm afraid that the black-parachute operation we rooted out was made up of more than the one or two we at first thought."

Felicity spoke up. "That came from us, in London, actually," she said. "We, ah, got wind of an operation to plant half a dozen GRU agents on our island, and they chose that means of entry. Really, you'd think they could just issue a few more diplomatic passports and give them spurious titles at their embassy."

"But you would have known immediately," Roger said. "Whereas, if they'd pulled off the black-parachute operation without incident, they would already be infiltrating into the country, and we'd have no idea. So, Stone, at the price of your ankle and Felicity's car, we have extinguished a nest of spies."

"If that's so, Roger, why are you still concerned about our safety?"

Roger shrugged. "We've accounted for all of them. We've

increased Felicity's security, as well, not to mention my own, just in case there are more."

"Well, I hope they're not on the estate as we speak, bumping into our guard." Stone took out his cell phone and pressed a button. "It's Barrington. Our situation has been resolved, so you may stand down and return to London. Anyone you encounter here tonight will be a friendly." He hung up. "There, I hope that prevents heads being broken."

"As do I," Felicity said.

They were called to dinner at a table set before the fireplace. Stone was allowed to taste the wine, then food was served.

When the servants had delivered the main course and retired, Roger leaned in. "Stone," he said, "it's my understanding that you have an airstrip on your property that will accommodate a fairly large aircraft."

"That is so," Stone replied warily. "Why does that interest you—and Dame Felicity—Roger?"

"We are planning a training exercise over a period of two, perhaps three, weeks that would involve both amphibious aspects and airborne, and it occurs to me that your property, situated as it is in a quiet area on a navigable river and with its own airstrip, might be an ideal base for our operations."

"Roger," Stone said, "I'm sorry to tell you that it would be a great deal less than ideal where my neighbors are concerned. We've taken pains not to create a noise problem hereabouts. The neighbors have been accustomed to an airplane landing and taking off now and then—on less than a weekly or even monthly basis—and I would not like to test their patience further. Also, as you may have heard"—he glanced at Felicity, who avoided his gaze—"my partners and I have bought the immediately neighboring property and established a country hotel there. Our guests would not welcome noisy aircraft and helicopters outside their windows, nor assault boats roaring up and down the Beaulieu River, so what you suggest is simply not possible."

"We had hoped to keep it all in the family," Roger replied, obviously disappointed.

"If that's what you'd like to do, then Felicity has a larger property than mine. It's only just across the river, as you discovered tonight, so perhaps she would be pleased to host your little party."

"Now, now," Felicity said, throwing up a hand. "Let's not get carried away." She took a swig of her wine. "Roger, put that notion out of your mind."

"Quite," Roger said, returning to his dinner.

They finished dessert and port and Stilton, then the guests made their goodbyes and departed, driven back to their boat by Stan, in the golf cart.

Stone and Rose made their way upstairs to bed and had just fallen into each other's arms when Stone disengaged for a moment.

"Tell me," he said to Rose. "Are you a party to this little scheme of Fife-Simpson and Dame Felicity's?"

"I'm sorry, I don't know what you mean," she replied, retreating to her side of the bed.

"Well, it occurs to me that, in addition to being a physician, you hold military rank."

"I have a reserve commission," she replied, "in the Home Guard. They helped pay for my surgical training."

"It also occurs to me that Roger and Felicity were discussing what must be a highly classified operation in your presence, as if you were cleared to hear it. I don't know about Roger, but it's very unlike Felicity to discuss something like that in an unclassified environment."

"That seemed to be Fife-Simpson's decision," she replied. "And, you may recall, Dame Felicity spoke only to scotch the idea."

"Then is it not true that your employer is a certain intelligence service, rather than a London hospital?"

She reached for his nether region and fondled him. "I can neither confirm nor deny your conjecture. I can, however, help you forget that you asked."

"That is certainly a possibility," Stone said, moving closer to give her easier access.

She kissed his ear, then used her tongue. "I thought you might think so," she whispered.

11

The next morning they were having breakfast in bed when Rose said, "You're very quiet this morning."

"I suppose I am," Stone said. "My discovery that you are playing on Dame Felicity's team has confused me."

"How so?" she asked.

"Well, are you here in my house and my bed and my pants because you have made that choice, or because duty requires it of you?"

"That's an insulting question," she replied.

"I'm sorry if it seems so. As I said, I am confused, and while in that state, should not be required to make discerning judgments about the emotional state of others."

"Would you like me to go?"

"I would not. I would merely like you to familiarize me with your current state of mind and your intentions."

"My current state of mind is serene," she said, "when I am not being asked annoying questions."

"And your intentions?"

"Honorable."

"May I assume, then, that your presence in my bed and pants

is entirely voluntary, rather than specified in paragraph six, line two, of your marching orders?"

"You may assume that my presence in your bed and pants is not only voluntary, but enthusiastic, and unrelated to any orders issued to me by my superiors, if such exist. Would you like a demonstration of that enthusiasm?"

Stone smiled. "Yes, please."

She rolled him onto his back, took him into her mouth, and did not stop until he screamed, "Uncle!"

"I trust that settles your mind," she said.

"Entirely," he replied.

Stone's phone rang and he grabbed it from the bedside table. "Hello?"

"It's Dino."

"Good God! What time is it in your world?"

"Sometime after midnight," he replied. "Viv has been summoned to London for a few days of business consultations. Would you be annoyed if I parachuted into your current location for that time?"

"I would be delighted to see you both," Stone said.

"Then look for us on your airstrip late in the afternoon."

"We will be ready to receive you."

Dino hung up.

"Are we going to have company?" Rose asked.

"We are indeed: my best friends, Dino and Vivian Bacchetti. She has business in London, but he does not."

"May I assume that they will have their own room?"

"You will not be required to share a bed with them."

"I must tell you that, according to the gossip, Dame Felicity is, shall we say, impartial where the gender of her bed partners is concerned. I was a little afraid that more would be expected of me than I might be willing to give—not that she is unattractive."

"I can neither confirm nor deny those rumors," Stone said. "But I can tell you that the Bacchettis have no such inclinations, so the only hand you may expect to land on your knee will be mine."

"I don't want to seem a prig," she said. "I have, on widely separated occasions, dabbled in that sort of thing, and with pleasure. But Felicity is not my type, whatever that is."

"Got it."

In the late afternoon, Stone got a satphone call from an airplane.

"Yes?"

"Ten minutes out," Dino said, then hung up.

Stone and Rose got into the Cayenne and drove down to the airstrip in time to watch the big Gulfstream settle onto the runway, then taxi to the ramp. Stone pulled the car up to the aircraft and introduced Rose to the Bacchettis while the plane's crew loaded their luggage into the SUV. Moments later they were back at the house, and the Gulfstream was climbing.

They settled into the library while Geoffrey, the butler, served drinks.

"Why are you limping?" Dino asked Stone.

"A slight accident," Stone replied.

"One that totaled a quarter-of-a-million-pound motorcar," Rose added.

Stone explained what had happened.

"So how did your training go?" Dino asked. "Was it as bad as I told you it would be?"

"Nearly," Stone said, "but I'm getting through life with only an Ace bandage on my ankle, though I've had to give up tap-dancing for a while."

"Were you able to keep up with the younger kids?"

"The younger kids were in their thirties," Stone said, "and pudgy."

"Have you learned how to be a British spy?"

"Only the rudiments."

"I could still take him with a knife," Rose said.

"I should explain that Rose, in addition to being a surgeon, may be one of Felicity's flock. We can't be sure."

"Is that convenient for everybody?" Viv asked.

"Well, if she is of that flock, that means she gets paid for being here," Stone said.

"You should get a bonus for putting up with Stone," Dino said.

"Oh, he has his uses."

"I won't explore that," Dino said. "Tell me, are the two of you still in mortal danger?"

"Our fearless leader seems to believe that he bagged them all," Rose said. "But now that you mention it, he didn't actually claim to have done that."

"Should I go armed?" Dino asked.

"Why not?" Rose said. "I am."

"You are?" Stone asked.

She produced a small 9mm pistol.

"Cleverly concealed," Stone said.

"Don't ask where."

"I'm going to need to search you more thoroughly from now on."

She laughed. "Anytime."

"Well," Viv said, rising. "I'm going to have a little nap before dinner." She looked at Dino. "And you, my darling?"

"Sorry," Dino said, rising. "I missed my cue."

"Drinks at seven, dinner to follow," Stone said.

Rose stood. "I could use a little nap myself."

"Got that!" Stone said, following her upstairs.

12

The following morning Stone was dressing when he got a phone call.

"It's Felicity. Can you pop down to your dock, alone, for a chat?"

"Ten minutes," Stone said.

"Perfect." She hung up.

"Rose, I have to go out for a bit. Will you excuse me?"

"Can't I come?"

"It's a private matter."

"Oh, all right. See you at lunch?"

"Sure. If you'd like to take a ride before then, invite Dino. When he was a boy his parents sent him to a dude ranch in Montana for a summer, to get rid of him, and he hasn't gotten over it yet."

"Perhaps I'll do that."

"Just press the button on the phone marked Stables."

"Right."

Stone went downstairs, got into the golf cart, and drove down to his dock, just in time to take Felicity's lines. "Good morning," he said.

"And to you. I have Bloody Marys already mixed. May I pour you one?"

"Thank you, yes."

She opened a thermos bottle and poured two glasses.

"What's up?" Stone asked, raising his glass and taking a sip.

"I wanted to speak to you about our newly minted brigadier," she said.

"Your new number two."

"Yes, but he was not my choice."

"Then what's going on, Felicity?"

She sat down next to him on the cockpit seat. "I appear to be under unusually intense scrutiny from above."

"From how far above?"

"At least the foreign minister, to whom I report, but probably the PM, as well, and possibly the whole of the cabinet."

"Then all that's left is the editorial board of the *Times*."

"That would not surprise me," she said.

"What have you done to warrant all this attention from your betters?"

"I've thought about it, and I can't imagine what."

"Oh, come on, Felicity. You are always at odds on four or five things with the government. Pick one."

"The strangest thing about all this is that I can't think of one that would so turn up the temperature. It is a peculiarly tranquil time at the Circus."

"All right, then why is Colonel—sorry, Brigadier Fife-Simpson, the instrument of their suspected displeasure?"

"I didn't even know the man six months ago," she said. "Then he was foisted upon me as director of training at Station Two, and he has, I must admit, done a very good job. The curriculum has been improved, and the failure rate among candidates has dropped markedly."

"You mean, even I passed?"

"Well, yes, but that wouldn't have surprised me." She placed a hand on his cheek. "I knew you'd do well, that's why I egged you on. What was your impression of the quality of the training?"

"High and intense. I haven't learned so much in such a short time for many years—not since I took a cram course for the New York State Bar in preparation for taking the exam. Mind you, back then I was merely learning what I had already forgotten during the years since law school."

"And the physical demands?"

"Demanding. Fortunately I was in pretty good shape—better than my classmates, who had been warming chairs for too long."

"Those classmates, my dear, were the crème de la crème of our recruitment."

"They were bright, I'll give them that, but pudgy. The only one near my age who gave me a run for my money was Fife-Simpson himself, who took part in the long runs, and he looks to be a few years older than I."

"He is three years older," Felicity said.

"Oh," Stone said. "I had to work hard to outrun him."

"And what parts of the training did you dislike?"

"The knife training, using real knives. That was excessive, I thought—closer to street fighting than military. Fife-Simpson could have gutted me at will, I'm sure, and there were times when I thought he might."

"Funny you should mention that," Felicity said. "Legend has it that when he was a young lieutenant in Northern Ireland during the Troubles, he walked into the wrong pub and was set upon by half a dozen IRA toughs. He killed two of them with a broken bottle and reduced the other four to whimpering lumps of flesh."

"I'm glad I didn't know that when we were training," Stone said.

"I'm glad he showed some restraint," Felicity said.

"Look, it sounds to me as though the powers that be have sent you a good man. Perhaps the thing to do is to use him well."

"I knew you would say something sensible like that," she replied. "Men!"

Stone laughed. "Would you rather they had sent you a bumbling idiot?"

"Yes, quite frankly. Bumbling idiots are easier to handle. They need only to be exposed. How would you handle this, Stone?"

"Either find a way to shunt him aside, or give him the toughest job you've got. That way he will either show himself to be inadequate to the task and humiliate those who sent him—or, he will solve your problem. I'd call that a win-win situation."

Felicity sighed. "I was hoping you'd suggest that I just have him taken out and shot."

"Then he wouldn't be any good to you at all."

Felicity kissed him lightly on the lips. "I wish they'd sent me you," she said.

"Tell me, had you ever met Rose before our dinner together?"

"No, she is apparently too junior for me to have had contact with her. Why do you ask?"

"Just wondering," Stone replied.

13

Stone went back to the house. On the way he saw Rose and Dino galloping across the meadow, making for the stone wall. He went into the house, to the library, lit a fire, found a book, and read while the butler set the table for lunch.

A few minutes later Viv came into the library, found a *Country Life,* and took a seat opposite from him. "It appears," she said, leafing through the magazine, "that this publication exists for the purpose of displaying fine houses to be sold by the wealthy to the rich. Oh, look," she said, holding it up. "An actual article—about cooking on those massive AGA stoves they have."

"When did you last cook something, Viv?" Stone asked.

"Right before I went into the Academy. Then after I met Dino, I couldn't cook anything Italian without insidious remarks about the cooking of his mother—who was, by the way, a vile cook. After that, I gave it up."

"Smart move. I had his mother's cooking once—just once— and you describe it accurately."

"This is typical," she said, holding up the magazine. "Five bedrooms and two baths. How does that work?"

"One for guests, I suspect. And a few years ago, they wouldn't have had central heating."

"And yet your house, despite its size, is quite cozy."

"But the gas bill would be enormous if the staff didn't turn off the heat when I'm not in residence. I have to give them a couple of days' notice that I'm coming."

Viv was quiet for a moment. "Rose seems nice," she said.

"Oh, she is."

"I didn't mean in bed. I meant, generally speaking."

"She is that, too."

"How did you meet?"

"I was involved in a minor accident in Scotland . . ."

"You mean the one in which you totaled Felicity's Aston Martin when it fell twelve feet off a bridge?"

"Well, yes."

"How did you happen to have Felicity's car?"

"She drove it up there on an inspection tour of the camp. She loves to drive. I was to drive it back for her. I like to drive, too."

"I'm sorry, how did the accident involve Rose?"

"I came to in their infirmary and she . . ." He stopped and thought for a moment. "I was going to say that she was in charge of treating me . . . but she wasn't. There was a male doctor in charge, but I didn't see him again after she arrived on the scene."

"What was she doing at a training camp for MI-6?"

"She was on a locum. That's where one doctor fills in for another, while he's on vacation."

"What was the place like?"

"Not what you'd call comfortable," Stone said. "In fact, the training seemed designed to make everyone uncomfortable. It was very military."

"And why would Rose want to do a locum at such a place?"

"You'd have to ask her that. Her reasons never came up in conversation."

"If I know you, Stone, there wasn't a great deal of conversation. On any subject."

"Now, now. I can be quite chatty, you know."

"Well, you're a great chatter-upper, as the Brits would say, but conversation?"

"You and I are having a very nice conversation, aren't we? And I'm holding up my end."

"I suspect that you spent most of your time holding up *her* end," Viv said, archly.

Stone laughed. "You remind me of Felicity sometimes."

"I'll take that as a compliment."

"You should."

The door opened and Rose and Dino came in, still in their riding clothes.

"Dino," Stone said, "where on earth did you find the riding gear?"

"In the village," Dino said, "at your suggestion, the last time I was here. I just left it in the closet when I went home, and when I came back, it was still there, cleaned and pressed."

Geoffrey came in and announced lunch, and they moved to the table.

"Rose," Viv said, "Stone was just telling me you did a locum at the training camp in Scotland."

"I did," Rose replied.

"And where are you based in London?"

"I'm on a sort of rotation," she said, "something like your judges used to be."

"You ride a mule from village to village?"

"I drive a mini from hospital to hospital," Rose replied. "Next week I start at St. George's for two weeks."

"Oh, yes, at Hyde Park Corner."

"That's the one," Rose said. "You know your London, Viv."

"As long as I have an *A to Z Guide* in my handbag," Viv replied.

"Did you have a good ride this morning?" Stone asked.

"Oh, yes," Rose said.

"I could hardly keep up with her," Dino added.

"I'm a farmer's daughter," Rose said. "There were always horses."

"Where was the family farm?"

"In Rutland, in the north of England. It's the country's smallest county."

"It sounds lovely," Viv said. "Does your family still live there?"

"Yes."

After lunch and some wine, everybody adjourned for a nap.

Viv, after Dino was asleep, called her London office at Strategic Services, spoke to her assistant and made a request, then she went back to the bed.

"What were you doing?" Dino asked.

"Oh, go back to sleep," she said.

"I was thinking, maybe a matinee?"

"Dino, do you know how long it's been since we had a matinee?"

"Well, we don't often have an afternoon in bed, do we?"

Viv rolled over and explored his crotch. "You're not kidding, are you?"

Stone and Rose had finished their matinee and were getting drowsy.

"Stone," Rose said, "do you think Viv likes me?"

"Sure she does," Stone said. "Believe me, you'd know it if she didn't."

14

tone woke later than usual and felt groggy. There was an empty brandy snifter on the bedside table, and he vaguely recalled Rose pouring them both one at bedtime. He got up, pulled on a robe, and made his way unsteadily to the bathroom, used the toilet, and splashed some cold water on his face, then returned to the bedroom. He had expected Rose to be asleep; there was an envelope on Rose's side of the bed, but no Rose. There was an empty snifter on her side, too.

He sat down on the bed, opened the envelope, and found a letter, handwritten on Windward Hall stationery.

My dear Stone,

Forgive me for sneaking out early this morning, but I had an e-mail, requiring me to be at St. George's in London today, so I called an Uber to get to the station.

I had a wonderful time at Windward and enjoyed meeting Viv and Dino. I'll give you a call later in the week.

Love,

Rose

There was a sharp rap on his door. "Stone?" Sounded like Viv.

"Come in," he called.

Viv came in, dressed for the day. "You're usually an early riser, aren't you?"

"Yes."

"Well, it's nearly ten o'clock. Are you all right?"

"I guess I slept a little too well," he said. "Have you and Dino had breakfast?"

"A couple of hours ago."

Stone picked up the phone and ordered breakfast for one.

"Where's Rose?"

"She had to go back to the hospital in London," Stone said, handing her the note.

Viv read it, then pulled up a chair next to his bed and sat down. "I'm not surprised," she said. She picked up the brandy glass on his bedside table and sniffed it.

"Why not?"

"Do you recall our conversation of yesterday? Rose's and mine?"

"Yes."

"Well, I was suspicious of some of the things she said, so I did some checking."

"Checking what?"

"To begin with, St. George's Hospital at Hyde Park Corner closed in the late eighties and moved to South London, to a place charmingly called Tooting. I called them, and they have no record of a Dr. Rose McGill. The building at Hyde Park Corner, which was a stately home called Lanesborough House before it was a hospital, was renovated, redone, and reopened as a hotel of that name in 1991. It's said to be the most expensive in London."

"That's odd," Stone said.

"Also, the county of Rutland is not the smallest in the country, as Rose stated. The Isle of Wight is."

"You'd think Rose would have known that, wouldn't you?"

"I would. I also had a check done of the property records in Rutland, going back a couple hundred years, and there is not now nor has there ever been a farm in the county owned by a family named McGill, Rose's name. Indeed, there is only one McGill family in all of Rutland. They have operated a betting parlor in Oakham for four generations and do not have a family member named Rose."

"Viv, I believe you're telling me that I have been had, in some sort of way."

"It would seem so."

"Maybe." Stone picked up his phone, found Felicity's number, and called her.

"Good morning, Stone," she said, after her call had been screened.

"Good morning, Felicity," he replied. "I wonder if you could check something for me."

"I'll try."

"Can you consult your records and see if MI-6 has an employee named Rose McGill?"

"One moment," she said. He could hear the tapping of computer keys. "Now," she said, "security regulations prevent me from confirming the name of an employee. However, I don't believe there is a regulation that prevents me from denying that such an employee exists. In fact, we often make such denials. I can, though, tell you honestly that we have no record of an employee by that name."

"You recall meeting her at dinner?"

"Of course. I'm not denying her existence, just her employment. You met her at Station Two, did you not?"

"I did."

"How?"

"She came into the ward while I was being examined by another doctor."

"What was his name?"

"I don't recall, but he was middle-aged and had a very handsome military mustache."

"Yes, that would be Major St. George, who is the only physician based at Station Two."

"Rose said she was doing a locum there."

"That term would be used only if she were replacing another doctor who was away from the station. Clearly, Major St. George was present."

"Clearly."

"Was Brigadier Fife-Simpson present in the ward at that time?"

"Yes, he came in to yell at me for wrecking your car—at least, I think that's what he was yelling about."

"Had you seen Rose before that meeting? In the dining hall, perhaps, or on the grounds?"

"No."

Felicity was silent for a moment. "I am inclined to think that Dr. McGill is a creature of the brigadier's," she said.

"Have you known the brigadier for long?"

"I had met him once or twice in passing, but I had never had a conversation with him until I drove up to Station Two in my erstwhile Aston Martin. Oh, incidentally, its replacement arrived this morning, a bit ahead of schedule, and it is indistinguishable from its predecessor. I thank you for ordering it."

"I trust the MOD paid?"

"Astonishingly, they did. I was prepared to do combat with them over that."

"Felicity, what am I to do about Rose McGill, if that, indeed, is her name?"

"Do you have her address and phone number?"

Stone thought about that. "No."

"Well, there doesn't seem to be anything you can do."

"I guess you're right."

"If you hear from her again, see if you can worm that information out of her, then I can investigate further. For the present, I think all this is best kept between us. I shall not mention it to the brigadier until I am on firmer ground. Now, I must run to a meeting on the Muddle East."

"Thank you, Felicity." Stone hung up and turned to Viv. "Rose McGill does not exist," he said, "at least, not for MI-6."

"I had rather thought she might not," Viv replied. "Shall I ask my people to track her down?"

"Maybe later. Right now, let's let Felicity deal with the situation." His breakfast arrived, and Viv made to go. "I'll be going up to London tomorrow morning," she said. "May I have a ride to the station?"

"Of course."

15

To clear his head, Stone ordered up the gelding and went for a ride. Dino and Viv declined to join him. He walked, then trotted the horse to warm him up, then eased into a canter. As the stone wall grew nearer he spurred the animal into a gallop. Clearly, the horse knew what was expected of him and he soared over the wall and ran until he was reined in.

Back at the house, Stone found his book in the library, then read until everyone was assembled for lunch.

"You're looking a bit more clear-eyed," Viv said.

"Yeah," Dino echoed. "I hear your girl slipped you a Mickey last night."

"It would appear so," Stone said.

"What are you going to do about that girl?" Dino asked.

"Nothing. Felicity will look into the matter when she feels the time is right."

"Don't you find this disturbing?"

"I find it baffling. I can't understand why she, or whoever she works for, would go to these lengths to deceive me."

"It's gotta be Fife-Simpson running her," Dino said.

"That's what Felicity thinks, but she's apparently in a delicate situation: Fife-Simpson has been pressed on her by her ministry, and she doesn't know why."

"It sounds as though they're going to dump her soon, and they want their own man there, ready to step in."

"My guess is that's what Felicity thinks, too, but she won't talk about it."

"Wheels within wheels," Viv said. "That's what these intelligence people are like. You never know what they're thinking."

The phone rang, and Stone took the call.

"Hi, it's Rose. I just wanted to apologize for leaving without talking to you, but they had three hysterectomies lined up and waiting at St. George's, and the surgeon called in sick."

"It's all right, I understand."

"Do you think you'll come up to London this week?"

"Yes, my London office has asked me to. Are you free tomorrow night?"

"I can do that."

"I'll book a suite at the Connaught. Bring your toothbrush."

"Sounds good. I think I can be there around five."

"By the way, what's your phone number?" Then she began talking to someone else in the room.

"Sorry, got to run; I'll see you tomorrow evening." She hung up.

So did Stone. "I didn't get her number," he said. He called Felicity.

"Yes, Stone?"

"I've heard from Rose. I'm going up to London tomorrow. I'll book a suite at the Connaught—she's meeting me there. Tell me, do you have some sort of concealable device I can use to re-cord her?"

"I can do better than that," Felicity said. "Let me book your suite at the Connaught. We have one there that is specially equipped. You won't have to do a thing, except talk."

"We'll go out for dinner," he said.

"Make an excuse to order from room service instead."

"All right. Let me know what you learn."

"All in good time," she said, then hung up.

"Felicity's service has a suite at the Connaught that's wired," he said to the Bacchettis.

"Be careful what you say," Viv said to him, "because your voice will forever be in the files of MI-6."

"Good point," Stone said. "Do you think I should confront Rose with her lies?"

"Heavens no," Viv said.

"Just give her all the rope she wants," Dino said. "Let's see what else she tells you."

"Right," Viv said. "If you start questioning her too closely, she'll get suspicious and clam up. Just let her talk."

"What else do I want to know about her?"

"Anything she tells you is likely to be a lie," Viv said. "But I have to tell you, she doesn't sound like a well-trained intelli-gence agent."

"Why do you say that?"

"She's already blithely told you things you could easily check out and disprove. A real pro would have a legend prepared that's all backed up."

"You could try getting her prints," Dino said, "on a wine-glass, or something. Where are you going for dinner?"

"Felicity wants me to order from room service."

"Do what Felicity says," Dino said.

"If the room is wired, just let the conversation flow, and Felicity will have it on tape."

"Right," Stone said.

16

tone drove the Porsche 911 up to London, figuring the car needed the exercise. He made it to the Connaught by four PM without getting arrested and turned the car over to the doorman for parking.

The MI-6 suite was better than he had expected; the rooms were large and well-decorated. Once the bellman had deposited his luggage and left, Stone stood in the middle of the living room and said loudly, "This is Barrington. I'm here."

A moment later his cell phone rang. "Yes?"

"Message received," a woman's voice said. "Good luck."

Getting lucky was what Stone had in mind. And now, for the first time, he considered that he and Rose would be performing for an audience, if only via audio. He tried to put it out of his mind.

Shortly after five o'clock his phone rang. "Hello?"

A man said, "Your companion is on her way up."

"Thank you." He hung up and waited. A moment later there was a rap on the door and he opened it to find Rose standing there, holding a small duffel.

"Hi, there," she said, snaking an arm around his neck and kissing him. "I declined the offer of a bellman," she said, pushing him inside and hipping the door shut. "I didn't want any witnesses." She backed him to the bed, and they were undressed and under the covers shortly.

Stone dismissed any thought of aural witnesses and turned his attention to gratifying her in every way he could think of. Finally, they were lying in each other's arms, spent and sweating.

"I didn't offer you a drink," Stone said.

"I didn't give you time."

"Would you like one now?"

"Yes, please." She released him; he went to the bar and poured them each one.

She plumped up their pillows and arranged them so that they could sit up. "That was spectacular," she said. "As always."

"It certainly was," Stone said softly.

"It's a pity we don't have a video for later viewing," she said.

"Negative," Stone replied. "The only recording should be in our memories."

"I have a very good memory," she replied. Soon, they had finished their drinks and were dozing.

Stone was shaken awake at seven o'clock. "What time is our dinner table?" Rose asked.

"My ankle is bothering me," Stone said. "Do you mind if we order from room service?"

"Not in the least." She kissed his ankle.

"Did you find that technique for healing in a medical textbook?" he asked.

"No, I made it up. Sort of a home remedy."

"Speaking of home, do you have an actual address and phone number?" he asked.

"Yes, I have a little flat in Ennismore Mews, in Knightsbridge."

Stone grabbed a phone pad from the bedside table. "May I have the address and your number?" he asked, handing her the pad and a pen.

"Of course," she said, scribbling.

Stone looked at the pad to be sure it was legible; it was. He read the address aloud, followed by the phone number.

"Didn't I give you that before?"

"No, you left my house like a thief in the night—and with no forwarding address."

"I apologize. Now you have it all."

"What's it like, performing three hysterectomies in a single day?" he asked.

She laughed. "You don't want to know. Men are not good at receiving that sort of information. Suffice it to say that the OR staff handled everything efficiently, and so did I. The worst thing was that I had to change gowns and scrub up three times."

"How did a doctor get involved with MI-6?" he asked.

"You already have my official denial that I am associated with such an organization," she replied.

"Do they recruit doctors?"

"How would I know, not being privy to their practices?"

"Oh, all right. Next time I see Dame Felicity I'll tell her I failed to worm anything out of you."

"The next time you speak to her, don't mention my name, or even my existence," Rose said. "I don't want me on her mind. I was shocked when she turned up with the col . . . sorry, the brigadier, in tow."

"Why?"

"Because I associated him with Station Two, which is the only place I had ever encountered him."

"Somehow, I thought you had known him before," Stone said.

"When I arrived at Station Two I reported to him, as everyone does, but I didn't see him again except on the ward, when he was screaming at you. The next time was at your table at Windward Hall."

"Whom did you replace at Station Two on your locum?" Stone asked.

"That's an odd question."

"I somehow thought there was only one doctor there—the one who doctored my ankle."

"The one you met. He came back from his leave a day early."

"Why did I never see you around the station before I was in the clinic?"

"Because I was in the clinic. That was where the work was."

"I guess that makes sense. What sorts of things did you treat during your locum?"

"The only other patient I saw was the fellow you shared the ward with, the one with a broken leg," she replied. "I was told that they rarely admitted anyone who was sick. Nearly all the admissions were of injuries suffered during training."

"Has anyone ever died in training?"

"If anyone has, I wasn't told about it. I did hear that we came close to losing you by drowning. It was a good thing the truck with the winch happened along when it did."

Stone found the room service menu and shared it with her. They ordered dinner and a bottle of wine.

"I'd like a shower before dinner arrives," she said. "Join me?"

"No, thanks. I don't want to get caught in there with you by a room service waiter," Stone said. "We might shock him."

Dinner arrived in due course, and two waiters set up the table and served them.

Stone couldn't think of anything else to ask Rose, and they dined quietly.

"Have you run out of questions?" she asked.

"You've worn me out," Stone replied.

"I will again." And she did.

17

Stone woke the following morning with the sound of the shower running in the background, and he joined Rose there. They spent a quarter of an hour soaping and scrubbing and whatever else they could think of, then they toweled each other dry, and Stone ordered breakfast and the papers, then he got into a robe to prepare for the arrival of room service.

Rose, on the other hand, came out of the bathroom entirely naked, toweling her hair. The doorbell rang, and she jumped under the covers.

When the waiters had departed they sat down at the table, Rose still naked.

"Be careful not to spill any hot coffee," Stone said.

She tied a napkin around her neck. "There. All safe."

"What time are you due at work?" he asked.

"Nine."

"Did you drive?"

"No, I took a cab. I imagine the doorman can get me another."

"I imagine so, too," Stone said. He tried and failed to ask her further questions.

Shortly before nine, now fully dressed, Rose grabbed her

coat and her duffel and kissed him goodbye. "When are you coming back?"

"When are you coming down?" Stone asked.

"Next week perhaps. I'll call you."

"Do that." He kissed her and she left.

Two minutes later, his cell phone rang. "Hello?"

"It's Felicity."

"Good morning, did your people get anything?"

"They got a great deal," she said, "but not much of value. You didn't ask the right questions."

"You didn't give me a script," he replied, "and I didn't want to appear to be grilling her. I did the best I could."

"Yes, well, we're all aware how well you did," she said.

"You're smirking," Stone replied. "What do you mean by that?"

"I mean the video was extraordinarily good. We had half a dozen angles, too."

"Video? What video?"

"Oh, there are cameras everywhere. Would you like to know what you had for breakfast, or what wine you drank last night?"

"You didn't tell me that, Felicity. You said there was only audio."

"I said no such thing. I said the suite was wired. We even got good footage of your time in the shower this morning."

Stone checked his memory against that statement. "Shit," he said. "I won't do that again without some agreed ground rules."

"Oh, come on, my dear. You came off beautifully—so to speak."

"Now what?"

"Now you are free to wander London as you will. And there won't be a bill from the Connaught—our treat."

"What's your next move with Rose?"

"Well, we're following her taxi as we speak, and we'll check out the Ennismore Mews address. Would you like to have lunch a little later?"

"Why not?"

"I'll be in your neighborhood. Shall we do it at the Connaught? One o'clock?"

"Fine." He hung up

Stone got dressed and left the hotel. He stopped into his tailor's, Huntsman & Sons, and had a fitting of some things he had ordered earlier, then he stopped by Turnbull & Asser and chose some neckties and a couple of nightshirts. He arrived back at the Connaught and found Felicity waiting for him in the restaurant.

"What did you do with yourself this morning?" she asked, as he sat down and tucked his shopping bag under the table.

"Tailor, shirtmaker. My goal is to have a complete enough wardrobe here that I don't have to travel with luggage, except a briefcase."

"An admirable goal," she said. They ordered. "Would you like to hear what our surveillance produced?" Felicity asked.

"Yes, please."

"She went to the Ennismore Mews address, changed clothes, then went shopping. While she was gone, her mail was read by MI-6. Just some catalogs and a couple of utility bills."

"In what name?" Stone asked.

"Margot Balfour," Felicity said.

"Nice name."

"The deed for the mews house is in that name, too, so she owns it."

"Has it occurred to you that she may be renting from Ms. Balfour?"

"Don't be annoying, Stone, and don't underrate us."

"So, you know that her name is Margot Balfour?"

"We do. She is a real person, as opposed to Dr. Rose McGill. And people named Balfour own a farm in the county of Rutland, and the name appears on the medical register."

"Where else did she go besides home?"

"Harvey Nicks, Harrods, a couple of shops in Beauchamp Place."

"Perhaps you can answer me this, without violating the Official Secrets Act," Stone said. "Can a woman employed by MI-6 afford to shop at those establishments?"

Felicity rolled her eyes. "Yes," she replied. "If she has a private income."

"And are the Balfours of Rutland County well enough off to endow her thus?"

"They are important landowners in that county and have been for two hundred years."

"So, Daddy and Mummy don't feed the chickens and milk the cows?"

"Her father is the cousin of a local duke and is a member of White's and the Garrick Club. Her mother is a bulwark of half a dozen Rutland charities. She has a sister who seems to be edging toward an aristocratic marriage."

"My goodness," Stone said. "Ms. Balfour seems to be too good for MI-6, doesn't she?"

"No one is too good for MI-6," Felicity replied. "Now, if you will excuse me, I have to go and see if that institution is still where it was this morning."

"Lunch is on me," Stone said.

"Of course it is," she said, opening her handbag and fishing out a computer thumb drive. "Here is the recording of your escapades of last night," she said. "It's the only one."

With that, Felicity flounced out to her waiting car.

18

Stone had nothing further to keep him in London for the remainder of the day, so he got his things and asked for his car. On the drive down to Windward Hall he reviewed his evening and morning and decided he knew not much more than he had the day before, save a new name. Everything else he knew was the same.

Back at Windward Hall he gave the car and luggage to Stan, then went to the library. Dino was asleep on the Chesterfield sofa, a light blanket over his feet. Stone found his book on the mantel—a new biography of Winston Churchill by Andrew Roberts—and sat down to read, pleased to see that he had passed page five hundred in a book of more than one thousand pages. He was immediately sucked back into the existence of the greatest Englishman as he became prime minister during World War II.

He had read another twenty-five pages when Dino stirred, then sat up, rubbing his eyes, seeming surprised to find Stone there. "How did you sneak in here without waking me up?"

"I didn't sneak in, but I did try not to wake you, and I didn't."

"Then why am I awake?"

"You are awake of your own volition, since I've been sitting here for an hour. Is Viv still in London?"

"Yes. How long were you in the bugged suite?"

"Yesterday afternoon and evening. We ordered dinner from room service. Rose left before nine this morning."

"Now, let me get this straight," Dino said. "You agreed to have yourself filmed while fucking Rose?"

"Dino . . ."

"You can't tell me that you spent hours with Rose in a room with a bed without fucking her and vice versa."

"I'm not telling you that."

"So, MI-6 now has what most people would call a 'compromising sex video' of you and Rose together?"

"They do not."

"What did you do? Pull the covers over your head?"

Stone retrieved the thumb drive from his jacket pocket and tossed it to Dino. "This is the only copy. Felicity gave it to me."

"And you believed her?"

"Believed what? It's all right there in your hand."

"You believed there are no copies?"

"If there were, I don't believe Felicity would have bothered to lie about it." Stone stood up. "Excuse me a minute." He went into the attached powder room and used the facilities. When he came out, Dino was gazing at his iPhone and laughing. "This is hot stuff, Stone!"

"Dino, you can't watch a thumb drive file on an iPhone."

"You can watch *this* one," he said. "It has a compatible fire-whatchacallit-plug."

Stone walked over to where Dino sat and looked over his

shoulder, then he snatched the phone away from him, unplugged the thumb drive, and gave him back the phone. "You're disgusting!"

"Some folks would say that what I just watched was disgusting, but not I. I thought it was great!"

Stone put the thumb drive into his pocket, sat down, and picked up his book. It wasn't all that easy, because the book must have weighed ten pounds.

"I especially liked the part where your head disappears between her legs," Dino said.

"Dino!"

"I'll bet all the spooks at MI-6 are watching it right now," Dino said, "passing it around the shop."

Dino's phone rang, and he picked it up. "Bacchetti. Hey, sweets, how's it going up there?" A pause. "Okay, what train will you be on? Good, I'll have Stan meet you at the station. Oh, and when you get here, have I got a surprise for you!" He hung up. "Viv has finished her business and is taking a train back down here. She'll get in at six-fifteen, so will you ask Stan to meet her?"

"Sure," Stone said, picking up the phone and paging Stan. He gave him his instructions, then hung up. Then his phone rang.

"Hello?" It was Felicity. "Hello, Felicity. He listened for a moment. "Viv is going to be on the same train, so find her, and the two of you can have a chat on the way down. Why don't you come to dinner and stay the night? See you then." He hung up. "Felicity is coming down on Viv's train, so she'll be here for dinner."

"And the night," Dino corrected him.

"Well, yes."

"Here's a thought: you can watch your video together. I expect that will get Felicity going."

"Felicity does not require that sort of stimulus," Stone said.

Felicity and Viv came downstairs together, after having freshened up, and entered the library.

Stone and Dino, freshly changed into suits, stood to welcome them.

"How nice to see you again—and so soon," Felicity said, kissing Stone on the ear and letting her tongue flick about.

"Stone and Felicity had lunch in London," Dino explained to his wife.

"You could have driven down with me," Stone said.

"I didn't know until I got back to the shop that I would be free," she said.

Stone poured everyone a drink, and they sat down around the fire.

"Oh," Viv said, "I have news."

"Tell us," Stone replied.

"I had a couple of my people look into the background of your friend Rose, and they came up with an address in Ennismore Mews, Knightsbridge. She lives in a little house there, formerly owned by one Lady Margot Balfour."

"Rose actually told me about that," Stone said, "but without the Lady Balfour part."

"It seems," Felicity said, "that Ms. McGill is, in fact, Lady Margot Balfour."

"No, no," Viv said. "The good lady was supposed to have married the 4th Viscount Oakham last spring . . ."

"But she didn't," Felicity interjected.

"Well, no, she could hardly do that," Viv said, "since her car was T-boned by a gasoline delivery truck when she was on the way to her rehearsal dinner. She and her maid of honor were killed instantly."

19

elicity was, for once, speechless.

"Did I say something wrong?" Viv asked.

"What is your source for that information?" Felicity finally asked.

"A researcher at my London office found a *Times* obituary," Viv said.

"You said this was last spring?"

"April, I believe."

"Looks like somebody forgot to change the name on the Ennismore Mews deed—and the utilities," Stone said.

Viv looked at her watch. "My office is closed," she said. "I'll speak to them again tomorrow."

"My office *never* closes," Felicity said. She stood, walked to where her handbag lay on the sofa, retrieved her phone, and began using it. "Call me the minute you sort this out," she said finally, and hung up.

Stone held her chair for her.

"My people are digging further," Felicity said.

"Have you spoken to Brigadier Fife-Simpson about Rose?" Stone asked.

"I'm not ready to bring him into this," she replied. "And I've instructed my staff to that effect."

They had dessert and were on coffee and brandy when Felicity's handbag rang. She dug out her phone, sat before the fire, and spoke for a few minutes, then hung up. The others joined her.

"Well?" Stone asked.

"Here it is," Felicity said. "Lady Margot Balfour is, indeed, deceased. She had a younger sister named Rose, who, while she was at Oxford, was married to a fellow medical student named John McGill. She divorced him two years ago, and has continued to use his name, but is still listed as Rose Balfour on the medical register. She was also named in her sister's will as sole heir, so she now owns the Ennismore Mews house, or will when the estate is finally sorted out."

"So Rose has not been lying?" Stone asked.

Viv spoke up. "There remains her contention that St. George's Hospital is still located on Hyde Park Corner, which it has not been since 1989."

Stone turned to Felicity. "And do you still contend that MI-6 does not employ a Rose McGill?"

"According to our records," she replied.

"Or a Rose Balfour?"

"That is another question, which I cannot confirm or deny."

"Ahh, I'm relieved to hear that."

"Why are you relieved that she won't confirm or deny it?" Viv asked.

"Because that means that there is a Rose Balfour in their employ."

"Oh, all right," Felicity said. "I'll tell you this much: she became an MI-6 asset while a student at Oxford."

"Only an asset, not an agent?"

"I can neither confirm nor deny that."

Everyone groaned.

"I cannot, at my whim, revise the Official Secrets Act," Felicity said primly.

"Of course not," Stone said, "even when you're among friends."

"I am among friends, for this purpose, only when I am alone in my office," she replied. "That is not to disparage any of you, but in my work, good practice demands extreme caution."

"We entirely understand," Stone said placatingly, while he replenished her brandy.

"And when are you seeing Rose, Stone?" Viv asked.

"This weekend."

"When, this weekend?" Felicity asked.

"She said she'll call me when she gets her schedule sorted out." He leaned over and whispered, "We're on safe ground tonight."

"I heard that," Dino said.

"No, you did not," Stone replied, fixing him with his gaze.

"Right, I didn't hear that, I just assumed it."

"Never assume," Felicity said.

"You know," Dino said, "if I never told anybody anything in my office, and if I didn't assume a lot, I'd never get anything done."

"It's not about what you do," Felicity said, "it's about what you don't do."

"I'll try and remember that," Dino said.

Felicity put the back of her hand to her lips and yawned. "If you'll all forgive me," she said, "I believe I will get some rest."

"Let me show you the way," Stone said, rising.

20

Brigadier Roger Fife-Simpson rapped sharply with his heavy umbrella handle on the gray steel door in an alley off Charing Cross Road. A tiny window in the door opened. "Fife-Simpson," he said to the eye behind the door.

"Wrong address," a muffled voice said sharply, and the window closed.

Fife-Simpson rapped again, this time harder. The tiny door opened. "Yes?"

"I work here," the brigadier replied.

"Name?"

"Brigadier Roger Fife-Simpson."

"One moment," the voice said, and the tiny door closed again.

The brigadier, who was not accustomed to being kept waiting on a doorstep, stood tapping a well-shod foot. Half a minute passed, and he put umbrella to steel once again.

This time, the big door opened, and a man wearing the black uniform of a commissionaire, an association of retired military people who provided reception and security services to businesses and some government officers, ushered him in. "Briefcase and umbrella on the moving belt," he said, pointing. His uniform sleeve wore the stripes of a master sergeant.

Fife-Simpson set them down and watched them stop under a machine of some sort, then watched as the two objects were x-rayed.

"Hat," the commissionaire said, removing it for him, turning out the lining and feeling it everywhere, then handed it back to him. "Overcoat off, please," the man said.

Fife-Simpson shucked off the garment and handed it to him.

The man felt every square inch of the coat, then handed it back to him and gave him a very thorough frisking, not forgetting his crotch.

The commissionaire handed him a slip of paper. "Collect your things. Elevator to the sixth floor, turn left, end of the corridor," he said.

Fife-Simpson collected his things, then got on the elevator and pressed the button, glancing at the paper. *Room 630.* The elevator arrived and opened, and he turned left and marched down the corridor. The door straight ahead of him opened before he could reach for the knob, and a middle-aged woman in a frumpy business suit greeted him. "Good morning, Mr. Fife-Simpson," she said.

"Brigadier Fife-Simpson," he replied. He then noticed that they were standing not in an office, but a kind of library, lined with steel shelving and with a matching conference table in the middle of the room, surrounded by a dozen steel chairs.

"Have a seat," the woman said. "Your office is not ready just yet. Someone will come for you." She stepped out of the room, closing the door behind her and leaving Fife-Simpson alone.

The brigadier looked around the room in disgust. He hung his British Warm coat on a peg beside the door, along with his umbrella, then set his briefcase and trilby hat on the table and sat down. He opened the briefcase, extracted a copy of the *Daily Telegraph*, and began reading the newspaper. Waiting was a skill best learned in the Royal Marines, he thought, where much of it was required.

Twenty-one minutes later the door was opened by a younger, better-dressed woman. "Good morning, Brigadier," she said. "If you would come with me, please."

Once again, Fife-Simpson gathered his things and followed her at a quick clip down the hallway. As they passed a set of elegant double doors on their left, she said, without slowing down, "Director's office," then led on to the end of the hallway, where a single door was marked with a shiny brass plate, reading DEPUTY DIRECTOR. She opened it, revealing an oak-paneled room with a desk, two chairs, a small conference table at one end with four more chairs, and two doors to his right. There was also a sofa, suitable for napping, he observed.

"Closet and loo there," she said, pointing. Then she took his coat, hat, and umbrella from him and hung them in the closet. She produced a medium-sized buff envelope and shook the contents out onto the desktop. "Your credentials," she said, hanging a plastic card—with his photograph, rank, and name— around his neck by a ribbon. She handed him a British passport, bound in red leather. "Your diplomatic passport," she said. "Sign it, please." She handed him a pen.

He opened the passport, read it to see that the information about him was correct, then signed it and returned the pen to her.

She handed him a printed sheet of paper. "Please take this to the armory, in subbasement two, where you will be issued with a weapon." She indicated two sheets of paper on the desk. "Please sign the document on the left, which is the Official Secrets Act, and the one on the right, which is a receipt for the ID card and the passport."

He signed them. "When may I see the director?"

"On Monday morning," she said. "Ten AM. She is away for the weekend."

"How may I contact her, if it should become necessary?"

"Call the main switchboard here, and they will locate her and patch you through. If she is available," she added. She walked to a bookcase, took a book from a shelf, and handed it to him. "This is a history of the intelligence services, combined with a manual of conduct for officers. You should finish reading it before Monday morning."

"Right," he said. "Do I have a secretary?"

"I am your secretary," she said. "My name is Marcia Cartwright; my office is next door, to your left, and you may ring or summon me by pressing the green button on your telephone. The red button is for the director."

"Thank you, Ms. Cartwright," he said.

"Please call me Marcia or Cartwright. We're informal here—most of the time. The director's secretary is Mrs. Prudence Green. She prefers to be addressed as Mrs. Green."

"Thank you again," he said, then sat down at his desk, waited for her to close the door, then opened the book she had given him and began to read.

....

Two hours passed, then he closed the book, picked up the weapon requisition, and made his way down to subbasement two. The door to the armory stood open, revealing a wooden counter backed by a heavy steel screen. He walked in, found a bell on the counter, and rang it.

A uniformed Royal Marines master sergeant became visible through the screen, then opened the door. "Brigadier Fife-Simpson, I presume, sir," he said.

"Correct," the brigadier replied.

"Welcome to MI-6, sir," the man said. "How may I help you?"

Fife-Simpson put the requisition on the countertop. "I wish to be armed," he replied.

"Of course, sir. What sort of weapon did you have in mind?"

"Something small, light, and concealable, perhaps a .380 semiautomatic."

"I believe I have just the thing, sir," the man said. "One moment." He disappeared through the screen and returned with a wooden box. "Here we are," he said, opening it. "A Colt Government .380, small, flat, and light. And a small, but effective, silencer."

"Perfect," the brigadier replied.

"What sort of holster do you require, sir?"

"Shoulder, I should think."

The sergeant disappeared again and returned with a cardboard box. "If you'll just slip off your jacket, I'll fit it for you, sir."

Fife-Simpson did so, and the sergeant slipped him into the leather and adjusted the straps. "How's that, sir?"

The brigadier shoved the pistol into the holster. "Perfect," he said.

"As to ammunition, would fifty rounds do you?"

"That would be good."

"Any preference, sir? We like the Federal Hydra-Shok."

"Very good."

The sergeant left and returned with a plastic box; he removed the pistol from its holster, popped the magazine, and loaded it and the spare in the box speedily. He tucked the pistol back into its holster, then inserted the spare magazine and the silencer into their receptacles on the holster. "There you are, sir. Is there anything else you'd like?"

"I'd like a knife, please. A switchblade, if you have it."

"Of course, sir." He left and returned with another wooden box, containing a six-inch-long knife. He flicked it open and handed it to the brigadier. "Careful with it, sir. It's razor-sharp. You could shave with it, in a pinch. And the blade is five and three-quarter inches."

Fife-Simpson hefted the knife, felt its blade, folded it, and slipped it into a hip pocket, where his tailor had made a place for it.

"Sign here, sir," the sergeant said, handing him the form and a pen.

The brigadier signed it, slipped on his jacket, and picked up the ammunition box. "Thank you, Sergeant," he said. "Good day." He left the room and marched back to his office, where he found on his desk a roast beef sandwich and a thermos of coffee and a note from Cartwright. *There's a canteen on subcellar 3, if you prefer.*

21

Stone awoke the following morning to see Felicity coming out of her bathroom adjusting her clothing. "Must flee," she said. "I had a text a few minutes ago, and my presence is required in London."

Stone rang Stan and asked him to transport her to the dock.

Felicity bent over and kissed his penis. "Thank you for a lovely evening," she said to it.

"You are most welcome, as always," Stone replied.

She kissed him lingeringly on the lips and departed.

Stone rang downstairs for breakfast.

Dame Felicity arrived in the little alley off Shaftesbury Avenue and pulled up to the steel door. As she stepped from her car the door opened, and the commissionaire greeted her. "Good morning, Director," he said, giving her a little bow. "By the way," he said, "your new deputy arrived yesterday."

"So I've heard," Felicity said. She took the elevator to the sixth floor and, noting the closed door at the end of the hallway, opened her own door and walked in. Her two secretaries rose and greeted her; Cartwright followed her into her office.

"Director," she said, "Brigadier Fife-Simpson arrived yesterday and is waiting in his office to see you. Shall I summon him?"

"Not yet, my dear," Felicity replied. "Not until I've thought of something for him to do. Do you have any ideas?"

"How much substance are we talking about?" Cartwright asked.

"Not very much."

"I see. May I have a few minutes to think about that, ma'am?"

"Of course. Let me know when you've come up with something."

As Cartwright reached her desk, her phone rang, and she picked it up. "Good morning, Director's office."

"This is Brigadier Fife-Simpson," a gruff male voice said.

"Good morning, Brigadier. How may I help you?"

"I wish to see the director at the earliest possible moment."

"The director is occupied at the moment and has a full schedule for today. Let me call you back when she can fit you in."

"Right." He hung up.

"Mrs. Green," Cartwright said to the other secretary, "think of something for Fife-Simpson to do."

"Go bugger himself, perhaps?" she replied.

"As much as I'd like to suggest that, perhaps not."

"Oh, well. You asked."

Mrs. Green had a thought. She rapped on the director's door, was told to enter, and she entered. "I've had a thought, Director," she said.

"Pray tell me."

"Perhaps an inspection tour of some of our stations?"

"Primary stations, or secondary?"

"Perhaps both?"

"It's a lovely thought," Felicity said, "but he might twig to what we're doing. However . . ." She thought for a moment. "Please get me Lance Cabot."

"Of course, Director," Mrs. Green said, smiling. She went back to her desk, placed the call, then announced to the director, "Mr. Cabot for you on the overseas line."

Felicity picked up her phone. "Lance, how are you?" she asked brightly.

"Very well, thank you, Felicity. And you?"

"Oh, very well. Lance, are you acquainted with a Brigadier Roger Fife-Simpson?"

"I seem to recall a colonel by that name."

"He's been promoted."

"Sort of a ramrod type?"

"That's the one. He's been appointed my new deputy."

"Somehow I feel that you did not select him."

"You might say that," Felicity said. "He'll be doing a bit of orientation with our outlying stations, as well as with our allies."

"Ah, I see."

"And I was wondering if one or more of your people might, ah, orient him for a week or so."

"I expect I can find someone to handle that—someone I don't like very much."

"Ideal," Felicity said. "May I have him arrive at Langley the day after tomorrow?"

"Certainly. I'll be leaving that afternoon. I can see him in the morning, then hand him off to a minion."

"How perfect," Felicity said. "I'll tell him to report to you at ten AM."

"I'll have staff accumulate some reading for him, then give him the ten-cent tour."

"Wonderful. Are you coming my way?"

"As a matter of fact, I am," Lance replied.

"May I entertain you at lunch?"

"That would be delightful. Thursday all right?"

"One o'clock at the Reform Club, then?"

"See you there."

"Fly safely." Felicity hung up and buzzed Cartwright. "I'll see the brigadier now," she said.

Fife-Simpson was started from a doze by a buzzing noise. It took a moment for him to realize that it was coming from his telephone, and he picked it up. "Yes?"

"Brigadier," Cartwright said, "the director will see you now." She hung up.

Fife-Simpson leapt to his feet, got into his suit jacket, checked the mirror on the back of the door, then trotted down the hall. He was shown into the director's office immediately.

"Good morning, Brigadier," Felicity said, indicating that he should sit.

"Good morning, Director," he said, taking the chair opposite her.

"First of all, may I welcome you to the service?"

"Thank you, ma'am."

"I have a task for you, which I believe you will find enlightening. It's the sort of thing I would ordinarily do myself, but I find myself a little overwhelmed at the moment."

"Whatever I can do, Director."

"Good. Pack a bag and present yourself, at ten o'clock in the morning the day after tomorrow in Langley, Virginia, to Lance Cabot, the director of central intelligence, at CIA headquarters."

Fife-Simpson sat up straighter. "And what am I to do there?"

"You are to look and listen, ask questions, and, if necessary, answer some, from a selection of the Agency's people, with an eye toward assessing the current relationship between the CIA and our service, and looking for ways to improve it. Stay as long as you need to, and on return, write a report summarizing your observations and your suggestions, for my eyes only. I may see fit to distribute it to a short list of our people at a later date."

"I'd be very happy to, ma'am," he said.

"And while you're over there, pop into our embassy in Washington, pay your respects to the ambassador, and have a talk with our station chief and his deputy. Find out what they're working on, and see what, if anything, they need to do their work better."

"How long should I stay, Director?"

"As long as it takes. Cartwright will arrange your schedule and book your airline seat and hotel accommodations. You should probably stay in D.C., since Langley is in a more rural setting."

The brigadier stood and nearly saluted, but caught himself. "Thank you, Director. I'll report upon return."

"Very good, Brigadier," she said, then turned to open a file and gaze at it, dismissing him.

Fife-Simpson marched out. Felicity breathed a sigh of relief.

22

Stone was reading in the library the following day when Rose let herself in, then sat in his lap. "Watch out for Winston Churchill," he said, moving the book to a side table. "You could bruise yourself."

She kissed him fulsomely. "I'm glad to see you," she said.

"I'm glad to hear it," he replied, kissing her back. "Your arrival was the signal to the staff to get lunch ready. Would you like something first?"

"Perhaps a glass of sherry."

Stone got up, took a decanter from the bar, and poured her a glass.

"Mmmm," she said, tasting it. "Delicious. What is it?"

"It's a dry Oloroso," Stone replied. "Called Dos Cortados."

"I thought Olorosos were sweet," she said.

"Most are, this one isn't." He poured himself one, and they settled into the Chesterfield sofa.

"Tell me," she said. "I've heard from a friend or two that someone has been asking questions about me. Would that have anything to do with you?"

"I expect it has something to do with the fact that I have

two very good friends who want to know all about everybody who has anything to do with me."

"I expect I can guess who they are."

"I expect you can."

"Was there anything they didn't tell you that you want to know?"

"A great deal, but right now only one thing."

"And what is that?"

"Why did you place St. George's Hospital at Hyde Park Corner?"

"Well, I didn't want to tell anybody that I'm working down at Tooting," she said, laughing. "Hyde Park Corner sounds so much better."

"Perhaps to anyone who doesn't possess an *A to Z Guide*," Stone said. "I'm surprised to know that you haven't been trained to lie better than that."

"They didn't train me to lie at medical school."

"Then that explains why you do it so badly."

"I expect so."

"I'm curious, though. Why did you hang on to your married name when you were divorced?"

"Because I didn't want my fellow students and professors to know that I was being divorced," she said. "I just didn't want to explain. However, I can tell you that I recently signed a number of letters to various organizations, including the medical registry, informing them that my name has been changed to Mary Rose McGill Balfour, and to correct their records to that effect. I left the McGill in there so that anyone looking for me by that name might find it."

"How transparent of you," Stone said. "So now you're a farmer's daughter again?"

"I always was."

"The only McGill in the county of Rutland is a bookmaker."

"That must have confused your nosy friends."

"Momentarily."

"Do you have any other names besides Stone and Barrington?"

"My middle name is Malon, which was my father's Christian name, but I never used it, because each time I did I had to explain that it was pronounced *May-lon*."

"Good thinking."

The table was set, and they were called to lunch. "Where are Dino and Viv?" Rose asked.

"They went riding and took a picnic lunch with them."

"Good. I have you all to myself."

"Entirely."

"Any other questions?"

"How does MI-6 list your name in their records?"

Rose sighed. "I suppose they would have listed it somewhere as Balfour. I was a student at the time. Mind you, if they knew you knew that, they'd take you out and shoot you."

"That's what they'd like you to think," Stone said. "What did you do for them as a student?"

"Watched out for communists, of course. They still haven't recovered from that nest of spies at Oxford and Cambridge. Kim Philby is a name that still raises temperatures at MI-6."

"Did you report any communists?"

"Only two, and they were both well-known to be members of

the Young Communist League, so I wasn't really giving anything away."

"Did they ever call on you for other services?"

"They keep a list of medical types that they believe to be reliable. Once, at their request, I removed a bullet from a young man's arse."

"One of theirs or one of yours?"

"I never asked, and they never told me. As soon as I had stitched him up and given him a dose of antibiotics, they spirited him away. I never saw his face, since I was working at the other end."

"How did you fall into the clutches of Roger Fife-Simpson?"

"I met him at Station Two a week before I met you. The service asked me to go up there and give some basic wound-repair instruction to a small group of spies-in-training—applying tourniquets, setting broken limbs, stitching up oranges, that sort of thing—nothing an Eagle Scout couldn't handle."

"What do you think of the man?"

"I think of him very little. I don't suppose I spoke to him or was spoken to more than three or four times, including dinner here."

"Felicity thinks you are his creature," Stone said.

"Hardly. He's not the sort I'd like to be the creature of. There was talk about him in the mess. He's apparently a very efficient killer with almost any sort of weapon. There was a story about him dealing with some IRA types in Belfast."

"I heard that story. Impressive, if true. Do you know what he did before landing at MI-6?"

"Not a clue. I had the impression at dinner that the landing wasn't Felicity's idea."

"I have that impression, too."

"He must have some connections in the government, though—probably the Foreign Office, since someone there foisted him upon Felicity."

"Where did you hear that?"

"I didn't. I just figured it out. Perhaps I'm wrong."

"Perhaps not."

"Do you see Dame Felicity often?"

"When we're both in residence down here."

Rose leaned forward on her elbows. "Is she very good in bed?"

Stone was saved from that question by Dino and Viv, returned from their picnic, joining them for coffee.

23

Lance Cabot was in a meeting with an operations team about to embark on a mission when he was handed a note. *A Brigadier Fife-Simpson to see you*, it read.

"Tell him to wait," he said, then continued with his meeting.

Forty minutes later the meeting broke up, and he buzzed his secretary. "Send in the brigadier," he said.

A moment later they were shaking hands. Fife-Simpson was dressing a lot better than the last time he had seen him, Lance thought.

"Lance, how are you?"

"Very well, Roger," Lance replied, waving him to a seat. "Coffee?"

"I had some while I was waiting," Roger replied.

"Yes, sorry about that. I was sending a couple of young men off to their deaths."

"I don't suppose you could tell me about their mission."

"You 'don't suppose' correctly," Lance said. "First, we'd have to clear you from your birth to this date, and you know how long that sort of thing takes."

"Well, yes, I suppose I do," Roger replied.

"Tell me, how long did it take to clear you at MI-6, after Admiral Sir Timothy Barnes shoved you down their throats?"

"Well, I don't think it was quite like that," Roger replied uncomfortably.

"Of course it was, Roger," Lance replied. "You don't actually think Dame Felicity was glad to see you, do you?"

"Dame Felicity has been very cordial," Roger said stiffly.

"You and Sir Tim were at some school or other at the same time, weren't you?"

"Yes, we were midshipmen at Dartmouth. He chose the Royal Navy, I chose the Royal Marines."

"And now he's First Sea Lord, I believe?"

"That is correct."

"In a perfect position to throw a bone to an old midshipman chum."

"I suppose you could put it that way."

"The way I heard it was that you were about to be passed over for promotion for the second time, which would have necessitated retirement, when Sir Tim saved your ass, pulled you back from the brink. Did you once save his life, or something?"

"Something like that," Roger replied.

"No, no, not his life, his career, wasn't it? Sort of the same thing, I guess."

"I'd rather not go into that."

"Why not? Being queer isn't a crime in Britain anymore—though it is, perhaps, a no-no for a high-ranking military member of the government. Whose arm did old Tim twist? The foreign minister's, perhaps? After all, MI-6 comes under his purview."

"Lance, I don't think you should bandy about notions of that sort," the brigadier said. "They might come back to bite you on the arse."

"Of course, you're right, Roger, and I try to keep my ass out of the way of people like Sir Timothy."

"Good. I'm looking forward to seeing a bit of your shop," Fife-Simpson said, desperately trying to change the subject.

Lance scratched his head. "There was another incident in which you and Sir Tim participated, I believe. Let's see, what was it?"

Lance's phone buzzed, and he picked it up. "Send her in, please." He hung up and turned to Fife-Simpson. "One of our brilliant young ladies is going to be your shepherd in our meadow."

Fife-Simpson was vastly relieved that Lance had been interrupted.

There was a rap on the door, and a middle-aged woman with a cropped haircut and dressed in a baggy tweed suit entered the room.

"Ah, here we are," Lance said. "Meg Tillman, this is Brigadier Sir . . . Excuse me, I'm getting ahead of myself . . . Brigadier Roger Fife-Simpson, the shiny new deputy director of MI-6, an organization that has never had a deputy director until the brigadier came along and impressed everybody. Roger, Meg is known around our shop as one of our brightest minds, and she is an expert on our history and mission. She's going to give you the two-and-a-half-dollar tour of both Langley and Camp Peary, our training facility, and answer all your questions."

Lance stood up. "Oh, I remember the other thing now. You and Sir Tim served in Belfast together, didn't you?"

"We did. We were both young lieutenants at the time." He made to move toward his guide, but Lance held him back.

"Let's see, as legend has it, you two young fellows were in search of—how shall I put it?—just the *right* sort of bar . . . weren't you? And you somehow got it wrong and ended up in a nest of IRA vipers and were set upon. You managed to occupy their attention long enough for Lieutenant Tim to fetch a squad of British military policemen, and they got to you in the nick of time, just before the Irish would have cut your balls off."

"That's not quite the way it happened," Roger said, blushing.

"Oh, of course it was. I was in Belfast at the time, at the Royal Ulster Hospital's casualty ward, getting a flesh wound attended to, when they brought you in. You were a mess. Sir Tim was very upset about it, I recall, and you spent a few days in hospital, closely attended by your friend."

"It was quite different . . ."

"Well, Meg," Lance interrupted, "off with you both, and don't skip anything. I expect the brigadier would love to see our technical services shop—the Brits always love that." He leaned over and whispered, "In your travels, be sure and introduce the brigadier to Mr. Wu at Camp Peary." He shooed them out the door and shut it behind them, then heaved a great sigh of satisfaction.

Lance dug out his cell phone and looked up a number. "Hello, Stone?"

"Yes, Lance," Stone replied.

"Where are you?"

"In England," Stone said.

"Oh, that's right, that's why I'm calling. I'm headed to London this evening, and I wondered if I could drop down to the Beaulieu River and see your magnificent house there this weekend. Can you put me up?"

"Of course, Lance. Call me from London and give me your arrival time, and I'll have you met at the station."

"Not to worry, I'll be driving, or, rather, driven. Look for me in time for drinks on Friday. Shall I bring a dinner suit?"

"I suppose so. Shall I invite Felicity?"

"Please do. I'll have some amusing stories to tell you both about a mutual friend who's visiting us as we speak."

24

O n Friday, a Strategic Services Gulfstream 4 picked up Dino and Viv for the trip back across the Atlantic. "This is a bit of a demotion from the G-600, isn't it?" Stone needled Viv.

"I'm told it will go the distance, and that's all we require," she replied, kissing him goodbye. "I feel better leaving you in the clutches of Rose, since we made an honest woman of her."

"Come now, she was always an honest woman. We just had to find it out." He gave Dino a hug, slapped him on the back, and followed him aboard the aircraft. "Nicer than I thought," he said, looking around the cabin, "and you have only a couple of companions to share it with." There were two other Strategic Services executives aboard.

"I'll live," Dino said. Then Stone deplaned and drove away with Rose in his golf cart, as the G-4 taxied to the end of the runway for takeoff.

"Viv must be pretty high up in her company," Rose said, "to be picked up at a private airstrip for a transatlantic flight."

"She is the number-two person, after Mike Freeman, who is chairman and CEO. It doesn't hurt that Dino is the New York

City police commissioner, and as such, he's the sort of person worth doing favors for."

"Did you build the airstrip?"

"No, the Royal Air Force was kind enough to do that during World War II. They used it to test new bombers and fighters, and to launch aircraft flying to France to parachute members of the Special Operations Executive into that country, to execute skullduggery against the Nazis."

"Did the Germans ever bomb it?"

"No, it didn't appear on any aeronautical charts, and it was heavily disguised in the daytime by fake farmhouses and hayricks on wheels that could be rolled away after the sun went down. Clever people, you Brits."

"What shall I wear to dinner this evening?"

"It's black tie for me, so dress accordingly."

"Do we have guests?"

"We do: Dame Felicity and a gentleman named Lance Cabot, who some say is not a gentleman. He is the director of Central Intelligence for the U.S. and, as such, the director of the CIA."

"Spooky dinner," Rose said.

"Well put."

Brigadier Roger Fife-Simpson stepped into a large, well-lit room that appeared to be a laboratory, except for the many objects lining its countertops. He was introduced to the director of technical services by his escort, Meg, and handed a small black case. "Open it," the director said. Fife-Simpson released the two latches and found inside a clarinet, broken down into its pieces. "I'm afraid I don't play," he said.

"Now press down firmly on the mouthpiece in its cap."

The brigadier did so, and the inside of the case flipped up to reveal another compartment underneath. Inside were a small pistol, a magazine, three metal tubes, and a slim telescopic sight. The director screwed the three pieces together, snapped the sight into place, and then handed the assembled weapon to Fife-Simpson. "There you are," he said, "perfectly equipped for an assassination."

The brigadier sighted around the room. "How accurate is it?"

"To a hairbreadth," the director replied. "Oh, and here's something else we've developed." He handed his visitor a handsome fountain pen.

Fife-Simpson unscrewed the cap, inspected the pen closely, then felt the nib. He snatched his hand away. "It stung me," he said.

"Sorry about that," the director said. "Don't worry, it's not the cyanide version." He turned to an assistant. "Antidote, please," and the young man began rummaging through drawers.

"I'm sorry this is taking so long," he said to the brigadier. "I expect you're feeling drowsy."

Fife-Simpson responded by sagging into Meg's arms. She and the director transferred the limp form to a sofa on one side of the room. "I'm afraid he'll be out for half an hour or so," the director said.

"Oh, good. I can use the rest," Meg said.

The director received a capped syringe from his assistant and handed it to Meg. "Stick him with that when you're ready to have him back. It works quickly on any part of the body and can be administered through clothing." He went back to work, and Meg sat down on the unused end of the sofa, glad for some rest from the brigadier.

....

Lance arrived at Windward Hall from London as evening fell. Stone and Rose came out the front door to greet him. Stone introduced Rose to Lance. "We're just going down to fetch Dame Felicity," he said. "Come with us."

They got into the golf cart and drove the quarter mile to the dock, where her boatman was just making fast the boat's lines. Stone helped Felicity ashore, and since everyone now knew everyone, introductions were unnecessary.

Back at the house, Geoffrey served them drinks.

"Thank you for taking the brigadier off my hands for a bit," Felicity said to Lance.

"Speak of the devil," Lance said. "I had a call a few minutes ago saying that Fife-Simpson was just rendered unconscious in our technical service department by a sting from a hypodermic disguised as a fountain pen—inadvertently, of course."

"Of course," Felicity replied.

"They'll bring him around soon."

They were called to dinner, and an old claret was uncorked, tasted, decanted, and poured.

"You said on the phone that you had met Fife-Simpson before?" Felicity asked.

"Yes. The first instance occurred in the casualty ward of a Belfast hospital. I had been observing the work of the Army and Royal Marines in the city and received a superficial bullet wound for my trouble, and while I was being treated, Fife-Simpson—a lieutenant at the time—was brought in. He had been badly beaten, and a friend, another lieutenant, was very concerned. The friend told me that he and a squad of military policemen had extracted young Roger from the clutches of an IRA scrum. The lieutenant said that Fife-Simpson had asked to be taken to a gay bar, but there was a mix-up. The lieutenant, by the way, was to become Admiral Sir Timothy Barnes, now serving as the First Sea Lord."

"Oh, is the brigadier gay?" Felicity asked.

"I don't think so. Rather, he is a gay basher, or, as some say, a gay trasher, who has helped along his career in the military by forming friendships with homosexual officers. Then, when it suited him, to gently blackmail his way into better fitness reports and promotions."

"That is disgusting," Felicity said.

"Do you know, Stone," Rose suddenly interjected, "the brigadier asked me if you were gay."

Felicity and Lance burst out laughing.

"Don't worry," Rose said, placing a hand on Stone's arm, "I'll give you a good report."

More laughter.

25

hey were on port and Stilton when Lance surprised Stone, and possibly everyone else, by asking Felicity, "Do you wish the brigadier returned to your service in one piece?"

"My desires conflict with my duty," Felicity said without missing a beat, "as it is seen to be by my betters."

"You surely must not wish to have your service used as a dumping ground for the unsuitable," Lance said.

"Certain members of the government find us useful for that purpose, at least on this occasion. What would you do in my position, Lance?"

"My service would regurgitate that man into the lap of whoever sent him to me."

"We British are less direct," Felicity said, "especially when dealing at the ministerial level."

"Do you suspect the foreign minister? Specifically, I mean, not as part of a group."

"I would not be shocked to find his fingerprints on the transfer document."

"Put another way: Do you think the FM has something to fear from his freshly minted brigadier?"

"The FM has been married to the same woman for more than thirty years, and during that time, has bestirred himself to sire a single son and heir, now twenty-eight, a chinless wonder who is employed in the nether ranks of his ministry, as a kind of greeter and handler of visiting dignitaries from beyond Calais."

"And what has been scribbled in the margins of your file on the FM over the years?"

"Let me put it this way," Felicity said. "There have been no rumors of women in his life."

"I see."

"I expect you do, Lance."

Lance sipped his port and nibbled at his cheese. "Is there a member of his staff who has outlasted all the others over time?"

Felicity thought about it. "There is," she replied. "One Sir Ellery Bascombe, a baronet, who was in the FM's class at Eton—and who has personally attended him ever since the fourth form. I've heard them referred to, once or twice, as 'the old married couple.'"

"And does Sir Ellery have any naval connections?"

"After Eton, the young man was not able to find a place at a suitable university, so the family sent him off to Dartmouth, where he was a classmate of Timothy Barnes—and Roger Fife-Simpson. He graduated, after a fashion, but was not commissioned, so the FM, then a party functionary, took him in. He has been a body man to his mentor, now the FM, in one form or another, since that time."

"Does he travel with the FM?"

"Nearly always."

"Ah," Lance said. "Perhaps you have found your way to the heart—or the jugular—of the foreign minister."

26

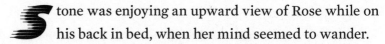tone was enjoying an upward view of Rose while on his back in bed, when her mind seemed to wander.

"Why, do you think," she asked, in the midst of regular movements, "that Lance Cabot would speak as he did about the brigadier in our presence?"

"Yours and mine?" he asked.

"Yes. I can well understand why he would make those remarks to Felicity in private, but why also to you and me?" She stopped moving.

"Pardon me," Stone said, "but may we delay the discussion of Lance's motives, which are always obscure, for a few minutes?" He gave her a little thrust to bring her mind back to the business at hand.

"Of course," she said, responding to his action. She concentrated her mind until they had both reached the peak of their desire and then descended rapidly.

"Now," she said, tucking her head into his shoulder, "where were we?"

"Lance's motives," Stone replied, still panting.

"Which are always obscure?"

"Always. I think it's the nature of his work that causes him not to want anyone to know all of what he is thinking at any given moment."

"What do you think he was thinking?" she asked.

"First," Stone said, "I think he wanted to give Felicity the ammunition she might need to deal with the brigadier."

"Obviously. And beyond that?"

"Beyond that is the no-man's-land of Lance's consciousness."

"I think Lance knows the brigadier much better than he has admitted to us," she said.

"That's an interesting observation," Stone admitted.

"After all," Rose said, "he did offer to dismember the man."

"I think that was most probably metaphorical."

"Do you think Lance incapable of cutting someone into pieces?"

"Personally? Probably not. I do think him capable of ordering someone else to do it, though in the subtlest sort of way."

"So do I," Rose replied.

"On such short acquaintance?"

"I'm rather good at making accurate assumptions about people on short acquaintance," she said. "You, for instance."

"How so?"

"I learned a good deal about you from the way you handled Fife-Simpson while flat on your back in a hospital bed."

"I confess, I don't like being pushed around."

"Hardly anyone does, but you engaged him in a way he was unaccustomed to, and set him back on his heels. That requires character. But you didn't engage him physically."

"Well, I thought I had a broken foot," Stone said.

Rose laughed. "Discretion is a part of character, too, as well as valor."

"I'll try to remember that."

"Tell me, have you often engaged in physicality?"

"Didn't we just do that?"

"I was referring to fighting."

"I was a police officer for many years, and as such, I had to be ready to meet physical resistance. People don't like being handcuffed and stuffed in the back of a police car, and they often resist."

"How did you handle that?"

"As quickly as possible. I learned early on that, in a fight, the first blow is very important. Properly struck, it discourages further argument."

"That's good advice," she said. "I'll keep it in mind."

"Are you planning to fight someone?"

"Not at the moment, but you never know."

"I'll tread carefully around you, then."

"Not too carefully, please."

And a moment later, they were back at it.

Lance finished a late lunch, got out his cell phone, tapped in the code to scramble the signal, and called CIA headquarters.

"Meg Tillman," a husky voice said.

"Is our guest still with us?"

"He is, and bored rigid, I should think. He plans to drive back to D.C. at midday."

"Before he departs, take him down to Camp Peary, equip him with protective gear and a knife of his choice, and introduce him to Wu. When he's done there, send him on his way with a hearty handshake and a slap on the back."

"Understood," she replied. "I think I speak for all the people he's met when I say, 'good riddance.'"

Lance laughed, then hung up.

Meg put away her phone and went to find the brigadier, who was in the break room, finishing a cup of tea. "Do you have time for one more visit?" she asked.

"To where?"

"Our training facility. The director thought you might enjoy meeting someone there."

Fife-Simpson sighed, put down his teacup, and followed her from the building. They crossed a hundred yards of well-kept lawn and entered another building.

"We've heard that you prefer the knife as a weapon," Meg said, "and we thought our approach to attack and defense might interest you."

"Of course," Fife-Simpson replied.

She took him into an equipment room and supplied him with a thick canvas jumpsuit and a protective upper-body garment that, when zipped up, gave him a shield from his chin to his crotch, and the sleeves of which stopped below his knuckle. "Suit up. You can put your things in a locker, there. I'll be waiting through that door." She pointed.

Fife-Simpson liked the garment he was donning; he thought it might soothe the fears of some of his students at Station Two. He opened the door and stepped into a room of about twelve by eighteen feet, with a thickly padded floor and walls, up to about six feet. Meg was sitting on a bench at his right, and she stood up and beckoned him to a cabinet, opening the doors to reveal a couple dozen knives and other hand weapons.

"Please select something," she said.

Fife-Simpson chose an ordinary-looking, but very sharp, field knife. "This, I should think," he said.

"Good," Meg replied. "Now, may I introduce you to Mr. Wu?"

Fife-Simpson turned and found an Asian man standing in the center of the room, dressed in gym shorts and nothing else. He appeared to be unarmed, and the brigadier had not heard him enter. The man beckoned, then pointed at a spot on the padded floor, about six feet in front of him.

Fife-Simpson walked out onto the floor and stopped.

Wu stood, feet slightly apart, empty hands at his sides. He had thick, cropped black hair and bland features. He beckoned with both hands. "Attack me, please," he said.

Fife-Simpson shook his head and said, "You are unarmed. I have you at a disadvantage."

"Perhaps not," Wu replied. "Attack me, please," he repeated.

Fife-Simpson felt a trickle of fear run down his bowels, but he shook it off, assumed a fighting stance, and circled to his left.

Wu turned with him, but made no other movement.

Fife-Simpson feinted a couple of times, but Wu had no reaction. Oh, what the hell, Fife-Simpson thought to himself, and lunged at the man's face. He was very quick, but Wu was quicker. He caught the brigadier's wrist, and Fife-Simpson found himself on his belly, his own knife blade pressed against his throat. What the hell was that? he asked himself.

Wu took the knife away and stood up, beckoning Fife-Simpson

to do the same. He tossed the knife to the brigadier, who caught it blade first, cutting his finger.

"Again," Wu said, beckoning.

Fife-Simpson was angry and embarrassed now and did not hold back. He feinted, and tossed the knife from one hand to the other, a maneuver that usually worried his opponents.

Wu simply caught the knife in midair and tossed it back to his attacker, who was struck in the chest by the blade.

Fife-Simpson was grateful for the protective gear now, because without it he would have had a knife blade in his heart. Wu was still beckoning with both hands.

The brigadier recovered the knife and, with no hesitation, flung himself feet first into a leg tackle, bringing Wu to his knees, but no further. There was the flash of a hand and Fife-Simspon found himself flat on his back, with the knife blade laid against his cheek, the tip a quarter-inch from his eye.

Wu looked at Meg questioningly. She gave him a slight nod.

Fife-Simpson was yanked to his feet, and the knife was tossed to him again.

"Once more," Wu said softly.

Fife-Simpson was humiliated and furious now. He drew himself into a coil—his left arm before him, bent at the elbow, fist clenched—and flung himself at Wu, slashing back and forth, a maneuver designed to hit his opponent anywhere, and with enough force to mark his body and bring blood.

Fife-Simpson found himself flying through the air. He struck the padded wall with more force than he had expended, then collapsed in a heap. He felt a warm trickle down one side of his nose, which found his lips and tasted a little salty.

"Enough!" Meg called out.

Fife-Simpson staggered to his feet, blinded in one eye by blood.

"Over here," Meg said.

Fife-Simpson staggered across the matted floor to where she stood. A young man stood beside her, holding what appeared to be a fishing tackle case.

She stripped the protective clothing off him. "Lie down on the bench, face up," Meg said.

Fife-Simpson followed her every instruction instantly, and the young man spent several minutes suturing and then bandaging his forehead and finger.

A half hour later, Fife-Simpson was driving his car through the gate of Camp Peary and onto the public road, following instructions to the motorway back to Washington, wondering what the hell had happened to him, and why.

27

ver breakfast the next morning, Lance told Stone and Rose about Fife-Simpson's experience at the CIA and Camp Peary.

"Was he badly hurt?" Rose asked.

"His injuries were almost entirely to his ego," Lance replied. "I thought a little humility might help him in his instruction of trainees at Station Two."

"I was one of them," Stone said, "and I hope you're right."

"Who is this Wu fellow?" Rose asked.

"Probably the best street fighter in the world," Lance replied, "with or without weapons. I once temporarily gave that title to another of our instructors, but Wu brought a quick end to his supremacy."

"Where did you find him?"

"In the Army, where we find a lot of our operational people," Lance said. "During basic training he was housed in a barrack full of racist recruits who challenged him to fights. He worked his way through them in a matter of days. His drill sergeant, who was afraid of him, called an intelligence officer to the base.

After an interview, we whisked him away to Camp Peary, and we've never let him go."

"So, Fife-Simpson is not the fighter he tells everybody he is?" Stone asked.

"No, but he is hardly helpless," Lance said. "He is probably the equal of our average instructor at Camp Peary, and if you should ever be provoked into a fight with him, my advice would be to shoot him in the head immediately."

"I think I'll start by asking Felicity not to bring him to dinner again," Stone said.

Felicity was halfway through her morning at work when her secretary announced Brigadier Fife-Simpson.

"Ah, Roger, back from your travels? Is that a bandage on your forehead?" She waved him to a chair.

"Nothing serious," he said, "though it could have been."

"Could this be the result of an encounter with a person called Wu?" she asked.

"It was," he replied, "and I am not grateful to you for putting me in that position. I could have been badly hurt."

"Roger," she said reprovingly, "it is my information that you were armed with a knife, while Wu had only his bare hands to defend himself. And it is my recollection that, when training recruits at Station Two, you gave them actual knives for them to practice killing each other."

"I did that for their own good," he said primly.

"Then perhaps the people at Camp Peary thought you needed an attitude adjustment," she replied.

"I, indeed?" He sniffed. "I was trundled about their headquarters like a foreign tourist, then sent down to their training establishment and humiliated."

"Well, you were a foreign tourist, but I suppose I must apologize for them," Felicity said, mock-soothingly.

"I think you and Lance Cabot hatched this plot between you," he said. "I just want you to know it didn't work."

"May I remind you," Felicity said, "that I am your superior at this service?"

"And I am a brigadier general of the Royal Marines," he nearly shouted.

"Perhaps you are not aware," Felicity said coldly, "that my position here carries the military rank of full admiral?"

"I apologize," Fife-Simpson sputtered.

"As, indeed, you should. I expect you are also unaware that your presence in my service was pressed on me from above."

He reddened. "Perhaps it was believed that my presence here might lend some organization and weight to this service."

"We are quite well organized, I assure you, and we bear such sufficient weight that you might suddenly find yourself training recruits from south of Calais in how to be British officers and gentlemen. Would you enjoy that?"

"I would not," he muttered.

"Then perhaps you could suggest a more agreeable use for your presence here?"

Fife-Simpson was suddenly at a loss for words.

"Then go back to your office, think it over, and write me a memo on the subject of how you might be more important to our purposes," she said. "Good day."

Fife-Simpson got up and left the room, mustering as much dignity as he could manage.

28

ater the same day, Dame Felicity presented herself at the Foreign Office and was announced to the minister. She was made to wait a half hour before being admitted to the inner sanctum, which was not alarming but customary. On entering she found the minister at his desk, reading and signing documents, ignoring her. She took a seat.

"I don't recall asking you to sit," Sir Oswald said, still not looking at her.

"I don't recall being asked to stand," Felicity replied tartly.

Now he looked up at her and put down his fountain pen. "I have, less than an hour ago, received a letter of resignation from your service of Brigadier Roger Fife-Simpson."

"Well, the proper thing to have done would be for him to send it to me, then allow me to pass it up to you, but my relief is such that I will overlook the transgression."

"He says you tried to have him killed," the foreign minister said.

"Foreign minister," Felicity said icily, "if I had tried to have him killed he would now be in a box in the churchyard at the Royal Naval College, after having been accorded full military honors."

"I did not bring you here to joke," he said.

"What made you think I was joking?" she asked.

Sir Oswald slammed his pen down on his desk. "Goddam-mit, Felicity, I will not tolerate insubordination from you!"

"Then sack me!" Felicity riposted at a similar volume. "Or leave me to stock my service with the best people, not castoff blackmailers like that horrible little man! Those are your choices, do with them as you will!"

"What do you mean, 'blackmailer'?" Sir Oswald demanded.

"I don't think I have to explain the term to you, Ozzie, nor to your faithful companion since your days at Eton."

"How dare you speak to me that way!"

"I am forced to such daring," she said, "in the circumstances. Instead of your outrage with me, you should, perhaps, devote your energies to explaining things to the prime minister after Fife-Simpson has put a flea in his ear. I'm sure, given his past, that will be his next move."

Sir Oswald diverted his eyes and sagged a little. "All right," he said, "let us be frank."

"I don't believe I have been less than frank," Felicity replied.

He turned back toward her and made a placating motion with both hands. "All right," he said, "what do you have on Fife-Simpson?"

"Well," Felicity said. "Let me see." She was quiet for a moment. "Perhaps you have been regaled, at some point, with Fife-Simpson's story of how he killed two IRA men and harmed three others in a Belfast public house—this in his youth, of course."

Sir Oswald sighed. "He made sure someone else told me about that occasion."

"It never happened," Felicity said. "At least, not the way he tells it."

Sir Oswald leaned forward and rested his elbows on his desk. "Tell me," he said.

So Dame Felicity apprised the foreign minister of the true events on that day and cited her sources.

"Does Tim Barnes know about this?"

"Sir Tim was his companion on that day and saved his life by summoning a team of military policemen."

"Why were they together?"

"One of them, I'm not sure which, had expressed a keen interest in finding a pub he had heard about which catered to, shall we say, a more effete clientele than that found in your typical Belfast watering hole. They stupidly wandered into the wrong pub."

"And you think Tim has been a victim of Fife-Simpson?"

"Yes, and I believe he remains so. Why else would he press Fife-Simpson on you and, thus, me?"

"And after Tim saved the man's life!"

"Quite so."

"Then he must be dealt with," Sir Oswald said, slapping his palm on the leather top of his desk.

"Then he should be dealt with carefully," Felicity said.

"How?"

"I think it would be best for us not to converse on that topic again. We should just let nature take its course."

"Yes," Sir Oswald said, "but with a boot up nature's arse."

"Quite." Dame Felicity took leave of the ministry and got into her waiting car. She sat back as she was driven and allowed her mind to wander, in the manner that it wandered when it was required to dream up an operation. Her frontal lobe zeroed in on a house in Cap d'Antibes, in the South of France, which had been in her family since her grandfather's time. She had used it in an operation a couple of years before, which had allowed her to renovate it and wire it for video and audio at her ministry's expense, and since to maintain it with a two-person staff. She picked up one of her two phones, the scrambler one, and dialed a number from its contacts list.

"Barnes," a pleasant voice said.

"Scramble," Felicity replied.

"Scrambled," he said, after a moment.

"Tim, it's Felicity. How are you?"

"I'm quite well, Felicity. We very much enjoyed our evening at Windward Hall, and a note has gone off to Mr. Barrington to that effect."

"I'm so glad," she replied. "Tim, I suppose by this time that you have heard of the departure from my service of our mutual . . . acquaintance."

"Word has reached me. He was very upset, and when he gets upset, unfortunate events sometimes follow."

"My very reason for calling," Felicity said. "I believe I have found a way to avoid unpleasantness in this matter."

"How may I help?"

"Please write down this address and phone number." She dictated, and he copied.

"Got it. What next?"

"That is the address of a very pleasant house in Cap d'Antibes that we sometimes use as a safe house for friends of our firm who are in jeopardy of one thing or another. It is cared for by a houseman and his wife, a very good cook. I would like you to offer it to our acquaintance for a holiday, sooner rather than later."

"I can do that, and tell him that it belongs to friends."

"Yes, and their names are Sir John and Priscilla Dover. You served with him somewhere or other. I'll leave you to flesh out the details. The caretakers are Marie and Oskar."

"All right. Then what?"

"Apprise me of his arrival and departure dates at Nice airport. And tell him he will be met by a car and driver. Also, you might mention to him that spa services, including a particularly well-recommended massage therapist, are available on-site. There is a list of phone numbers in the center desk drawer in the library. You may also tell him that food and drink will be provided, and that there is a private beach for his use."

"You make it sound wonderful," Barnes said.

"On some other occasion, I would be pleased for you and your wife to use it."

"Thank you so much, Felicity," he said.

"Thank you for your assistance, Tim." She hung up as they pulled to a stop at the rear entrance of her service. Back at her desk she buzzed Mrs. Green.

"Yes, ma'am?"

"Take a letter to Brigadier Fife-Simpson."

"Please go ahead."

"'Dear Sir: Your resignation is accepted with immediate effect and without undue regret. Kindly deposit your credentials and weapons with the commissionaire on your way out.' Type that up for my signature, then deliver it to him. If he is out, leave it on his desk."

"Yes, ma'am," Mrs. Green replied, with a hint of pleasure in her voice.

29

ife-Simpson was sitting at his desk seething at his treatment by MI-6, the Foreign Office, and the Admiralty, when someone rapped sharply on his office door. Without waiting to be asked to enter, Mrs. Green opened the door and stepped forward, handing him an envelope sealed with red wax.

"What is this?" he demanded of her.

"For your eyes only, Brigadier," she said. "For immediate action." She stood waiting.

Fife-Simpson examined the envelope carefully, then broke the seal and unfolded the paper. As he read it, all expression drained from his face, leaving him with his mouth open.

"This way, please," Mrs. Green said.

He looked up at her. "What?"

"It says, 'with immediate effect,'" she replied. "This way, please."

He stuffed the letter into his pocket, got his coat and hat from the closet, and followed her down the corridor. "What about my personal effects?" he asked while they waited for the elevator.

"Cartwright will collect them and have them delivered to

your residence," Mrs. Green replied. The elevator arrived. "Good day," she said, holding the door for him.

He got out of the elevator on the ground floor and found the commissionaire blocking his exit from the building.

"Credentials and weapons, please, Brigadier."

Fife-Simpson handed over his ID and pistol.

"Holster and switchblade, please."

He took off his coat, got out of the shoulder holster, and fished the knife from his hip pocket, then laid everything on the table.

The commissionaire helped him back on with his jacket and coat, then handed him his hat and opened the door for him. Fife-Simpson stepped out into the street. "You are to forget this address," the commissionaire said, then slammed the door behind him and bolted it.

Fife-Simpson turned around and found a taxi waiting. His name was on a card taped to the windshield. He got in.

"I have the address," the driver said, closing the window between them.

Fife-Simpson got out of the cab in front of his building and took the lift up to his flat. He hung his coat and hat carefully in the hall closet, then walked into the drawing room, loosened his necktie, poured himself a large scotch, then poured himself into his favorite chair and drank half of his drink in a single draught.

His telephone rang, and he reflexively picked it up, even though he didn't wish to speak to anyone. "Brigadier Fife-Simpson," he said into the phone.

"Will you speak to the First Sea Lord?" a woman's voice said.

"Of course," he replied, brightening. This might be something good.

"Hello, Roger," a familiar male voice said. "It's Tim Barnes. How are you?"

"I've been better," Fife-Simpson replied.

"Perhaps what you need is a holiday. I have just the thing for you."

"Really?"

"Yes. Kate and I had planned a holiday at Cap d'Antibes, in the South of France, at a lovely place owned by some friends. However, as all too often happens, the Royal Navy has decided to put itself first, and we have to cancel. We have the house for a week. Would you like to have it, as our guest, starting tomorrow?"

"Ra-ther!" Fife-Simpson replied gleefully.

"All right. I'll have my plane ticket changed to your name. You're on British Airways 106 to Nice, tomorrow morning at eleven AM. There'll be a car and driver to meet you at the other end."

"Tim, this is just wonderful, and at a moment when it will do the most good."

"A couple named Marie and Oskar run the place, and she cooks like an angel. The house is stocked with food and drink, on us, and I've made an appointment for myself at five tomorrow afternoon for a massage. Shall I leave that in place for you?"

"Oh, yes, please."

"Very well, then. Have a wonderful holiday, and be sure to drop us a postcard."

"Thank you again, Tim."

"Don't mention it. Goodbye." He hung up.

Fife-Simpson leapt from his chair, tossed down the remainder of his drink, and went to find his luggage. When he was all packed he ordered in a pizza, opened a bottle of wine, and settled in for dinner.

Dame Felicity buzzed Mrs. Green.

"Yes, ma'am?"

"Find Sims in operations and send him up to me, please."

"Right away, ma'am."

Sims was a rangy lad of thirty-five whose suit never quite fit him, but who had a quick mind and a sly nature.

"Take a seat, Sims," Felicity said, and he did so.

"You remember the little op we pulled off at the place on Cap d'Antibes two years ago?"

"Of course, Dame Felicity. One of our better ones, I thought."

"All of our video and audio working there?"

"We keep it in good nick," he replied.

"Good. A man called Roger Fife-Simpson is arriving at the Nice airport tomorrow at two o'clock local."

"Would that be our brigadier?" Sims asked.

"Yes, our now late, lamented brigadier. Have him met and transported to the house. And, of course, let our people there know to expect him."

"Yes, ma'am. Do you wish him, ah, entertained?"

"Yes, please. He has been told to expect a massage therapist at five PM. Arrange that."

"Male or female?"

"Male, and make him handsome, muscular, and well hung."

"Is the brigadier that way inclined?"

"That remains between the brigadier and his psychotherapist," she said, "but don't bother with seduction, just give him a nap and use the opportunity to take some holiday snaps of the two of them in living color and in poses I'll leave to you and the masseur."

"Understood. And what disposition of the photographic material shall I make?"

"Everything for my eyes only, and don't hang on to the negatives. I want it all."

"I'll need a signed work order," he said. "How shall I characterize the operation?"

She handed him the blank form, signed. "Call it therapeutic." She sent him on his way.

30

rigadier Fife-Simpson stepped out of customs in Nice and into the main hall. He immediately spotted a man in a dark suit holding a sign bearing his name. He checked his watch. His flight had been forty minutes late, and customs had taken longer than he had expected. Roger handed the man his luggage and followed him outside to the curb, where a Mercedes awaited.

A half hour later, after a drive past many beautiful houses, the car turned into a driveway guarded by a high hedge and drove to the front door of a charming cottage, where two servants met and greeted him effusively and took his luggage inside. He was shown to a large, comfortable bedroom, where a massage table had been set up.

He was offered food and drink and opted for the drink, in order to keep the champagne buzz from the flight going.

"Your massage therapist is due in half an hour," Marie said. "There is a robe in your bathroom."

He unpacked, changed into the robe, and was seated in a cushy chair when Marie returned with his large whisky. "Enjoy," she said.

A few minutes later, his whisky gone, there was a knock on the door and a handsome, muscular, young man in a tight-fitting polo shirt entered, carrying a case. Fife-Simpson had expected a woman, but what the hell.

"Good afternoon," the young man said. "My name is Pierre." He set his case on the floor and indicated that Roger should mount the massage table, facedown. "Are you well today?" Pierre asked, helping him get comfortable.

"I'm a bit tired," Roger said.

"Perhaps what would help is a small injection of vitamin B-twelve," Pierre said. "I am licensed to administer it, and it will greatly enhance your massage experience."

"Oh, all right," Roger replied.

"Just a little pinch," Pierre said. Roger felt a stab in a buttock. "There, now just relax." He lowered the sheet and began rubbing Roger's back.

Roger took a few deep breaths, then drifted off.

Pierre pinched his other buttock, hard. "Feel that?" No response. Pierre went to the bed and pulled back the covers, then he lifted Fife-Simpson bodily and carried him there. He took note of the camera positions in the crown molding, then put on a baseball cap, the bill of which would shield his face from view. He stripped off his own clothing, massaged himself until he was engorged and camera-ready, then turned Fife-Simpson on his belly and began posing him in various positions.

Roger came slowly awake, lying on his back, as the masseur massaged his legs, then pulled the sheet over him.

"There," Pierre said. "Did you enjoy your massage?"

"Yes," Roger muttered. "Very nice."

"I will go now, and you may continue to rest, if you wish. Marie will put away the massage table later." Pierre closed his case, picked it up, and departed.

In London, back at the Circus, Sims opened the door to the operations room and admitted Dame Felicity.

"How did it go?" she asked.

"Perfectly," Sims replied. "Pierre gave us everything we could possibly want, not to mention what he gave the brigadier."

"Let me see the tapes." She took a chair and watched the array of monitors before her, each aimed at the massage table from different angles. The masseur entered the room, Fife-Simpson climbed onto the table, and, after a moment, the injection was administered, and he seemed to fall asleep.

Felicity watched with amazement, her eyes flicking from one monitor to the next, while Pierre, who had the largest penis she had ever seen, turned his attentions to his client. "My God," she said, after half a minute of this, then she stood up. "All right, I've seen quite enough," she said. "I'll leave you to it."

"Thank you for joining us, Director. Now we'll edit the raw footage, you should excuse the expression, into a harmonious whole and transfer it to our special website. Once done, I'll give you the code and password."

"Jolly good," she said. "I'll see the final cut on the website when you're done."

"I'll call you," Sims said.

....

Back in her office, Felicity phoned Admiral Sir Timothy Barnes. "Scramble," she said.

"Scrambled," Barnes replied.

"The brigadier arrived pretty much on schedule, and things went very much as planned," she said.

"I'm glad it went well."

"Tell me, Tim. Is Roger likely to come back to you for a favorable reassignment?"

"I think that's quite likely," Barnes replied, "given his past conduct."

"I think it might be appropriate if you found him a post in a setting somewhat less comfortable than the Scottish Highlands—something more remote, perhaps."

"I've been thinking about that," Barnes replied, "and we have an upcoming vacancy. Something that might cause him to consider retirement."

"Anything available at either the north or south poles?" Felicity asked, archly.

Barnes laughed heartily. "I wish," he said. "Oh, I wish."

"I'm sure whatever you have in mind will do very nicely," she said. "Let me know of his final disposition."

"I shall do so," Barnes replied.

She heard a knock on her door. "Hold on a moment, Tim," Felicity said. "Come in!"

Sims entered and handed her a slip of paper. "Here are the entry code and password to the website," he said. "Everything will be up and running by five PM. And, by the way, we're adding some dialogue to the audio—grunts and ecstatic groans."

She turned back to her phone conversation. "Tim?"

"I'm here."

"I'm going to read you the entry code and password to a highly secret website, created especially for this event. After five o'clock, you'll be able to view the brigadier's holiday video."

"That's grand, Felicity. I'll pass it on to the First Lord of the Admiralty and the foreign minister. I don't think it will need to go any further than that."

"That should be quite far enough," she replied. "When it has done its work we'll archive it, just in case it's needed in the future."

They both said goodbye and hung up.

31

Brigadier Fife-Simpson arrived back at his London flat, checked his mail, and found a request from the First Sea Lord that he appear at the Admiralty the following day for a reassignment interview.

At the appointed hour, dressed in his uniform, he reported to Admiral Sir Tim Barnes as instructed. He was greeted warmly by his old friend and given coffee, then Sir Tim got to the point.

"Roger," Sir Tim said, "I've been looking through our vacancy lists for a new assignment for you."

"I'm raring to go, Tim," the brigadier replied, being so bold as to address him familiarly, since they were alone.

"I've found you something—a command, actually, that while it may seem a bit farther south than what you're accustomed to, might be just the sort of assignment that could lead to greater things in the future. After all, a hardship post can look very good on one's record when, in the future, one comes before an Admiralty board. I expect you're aware that, now that you are of flag rank, promotions and reassignments require board approval."

Hardship? Fife-Simpson thought, a bit alarmed. "Farther south, did you say?" he asked.

"The Falklands, actually. That's as far south as one can go. You'd be in command of the detachment there."

The brigadier frowned a little. "How large a detachment?" he asked.

"Twelve officers and seventy of the lower ranks. All men, I'm afraid. The First Lord thought it best, for his own reasons, not to send women down there."

"And what does the detachment do there, sir?" He thought it best not to be familiar again.

"They guard the Falklands," Sir Tim replied.

"From what, sir?"

"Why, from reinvasion of the Argentinians, of course. You'll remember how hard it was dislodging them after they took the islands back from us the last time. We don't want that happening again, do we?"

"And the Admiralty believes it could prevent a reinvasion with eighty-two men?"

"Oh, we're much better armed and more responsive these days than back then," Sir Tim replied. "We could reinforce your contingent in days, not weeks."

"And how long is the posting, sir? It's temporary, I assume."

"No, it's a normal two-year rotation, possibly three, should difficulties arise." Sir Tim looked at him, frowning. "Is something wrong, Brigadier?"

"Not quite what I hoped for, sir," Fife-Simpson replied.

"Well, in these days of peacetime, our numbers have shrunk,

and so have the number of postings available. I might be able to find you something in West Africa, but the climate there is, shall we say, inhospitable, and the risk of tropical infections formidable."

"Thank you, sir, I don't think so. May I ask: Do I have another alternative?"

"Well, there's always retirement, I suppose." He looked at the file before him. "You've another year before being eligible for a full pension, though. Perhaps I could fudge that a bit, if you wish me to."

"May I have a few days to consider my options, sir?"

"Of course, Roger. Ring me as soon as you can and let me know your wishes in the matter. In the meantime, I'll see what might be done about the pension." He stood, signaling that the meeting was at an end. "I might be able to do something without board approval." As he spoke he tilted the file in his hand, and an index card fell out onto the coffee table. Sir Tim picked it up and looked at it. "Oh, yes, I was given this to hand to you by the First Lord. It appears to be a website. Something to do with the Falklands, I imagine." He handed it to the brigadier, who tucked it into a pocket, then saluted and left the room.

It had begun to rain. It took the yeoman at the front door a few minutes to find him a cab. By then it was coming down so hard that he got quite wet while getting into the taxi, which did not help to lift the depression that had befallen him on hearing of his new posting. The Falklands, for God's sake! It was the other end of the earth! Bleak and with no women. And two years of it, perhaps three!

....

Back at his flat, he shucked off the tunic and hung it in his closet to dry. As he did, he came across the card Sir Tim had given him. He flopped down in his chair. Retirement? What would he do in retirement? He had no civilian connections whatever, and no training that would qualify him for a job in the city or in the courts. He'd sold the family's country property after his father's death, and he still had that money, so he could live. He imagined his existence, and that depressed him further.

It became clear to him as he sat there that he was going to have to bring some pressure to bear on old Tim; it had worked before, it could work again. Maybe some administrative post at the Admiralty; that would be bearable. He picked up his laptop and turned it on.

As the screen came up it was occupied by a message, demanding a user name and a password. He was expecting nothing like that, so he attempted to exit and go to his e-mail, but it would not budge. He restarted the computer to clear it, but got the same message.

He looked at the card Tim had given him and tried typing in the entry code and password it contained. Instantly a photograph appeared: it was a medium shot of himself, naked and in bed with a man, whose face was obscured. He scrolled down and found half a dozen other photos, from different angles and himself in different poses. He shrank away from the computer, as if it were a poisonous reptile.

Mercifully, the video ended, but there was another on-screen message: Consider your options.

Fife-Simpson fell back into his chair. What he had seen on

screen had shocked him to the core. It was no longer a criminal act, but for an officer of flag rank, it would be a career-ender; whoever had sent the video was clearly threatening that it could get out.

Retirement was beginning to look better to him. Certainly, better than the Falkland Islands.

32

tone and Lance took a ride together at mid-morning. After jumping the wall Lance pulled up under a tree and got down from the saddle. Stone followed him. Lance sat down with his back against the tree. "Join me?" he asked.

Stone joined him.

"This might be a good moment for a little chat," Lance said. "I don't suppose the horses or their tack are bugged, are they?"

"I think not," Stone replied.

"I was thinking about our relationship," Lance said.

"'Relationship'?"

"Between you and the Agency. I think it has been valuable to both of us on occasion, has it not?"

Stone thought about that in terms of what Lance had done for him, not what he had done for the Agency. "I suppose so," Stone said. "At widely separated intervals."

"I was thinking that the relationship might be more satisfying, if the intervals were shorter."

"What, exactly, do you have in mind, Lance?" He was curious, but guarded, as he always was with Lance.

"Well," Lance said, "you have homes in places where we do

business, so to speak—New York, Los Angeles, England, and Paris. Perhaps it's just as well that you disposed of your Connecticut property."

Stone remained silent.

"Allow me to elucidate."

"Please do," Stone said.

"Because of your widespread holdings and your apparent ability to do business while visiting them, while doing not much work for Woodman & Weld . . ."

"Let me stop you right there," Stone said. "I do a great deal more work for the firm than you are, perhaps, aware of."

"I'm aware of a great deal," Lance said. "It's in the nature of what I do."

"You are sometimes underinformed, Lance," Stone said.

"I'm sorry, I didn't mean to cast aspersions on your practice of the law."

"Didn't you?"

"I'm merely pointing out that, in spite of being an important partner at your firm, you manage to have a great deal of flexibility in the way that you do your work."

"I suppose that may be true," Stone said, then immediately regretted it. He had given Lance a foothold, and Lance could do a lot with a foothold.

"I'm merely suggesting that we might formalize our relationship just a bit."

"How much of a bit?" Stone asked.

"Well, I believe that you might find more serious work with us a good deal more satisfying—even entertaining—than just being a consultant for the Agency."

"Are you telling me that your firm is more fun than my firm?"

"Oh, most definitely, Stone. We have such a good time, saving the world. Wouldn't you like to have a hand in saving it? At the end of it all, you might find your memories more gratifying than just having made it rain at Woodman & Weld."

"I grant you that making rain at a law firm is not the most fun you can have, but the material rewards compensate quite nicely."

"I know how much money you make there, Stone," Lance said, "and I know how much money you have tucked away. You could shift gears in your life quite easily and never miss a meal, as it were."

"I've thought about that," Stone said, "but retirement doesn't appeal to me."

"Then why not do work that is more important than just making money?"

"Let me be frank, Lance. Being at your beck and call, as a consultant, is preferable to being at the end of your leash, no matter how long a leash it might be."

Lance chuckled. "Let me tell you something you don't know about my management style," he said. "In dealing with my most important colleagues, I hardly ever give orders; it's my view that, if I can't persuade them that what I want done is the right thing to do, then we look for another way, one that, more often than not, is suggested by them. Then they go away happy and get it done."

"Let's cut to the chase, Lance," Stone said. "What, exactly, do you want me to do?"

"It's not just what I want," Lance said. "It's also about how you want to spend your life."

"And, in your view, how should I spend it?"

"I'm thinking of creating a new position at the Agency that might suit you very well."

"And what is the new position?"

"It doesn't have a name yet. It might be called something like 'senior colleague.' Perhaps you can suggest something better."

"I can't suggest anything until I hear a better description of the duties involved."

"The duties involved would be very much like the consulting you do for us now, only more frequent and with much more official weight, not to mention the perks and benefits of a full-time senior officer—salary, insurance, pension."

"I have never seen or heard a description of what I do now," Stone pointed out.

"And yet, you have been doing it for some years. This would be a senior position, somewhere between station chief and director. How about 'deputy director for special operations.'"

"And what are the 'special operations'?"

"Whatever you and I, in consultation, want them to be. There would be no administrative duties whatever, and you could maintain your current residences, plus something rather special in D.C."

"Something special?"

"You did a real estate swap with the Presidents Lee a few years ago, in which you gave title to the State Department of your house in Georgetown, for the use of the secretary of state."

"I did."

"It seems that the State Department no longer wishes to be a landlord, after the current occupant vacates. And it appears to me that she will be moving out later this year."

"If she is elected."

"She will have to resign as secretary of state before she declares herself a candidate—though she could continue residing in your house as long as you wish to have her there."

Stone was now stunned. Lance was serious.

"Also, if she should not win the election, I would be very interested to have her back at Langley in a very high position, one that would virtually guarantee that she would succeed me, if I should be invited to improve my situation elsewhere."

"I assume that you have your eye on something in particular?" Stone asked.

"I believe that, no matter who wins the election, I might be in a position to choose one or two other positions."

"Let's see, what might be suitable? Head of the National Security Agency? Perhaps even secretary of state?"

"That's very flattering, Stone," Lance said. He got to his feet and prepared to mount his horse.

"Think about it, and we'll talk later." He swung into the saddle, and Stone remounted and followed him.

In the late afternoon, as Stone sat in the library with his book, his cell phone rang. "Yes?"

"Is that the lord of the manor speaking?" she asked.

"Ah, Holly," he said, feeling a wave of warmth.

"I'm *absolutely certain*," she said, "that I told you there'd be an opportunity for us to rendezvous in England around now."

"Of course you did. I haven't forgotten. When?"

"I'll be popping over this weekend, and I expect I can manage a week or two between London and your Windward Hall."

"How will you be traveling?" he asked. "I mean, in what sort of aircraft?"

"Well, I don't rate Air Force One, but it will probably be a very nice Gulfstream 500 that various members of the Joint Chiefs of Staff have managed to corral for themselves."

"In that case, they can dump you right into my backyard."

"I have to jump?"

"No, there's a very nice seven-thousand-foot airstrip on my property, with GPS approaches. They can land, boot you and your luggage out, and take off again, unhindered, then fly to wherever they were going in the first place. Got a pencil?"

"Always."

He gave her the coordinates and frequencies for landing. "Pass that on to your pilots before you take off."

"That sounds delightful. I'll fly over tomorrow, then a car will whisk me to London on Sunday night."

"Then back here when you're done in London."

"Of course."

"Request an early-morning departure—that will get you here in daylight. And even if it doesn't, there's a beacon and runway lighting, pilot-operated on the common frequency."

"Duly noted. What clothes will I need?"

"Oh, a couple of ball gowns and your workout gear, I suppose. Don't forget your riding togs. I will introduce you to some horses. We'll have at least one black tie event, maybe two, so come equipped."

"I can do that."

"I'd suggest you leave your London gear on the airplane and have them deliver it to your hotel. Where are you staying?"

"In the Agency's suite at the Connaught. Lance was helpful."

"Speaking of Lance, I'll want to talk to you about him."

"Give me a hint?"

"Nope."

"Oh, all right."

"Call me at this number on your satphone when you're fif-teen minutes from touchdown, and I'll meet you at the airstrip."

"Wonderful. See you then."

33

The morning after his meeting with the First Sea Lord, Brigadier Fife-Simpson had another phone call.

"Hello?"

"This that Brigadier Fife-Simpson?" a woman asked.

"It is."

"This is Captain Helen Frogg. I'm calling on behalf of the Commandant General of the Royal Marines, General Sir Jeremy Pink."

"Yes?"

"You are requested to present yourself to the commandant at Naval Headquarters in Whitehall at three o'clock this afternoon."

"Yes, I'll be there."

"Thank you, Brigadier." She hung up.

Now there was a ray of hope in the gloom, the brigadier felt. Otherwise he would not be seeing the commandant. He took his uniform to the neighborhood dry cleaners and waited while it was pressed, then he returned to his flat and got into it.

....

At three o'clock sharp, the brigadier presented himself at the offices of the commandant, and, to his surprise, was not kept waiting but told to go straight in. He marched into the office, braced, and saluted. "Brigadier Fife-Simpson reporting as ordered. Good morning, Commandant."

Instead of being asked to sit, the commandant rose from his desk and directed the brigadier to the conference table at one end of his office, where there were some papers stacked, then told to sit. He did, and the commandant sat opposite him at the table.

"Now then, Brigadier," he said, "at the request of the First Sea Lord, I am presenting you with two options. First, there is the post of commander of the Royal Marine detachment in the Falkland Islands." His nose wrinkled. "I've served there, and I don't recommend either the climate or the landscape. The sailing is pretty good, though, if you have a yacht. Alternatively, I am pleased to tell you that, after the intervention of the First Sea Lord, the promotions board has, in your case, agreed to waive the thirty-year-service requirement for full retirement pay and benefits. Your choice is clear: If you wish to accept the Falklands posting, kindly sign the documents on your left. If you, alternatively, wish to accept retirement with immediate effect and full benefits, kindly sign the document on your right." The commandant took a fountain pen from his jacket pocket, unscrewed the cap, and laid the instrument on the table between the documents.

"Sir . . ."

The commandant interrupted him. "I assure you, Brigadier, there is no other posting available."

The brigadier picked up the pen, thought briefly of the Falklands, then signed his retirement document.

The commandant picked up his pen, screwed on the cap, returned it to his pocket, and stood, gathering and sorting papers.

The brigadier stood and saluted him.

The commandant offered him a handshake and thanks for his service.

Thus dismissed, the brigadier turned and, with an envelope containing his retirement documents and those explaining the terms, marched out of the office and into civilian life.

An hour later, Fife-Simpson sat in the bar of the Naval and Military Club, in St. James's Square, known to its members as the "In & Out." The brigadier was definitely Out and not In. Out meant more rain that day, and foolishly not having brought an umbrella with him to Whitehall and not having been able to raise a cab, he had been forced to walk the distance between the two.

"I say, Roger," a voice said. "Is that you?" A man in a business suit sat down on the stool next to him.

Fife-Simpson turned and looked at him. A colonel of his acquaintance. "Hello, Nigel," he said.

"You're looking a bit damp, there, you know? Surely the valet will press your uniform for you."

"Yes, he would, if I chose to spend an hour in his steamy back room. I don't believe they'd allow me to drink here in my skivvies."

"Ho, ho, ho, I imagine not. I read of your promotion in the *Telegraph*," Nigel said. "What have they got you doing now?"

"Well, I commanded Station Two, MI-6's training camp, for

six months. Then I was made deputy director of MI-6. Mind you, that's between you and me and the lamppost. They don't like us talking."

"And is that good work?"

"Not really. Not enough to do, so I packed it in—today."

"I hadn't realized you'd cracked the thirty-year mark."

"I hadn't, but the board made an exception," Fife-Simpson replied, then realized that he had just told this very talkative man that he had been sacked. "They offered me a command," he said quickly, "but I decided to pack it in."

"Oh? What did they offer you?"

Fife-Simpson scrambled for a plausible story, then gave it up. "What are you doing with yourself, Nigel?"

"Oh, I've got number 44 Commandos," he replied. "Not that we have a lot to do these days, except train." He glanced at his watch. "Oh, God, my wife is standing on a street corner at Harrods. I must flee." He clapped the brigadier on the back. "Cheerio," he said and then fled, leaving the brigadier to himself.

Fife-Simpson poured the remainder of Nigel's whisky into his own glass. Must be frugal from now on, he thought.

Then he thought again. With his pension and the income from his father's estate, he would be doing rather nicely—better than half again his pay as a brigadier. He polished off his drink. "Another," he said to the bartender. He could afford it.

He took his drink to a chair beside the fire and fell into it. He'd dry faster here.

Sometime later, someone shook his shoulder. "Excuse me, Brigadier, will you be having dinner?"

Fife-Simpson took a moment to reorient himself. It was dark outside, and still raining. "Yes, thank you. I'll go right in." He got unsteadily to his feet, and looked for the lavatory, then he went into a stall and threw up. He went to a sink and splashed water on his face, then regarded it in the mirror. He seemed to have aged since yesterday.

He went into the dining room and took a table alone, avoiding the common table where the unaccompanied dined.

As he picked at his steak and kidney pudding, clearheaded now, he began to look back on the past few months. He had put a foot wrong somewhere, and he tried to pinpoint when.

On consideration, he decided he should have stayed at Station Two. God knew it was not comfortable, but it was better than having nothing to do at MI-6 and a damn sight better than the Falklands. It was the gambit that got him made deputy director that had been his downfall, he reckoned. That and the business with the attack on the station and the wrecking of Dame Felicity's goddamned Aston Martin. He should have smoothed that over and stayed where he was for at least another year, before he prodded Tim Barnes to promote and reassign him.

Then, he realized, there was something else: that fellow Barrington, who had lost control of the car. That was the precipitating factor of his slide. It had shone too much attention on him at the wrong time. He felt nothing but hostility for Dame Felicity, too.

He began to think: there must be a way to make the bastards pay.

34

tone's phone rang late in the day on Thursday. "Fifteen minutes," Holly said, "and no fond embraces when I alight. They'll be watching us." He took the golf cart down to the strip and watched the skies. He didn't see the Gulfstream until it turned for the final runway approach. It set down gently as if it and the strip were old friends. Holly was at the top of the airstair door when it dropped, and a steward followed her with her luggage.

They drove back to the house, with Holly making all the ooh and ahh noises appropriate to the landscape and the house. Geoffrey took charge of her luggage and, once inside the front door, they shared a warm embrace and a wet kiss.

"Do you want to freshen up?" he asked.

"I did that on the airplane," she said. "It has wonderful facilities."

He gave her a tour of the main floor, finishing up in the library.

"This is marvelous," she said. "It's like the big brother of your study in the New York house."

He poured them each a Knob Creek, and they sat down before the fire. "Now," he said, "tell me everything."

"Well, I've been doing most of my usual work and campaigning myself to a frazzle the rest of the time. The polls are favorable, so what else can I tell you? Why don't you tell me about Lance instead?"

"All right, Lance came and stayed for a few days, and yesterday he sat me down and made me an offer before he left."

"What sort of offer?" she asked.

"A vague one that involved me becoming a full-time employee of the Agency with the rank of deputy director, but remaining in New York and pretending to do what I've been doing since I passed the bar."

"So he wants to turn you from a consultant into a . . . Well, let's call it an operative."

"Pretty much."

"Do you think you might enjoy that?"

"I think I might, but I need your advice. If I should take this on, is Lance going to drive me crazy?"

"No, Lance is too smart to do that, unless he wants to get rid of you. Lance is a good judge of people, and he'll understand what he can ask for and expect to get. Does a contract exist?"

"He's faxing one from London, he says."

"Let me read it—especially between the lines."

"Good idea."

"What do you hope to gain from accepting?" she asked.

"I hope that what I'm asked to do will be both personally satisfying and good for the country. I've always felt a little guilty about not serving in some capacity."

"You served New York City for fourteen years. Wasn't that enough?"

"Apparently not. There's still an itch, otherwise I wouldn't have become a consultant to the Agency."

"Have you enjoyed what you've done as a consultant?"

"I have, I'll have to admit."

"Then you might enjoy being an operative even more."

"You really think so?"

"I think Lance is bending way over backward to entice you, and that's a good sign. There are, after all, only two other deputy directors, one for intelligence and one for operations. Will they know you're aboard?"

"Good question. Lance didn't say."

"That's one of the things you should know. You don't want to start by stepping on powerful toes."

"There was something else in our discussion, just as vague as the rest. I had the impression that Lance thinks he might be moving onward and upward before too much longer. Will that be the case, if you're elected president?"

"As far as I'm concerned, Lance could have any intelligence or foreign policy job he wants, and I'd feel lucky to have him. But I haven't been elected yet, and Lance is going to have to be very careful not to incur the wrath of my Republican opponent, whoever he might be, if he wants to remain director of Central Intelligence in the event I lose."

"Wheels within wheels," Stone said.

"You have no idea," Holly replied.

35

tone and Holly spent the next day on horseback, taking the horses and a picnic lunch down to the Solent. "This is the body of water that separates the Isle of Wight from England," he explained. "We'll be crossing it later on a little trip to Cowes, which is England's yachting capital, for dinner at the Royal Yacht Squadron."

"How are we dressing?"

"Black tie, as always, on a Friday night at the Squadron. Felicity Devonshire is hosting a dinner party for us. Fortunately, the weather forecast is good. The Solent can be a choppy place with a strong wind from east or west."

"What time are we leaving?"

"Five-ish, in order to arrive in time for drinks before dinner."

"Stone," she said, changing the subject, "I've been thinking about Lance's offer to you, and I'm inclined to advise you to take it."

"Yes?"

"Yes, as long as you have a way out. I know that you see your own personal truth as self-evident, but in dealing with Lance you might find that at odds with what he wants you to do."

"I can understand that."

"As long as your contract reads that you can opt out anytime you're uncomfortable."

"I'll be sure that's in the contract. He's faxing it from London today, so perhaps we can have a look at it together when we get back to the house."

"You said he mentioned the rank of deputy director? Was there anything added to that?"

"He suggested 'special operations,' but he didn't seem set on it."

"That sounds too much like you'd be directing actual operations, and you have no experience with that."

"True enough."

"I'd suggest something vaguer, like 'senior adviser.' A mention of operations might ruffle other feathers."

"I'll keep that in mind."

"You'll want to watch out for the deputy director for intelligence, Hugh English."

"What's he like?"

"In his sixties, wears British tailoring, gruff, but he can be charming when he wants something. He's what the Brits call 'clubbable.' The Republicans in Congress love him because he's been leaking to them for years. If they win the election and Lance gets bounced, Hugh English is likely to get his job. As I said, don't underestimate him. He's capable of low cunning."

"What about the other DD? For operations?"

"That would be Finn McAdoo. He's the young comer, and because of that, Hugh English hates him. If I'm elected, and if Lance wants to move elsewhere, I'd likely choose Finn to replace him. You'll like him immediately."

....

After lunch they rode back to the house, where Stone found a multipage fax waiting for him in the library. "Here we go," he said. He read the pages, then handed them to Holly. It didn't take long to get through them.

"It's surprisingly benign," Holly said, "and it doesn't mention a title, though it mentions the rank."

"I noticed that."

"All you need is a sentence allowing you to resign at will, and the title, which should be descriptive of the job. He's not going to be able to keep this from the top-level people at the Agency, and the title will tell them where you stand."

Stone made a note about adding the out clause. His cell phone rang, and he answered it.

"Did you get the contract?" Lance asked.

"Yes. My adviser and I have just finished reading it."

"Is Holly there?"

"Yes, I'll put you on speaker."

"Any questions?"

"I want an out clause," Stone said.

"It will be my job to see that you never want out."

"Yes, but you may decide to move on to better things, and I don't want to be at the mercy of a director I don't know."

"Done. There's something else, though," Lance said.

"What's that?"

"I had conceived your role as a covert one, but on reflection I think it might be better if it became known. I wouldn't make a public announcement, just let the word get around."

"All right. It occurs to me that some people should know

from the outset: my secretary, Joan Robertson, and, of course, Dino and Viv Bacchetti."

"No problem there. Dino and Viv are both consultants already, as you know."

"I didn't know about Viv."

"Now you do. You can tell anyone you like, but be discreet."

"Lance, will you announce it inside the Agency?" Holly asked.

"I'll send out a selective memo. The right people will know."

"I'm sure you'll guard against Hugh English looking at Stone as a threat."

"Certainly. I'll reassure him."

"What about his title?" Holly asked.

"Did you have something in mind, Holly?"

"Perhaps something like 'senior adviser to the director'? Give him the rank of a deputy director but don't broadcast it."

"I like it," Lance said. "It won't rile Hugh English too much. Stone, what do you think?"

"Sure, fine."

"I'll get the thing retyped and fax it again in a few minutes."

"All right," Stone said, and hung up.

A few minutes later, the fax machine began spitting out pages. Stone read, signed, and initialed them in the appropriate places and faxed them back.

"Well," Holly said, "you're on the hook now. That's what we say about a newly acquired asset at the Agency."

"On the hook for what?"

"For whatever Lance wants from you."

"Interesting about Viv being a consultant."

"And a prized one," Holly said. "She's in an ideal position at Special Services to glean business information."

They were getting dressed for dinner when a package was delivered to the house. Geoffrey, the butler, brought it upstairs to Stone. It was small but hefty for its size. Stone opened it and removed a wallet containing a new ID and a badge, plus a box of business cards and an Apple iPhone. Stone had used one of these, briefly, in Paris. It had scrambling, encryption, and other capabilities At the bottom of the package was a Colt Government .380 pistol with royal bluing, ivory handles, a couple of extra magazines, a box of ammunition, and a soft suede holster. There was also a silencer and a place for it in the holster.

"Looks like you're in the spy business," Holly said.

36

Late in the afternoon Stone and Holly cast off his dock in his Hinckley 43 motor yacht and moved slowly down the Beaulieu River, careful not to make an excessive wake.

"This is a beautiful stretch of water," Holly said, gazing at the passing landscape, the farms, and country houses.

"I have to agree. That and access to the Solent were big parts of my decision to buy the place."

"I assume Felicity Devonshire brought it to your attention."

"And insisted I buy it. I didn't take much convincing."

They moved around a bend in the river and picked up the marked channel to the Solent. Shortly, they were running toward the Isle of Wight, a few miles away, at 25 knots. Stone pointed out the Squadron at the head of the harbor, a castle with a row of brass cannons out front. "Henry the Eighth build this to protect England from France. I don't think it was ever used for that purpose."

"And yet, the cannons are there."

"Those are used exclusively for starting and finishing races," Stone replied. They pulled into the Squadron's little marina, where a uniformed boatman waited to take their lines. After they had made fast and shut down, they walked the few steps to the castle's entrance, then to the front door. Down a hallway they came to the Lounge, where cocktails were served, and found the rest of their party waiting.

Stone introduced Holly to the First Sea Lord, Admiral Sir Timothy Barnes, and to the Squadron's commodore Derek Drummond and his wife, Hildy. Felicity introduced them to the other couple, General Sir Jeremy Pink and his wife, Nicole. A bottle of champagne was brought. They drank that, then were called to dinner in the next room. The Members Dining Room was large but comfortable; portraits of past commodores, some of them kings and princes, stared down on them. They sat at a round table for eight in the center of the room.

Dame Felicity raised her glass. "I think we should have a congratulatory toast to Stone Barrington, who has just become a deputy director and special adviser to the United States Director of Central Intelligence."

Stone was, at first, stunned, until he remembered that Felicity always seemed to know everything before anyone else.

Stone thanked them. "The appointment is only about two hours old," he said. "Dame Felicity continues to astonish me with her knowledge of all things."

"I'd understood that you were a lawyer, Stone," Tim Barnes said.

"There is no change in that regard," Stone replied. "I'll continue to be based in New York and remain active with my firm."

"What will you advise the director on?" Pink asked.

"That remains to be seen," Stone replied.

"Of course, you must be secretive about that."

"Not just yet, since I have not acquired any secrets."

"I should tell you, too," Felicity said, "if you don't already know, that Holly Barker is a former director of Central Intelligence, and that she is, currently, the American secretary of state. Also, it is rumored, she might be soon announcing her candidacy for the Democratic nomination for president." There was a round of quiet applause.

Holly bowed her head in acknowledgment, but said nothing.

The first course arrived and Felicity turned toward Stone. "Perhaps you have not heard that Brigadier Fife-Simpson has left Her Majesty's service and taken retirement."

Pink spoke up. "He declined a posting in the Falklands." There were quiet chuckles around the table.

"I should mention," Felicity said quietly to Stone, "that the commodore is a retired Royal Marine, and everyone here has signed the Official Secrets Act, so tales are not being told out of school."

"I've met the brigadier only a few times, but I can understand that everyone involved is relieved," Stone said, raising more chuckles.

"I hope to God that someone is keeping an eye on that fellow," Sir Jeremy Pink remarked.

"Someone is," Felicity replied drily. "He was most recently observed drunk, in the In & Out bar of the Naval and Military Club. After dinner, the doorman decanted him into a cab."

"Somehow," Pink said, "I feel the country is safer tonight."

They finished with an excellent vintage port, with Stilton, then were offered brandy. Stone drank lightly, as he was driving the Hinckley.

....

On the way back across the Solent, driving more slowly in the dark, Stone explained to Holly who Brigadier Roger Fife-Simpson was.

"Every military or intelligence service attracts a few people like that," Holly said. "I've known my share of them."

"I'm glad you missed the opportunity of knowing this one," Stone said.

"I heard from Lance about his visit to Langley and his encounter with Wu."

"I'm sorry I didn't get to see that," Stone said.

Back at Windward Hall, Stone found a note to call Joan. His cell phone had been off for the evening, but it was late afternoon in New York.

"Well," Joan said when Stone had raised her. "I've never known you not to carry your cell phone."

"I've got a new one, and it hasn't been activated yet."

"We got a call from Lance Cabot's office, saying that they want to install some equipment here tomorrow. What's that all about?"

"Lance has asked me to spend more of my time consulting with the Agency. I'm called a 'senior adviser to the director' now. I expect that work will be a secure line to the Agency."

"And a dedicated computer link, too," Holly said.

"I heard that. Holly's there, is she? My regards."

Stone passed that on. "By the way, you will soon undergo a background check for a security clearance, so I hope there are no skeletons in any of your closets."

"Not that they'll ever find," Joan replied.

"I wouldn't count on that. You'll have forms to fill out, so don't lie about anything, even to protect me."

"Who else knows about this?"

"Dino and Viv, but it's not a secret. There won't be a public announcement, so you won't have to field any questions from the media."

"The rumor is out there: I've already had calls from the *Times* and the *Washington Post*. I told them I didn't know what the hell they were talking about."

"You'll have to apologize the next time they call."

"Oh, all right. Anything else?"

"I'll call if I think of anything. We're going to bed now." He hung up and turned his attention to Holly, burrowing under the covers.

"Another minute, and I'd have been asleep," she said, reaching for him.

37

Brigadier Roger Fife-Simpson arrived at his usual pub, the Grenadier, in Wilton Row, as the five o'clock crowd had begun to diminish. He hated it when all the Millennials were jammed into the small bar after work; it was more pleasant in the early evening.

He sat down and motioned to Tom, the barman of many years' standing, for his usual large scotch, and it was delivered.

"Brigadier," Tom said, setting down the glass.

"Tom," he replied.

They chatted briefly, then a woman sat down a stool away from Fife-Simpson. She tried to hang her umbrella on the bar, but it slipped and fell to the floor.

"Let me get that for you," Roger said. He picked up the umbrella and handed it to her.

"Thank you so much," she said.

"May I offer you a drink?"

She smiled. "Thank you. A gin and tonic, please."

Tom brought the drink.

"I haven't seen you here before," Roger said. "Are you a local?"

"I'm a new local," she replied. "Just moved into the neighborhood yesterday." Her accent was straight, old-fashioned BBC—no detectable regional accent.

"Well, you've chosen the right pub," he said.

"And the right neighbor," she replied, offering her hand. "My name is Jennifer Sands."

"Roger Fife-Simpson," he said, taking the hand. She was blond, buxom, fair-skinned—late thirties, he thought. "Where did you live before?" he asked.

"In the country," she replied. "Oxfordshire."

"Did work bring you to London?"

"No, my work is portable. I'm a writer."

"What sort of writing?" he asked.

"Fiction, mostly short stories for literary magazines," she replied, "but I've started a novel."

"A major undertaking," he said, nodding sagely.

They continued that way for a few minutes. "Why don't we adjourn to the dining room for a bit of supper?" he suggested.

"That would be very nice," she replied.

He got them a table and menus, and they ordered.

"But enough about me," she said. "What work do you do?"

"I'm recently retired from the Royal Marines," he said. "As a brigadier general."

"That's impressive," she replied. "Were you a commando?"

"In my extreme youth," he replied. "My penultimate assignment was commanding the training academy for one of the intelligence services."

"Which one? I get them confused."

"MI-6, foreign intelligence."

"So, you were training spies?"

"I was."

"What did you teach them?"

"Everything from basic tradecraft to personal combat. It's a very vigorous course."

"How fascinating! You said that was your 'penultimate assignment.' What was your ultimate?"

"Deputy director of the service," he replied, in a mock whisper.

"That must have been fascinating!"

"It was rather dull, if the truth be known, after all the action of my earlier years. Most of which I can't talk about, of course."

"Were you a spy?"

"If I told you, I'd have to kill you."

She laughed as if she'd never heard the stale joke before.

They had another drink before dinner, then he ordered a fine claret with their food. By the time they got to the port, the brigadier was flying high, and Jennifer seemed to be as well.

"Where is your flat?" he asked.

"Just up the mews," she said. "Only a few steps away. Would you like to stop in for a nightcap?"

"I'd like that very much." He waved for the bill and paid, then they left.

There had been a little rain, and the cobblestones were shiny in the lamplight. She led them to a small mews house and unlocked the front door.

He looked around. There was handsome furniture and good pictures. "This is quite elegant," he said.

"A friend owns the leasehold," she said. "I rent from him." She went to the small fireplace and lit the gas flame. "Cognac?"

"Perfect," he said.

She poured them both a drink and settled onto the small

Chesterfield sofa before the fireplace, patting the seat next to her. "Come, sit."

He joined her, and they sat thigh to thigh. She turned toward him, brushing his arm with an ample breast.

"That felt good," he said.

She gave out a low laugh. "I'm glad you think so."

He turned his head, and her face was right there. She kissed him, then withdrew an inch. "Oh, I'm sorry. It's too soon."

"No," he said, "it's not too soon." They kissed again; her hand was on his thigh, his on her breast. He pinched the nipple, and she made a little noise. Her hand was higher up now, then it rested on his swelling crotch.

The action accelerated, and soon they were headed for her bedroom, shedding garments. For the next half hour they had the best sex Fife-Simpson had ever experienced, and soon he was sound asleep, snoring lightly.

Jennifer disengaged, used the bathroom, then came back to be sure he was still asleep. Having ascertained that he was, she gathered his clothing and examined the contents of all the pockets of his suit. She found his identity card, confirming his name and rank and noting his service number; she checked the credit cards, made a note of the numbers, codes, and expiry dates, then folded the garments carefully, laid them on a chair, and went to her desk, switching on her laptop.

She opened her e-mail program, tapped in an address, then entered two lengthy passwords to gain access to a chat page. She typed: **Stage one completed satisfactorily.**

An immediate answer came back. Have you surveyed the property?

Thoroughly. It's shut down for the night.
Send him away happy. Cultivate.
Certainly.

They signed off.

Fife-Simpson woke the following morning to the aroma of frying sausages. He could see her through the kitchen door, wearing only an apron. "I'll give you another sausage," he said aloud to himself. Then he got out of bed, his erect member leading the way.

38

The brigadier got back to his flat at mid-morning, after another roll in the hay with Jennifer Sands, plus a short nap. He slipped his key into the expensive Israeli lock that had been installed by MI-6, then turned it, and walked in.

"Good morning, Brigadier," a male voice said.

Fife-Simpson jumped, then saw the man in the armchair facing the door. His hand reflexively went to his hip pocket, where his knife resided.

The man in the chair raised a pistol and pointed it at him. "Now, now," he said, "none of that." He pointed at a chair with the pistol. "Please," he said, "sit, and let's have a chat."

Roger tossed his hat aside, slipped off his coat, and sat down. "What is this about?" he asked. "What do you want?"

"Just a chat, for the moment," the man replied. He had an upper-class British accent. "How was your evening out?"

"I'm sorry if I kept you waiting," Roger replied.

"Let's start over. First of all, you may call me Alex. Secondly, when I ask you a question, please answer it directly, instead of deflecting. It saves time. Once again, how was your evening out?"

"Entertaining," Roger replied.

Alex smiled. "Yes, I expect it was. Most entertaining. All you had hoped, I expect."

"Did you arrange it for me?" Roger asked.

"Not entirely," Alex replied. "I left that to Ms. Sands. These things are more effective when people follow their own instincts, and she enjoyed herself quite as much as you did."

"Give her my thanks when you see her," Roger said, drily.

"Oh, you'll see her again, and she will be just as happy to see you as last night."

"What do you want?" Roger asked again.

"First, I'd rather talk about what *you* want, apart from Ms. Sands, whom you have already won. What do *you* want, Roger? If I may call you that."

"Call me anything you like."

"Roger it is, then. There is an envelope on the table next to your chair," he said. "Open it."

Roger looked at the table, picked up the unsealed envelope and opened it. He found himself staring at a photo of himself and the French masseur. He grimaced in spite of himself, shoved the photo back into the envelope, and tossed it to Alex. "With my compliments," he said. "It won't do you any good."

"I'm still looking for what you want," Alex said. "If it's what's in the envelope, I can arrange that, too."

"Certainly not. I was unconscious when that was taken."

"Were you? Somehow, you seemed to be enjoying it. I have others, in other positions. Would you like to see them?"

"No."

"A pity, they are quite artistic, in their way. The lighting is very good. It was certainly an interesting beginning to your holiday in France, wasn't it?"

Roger didn't reply.

"Well, now, we were talking about what you want," Alex said. "Let's see, you have your full pension and the monthly income from the trust your father set up for you, because he didn't trust you to handle the money wisely. A difficult man, your father, eh?"

"You don't know the half of it," Roger muttered.

"So, you can live quite contentedly on your present income," Alex said, "if you're careful how you spend it. Perhaps if you shave a few drinks off your weekly consumption you could afford to continue seeing your shirtmaker every year or two, but not your tailor, of course. You'll have to be very careful with your clothes. You could stop getting caught in the rain, that would help."

"How long have you been following me?" Roger asked.

"For a great deal longer than you realize, Roger. You came to our notice for the first time when you began extorting your fellow officers, the gay ones, for career assistance. One of them was ours, you see. After that we followed you quite closely."

Roger slumped a bit in his chair now.

"I must say, we were very disappointed when you were sacked from MI-6. We were expecting great things from you."

"I'm sorry to disappoint you," Roger replied sourly.

"Dame Felicity turned out to be tougher than you had anticipated, didn't she? That's why she's where she is . . . and you're where you are."

Alex suddenly rose, walked to where Roger sat, and pressed his pistol lightly against Roger's temple. "Perhaps you didn't realize that this is your gun. You could quite easily become a suicide, you know. We've already written you a very nice note, to help the police and the Admiralty and the Foreign Office with their investigation. You might remember, from here on, that you're only a moment away from ending it all."

"I have no such intention," Roger said.

"Of course you don't. I just need to be sure that you are aware of your circumstance at all times." Alex returned to his chair and sat down. "Now, we were discussing what you want, Roger. How would it be if your income quadrupled overnight? That would bring your shirtmaker *and* your tailor back within reach. Or, if it were increased by a factor of, say, ten, the world would be your oyster. You could travel, even buy a holiday home somewhere warm in winter. You could take cruises—first class, of course. Your appeal to women would soar, I should think. How does that sound?"

Roger sighed. "Better than I would have thought. What do you want from me in return?"

"Information, Roger: your keen sense of observation, your friends still in government service, descriptions of places and systems."

"I'm not in a very good position for that these days," Roger replied.

"But you have a prodigious memory for detail, Roger, and that is a very valuable asset for a man in your position."

"And what is my position?" Roger asked.

"Precarious, at the moment," Alex replied. "But with your cooperation I would be very optimistic about your future. You should live, at the very least, another thirty years, long enough for inflation to outrun your income, and that would lead to penury. A bleak prospect."

"Don't think I haven't thought of that."

"Fortunately, I am in a position to make your future positively rosy."

Roger perked up. "And what would I have to do to ensure that?"

"Well, for a start, why don't we give you a nice holiday in a sunny place, all, ah, conveniences provided? We can also invite Jennifer to join you. She'd love that, and she knows how to show her gratitude."

"Ah, yes," Roger said.

"And let me dangle another prospect," Alex said. "You might find yourself materially contributing to the downfall, perhaps even the disgrace, of your nemesis, Dame Felicity Devonshire."

Roger couldn't help smiling.

"Something else: a more recent acquaintance of yours, Mr. Stone Barrington, has come to occupy an influential place in the orbit of the American CIA."

"Has he?" Roger asked, brightening.

"I thought that would interest you." Alex stood, walked over to Roger's desk, and returned his pistol to the drawer where he had found it. "Come, let's go."

"Right now?"

"Why wait? Your luggage is already in the car."

39

An elderly Mercedes sedan awaited them—a large one. Roger was put into a rear seat and found curtains drawn on the windows and on the partition between the driver and the passengers. Roger and Alex were the only two passengers aboard. The car moved off, and Roger soon gave up trying to follow the turns they were making. They were apparently in quite heavy traffic, starting and stopping a lot. Roger thought they might be moving through the south London suburbs.

After an hour or so they began moving faster and more steadily—on the open road, but not a motorway, he reckoned. More turns were made, and then the car came to a stop. Roger started to get out, but Alex put out a hand. "A moment longer, please."

Roger heard a motor start and something was squeaking.

"Now," Alex said.

Roger got out of the car and found himself standing in an aircraft hangar. A business jet of French manufacture, one with three engines, occupied the space.

Alex came around the car and opened the front passenger door. To Roger's surprise, Jennifer Sands got out. "Hello, Roger," she said, giving him a warm smile.

Roger could manage only a quick "Good morning."

The driver went to the car's boot and began handing suitcases to two uniformed aircrew, who stowed them in the airplane's rear luggage compartment.

"After you," Alex said to Roger.

Roger allowed Jennifer to precede him, then climbed the airstairs and entered a comfortable cabin. Alex indicated which seat he should take, then took his coat while Roger buckled himself in. The airplane had begun to move, apparently being towed. The curtains were drawn on all windows, and the cockpit door was closed, so he still could not see outside.

"Am I going to need a passport?" Roger asked Alex.

Alex patted his breast pocket. "It was in your desk drawer. I took the liberty. It was interesting that MI-6 neglected to reclaim your diplomatic passport."

After a short tow, the airplane stopped and an engine started, then another, then a third. They started to taxi. Roger tried to figure out which airport they were on. If they had gone south, it might be Biggin Hill, a former RAF station, which took business jets and was a port of entry.

The airplane trundled on for a few minutes, then seemed to make a left turn and stop. A couple of minutes passed, and the airplane moved on and made another left. Roger thought they must be on a runway. Confirming his judgment, the engines spooled up to full power, and the airplane soon left the runway. He heard the landing gear and flaps come up. Now they were climbing.

A uniformed stewardess came down the aisle. "Would you like a drink before lunch, Brigadier?" she asked.

"Yes, thank you. Your best scotch. No ice." The whisky she brought was very good, indeed. By the time he had drunk it the airplane had leveled off at altitude, and he was being served chicken Kiev. He wondered if that was a geographical hint. It was very good, though. The stewardess did something at a panel up forward, and the window shades rose. Roger looked outside and saw nothing but sea.

He finished his lunch, his tray was taken away, and the stewardess brought him a soft blanket and a pillow. He reclined his seat a bit and closed his eyes.

Roger was awakened some time later by a jerk as the landing gear came down. He checked his watch: they had been in the air for more than two hours. The airplane touched down, and he was able to see buildings and other aircraft, some of them wearing Russian insignia. They taxied to a halt on a ramp and were unloaded into another large car. They left the airport and drove along the sea for three-quarters of an hour, then pulled into a gated driveway, drove up to a large white house, and stopped.

Someone opened his door, and he got out. Alex led him into the house, down a central hallway to double doors that opened onto a terrace; beyond was a beach and the sea.

"Welcome to Crimea," Alex said. "This house once belonged to an archduke." He led Roger on a tour of the place, then took him upstairs to a large bedroom with a terrace opening onto the sea.

Jennifer had joined them. "Would you like me to stay here with you?" she asked.

"Yes, I would," Roger replied.

"You have a nap, and I'll unpack for you."

Roger stretched out on the bed and was soon dozing.

Roger stirred. The room was darkened, though there was daylight still coming through a crack in the curtains. He felt a hand on his crotch and did not disturb it. She unzipped his trousers and unbuckled his belt, then pulled his trousers down a few inches and took him into her mouth. She didn't stop until well after he had climaxed.

They had a shower together, then dressed for dinner, and went downstairs. Alex awaited them on the front terrace at a beautifully set table. A bottle of wine rested in a cradle, and a bottle of Talisker single malt scotch whisky, was next to it. Alex poured them all drinks. He raised his glass. "To new friends," he said. They drank.

Soon caviar arrived—Beluga, the real thing, half a kilo of it. Roger hadn't had any for many years, and he washed it down with iced vodka. Chateaubriand, the best part of the beef tenderloin, was the main course, served with Béarnaise sauce and haricots verts. Dessert was a delicious cake served with a dessert wine.

They took their cognac in the library, a large room with many bound books, mostly in French.

"What do you think of our little cottage?" Alex asked when they were settled.

"It's bloody marvelous," Roger replied, replete with food and drink.

"You will have access to it in the future," Alex said, "from time to time, if all goes well. And I've no reason to think it won't go well." He waited for Roger to respond but got only a contented groan. He pointed across the room. "There are the books in English. They were chosen by Kim Philby."

If Roger had been slow on the uptake that would have brought him up short. "Ah, yes," he said.

"Did you know Philby, Roger?"

"Oh, no. He was before my time. Everyone who knew him spoke of his charm and wit."

"He spent a number of holidays here. Once we had his friend Guy Burgess for a visit, but he was so drunk all the time I doubt if he remembered it later. He wasn't invited back."

Alex got to his feet. "Well, I'm going to turn in. It has been a long day. You two finish your brandy." He gave a little bow, then left the room.

Jennifer leaned over and whispered in Roger's ear, "Don't say anything in this house or on the terraces, unless you want it recorded," she said.

40

ennifer shook him gently awake at eight AM. He shaved and showered, then was called to breakfast on the terrace—lots of smoked fish, eggs, and salads.

"It's time to go downstairs," Jennifer said. "Alex is expecting you."

Roger took a seat across from Alex at a small table in the library, in a nook overlooking the sea. It was a windy day, and there were whitecaps to be seen.

"Now," Alex said. "You are being recorded, of course."

"Of course," Roger replied.

"I am going to ask you many questions," Alex said. "If you answer truthfully and give me your best recollections, we will not have to accomplish this interview by other means."

"All right," Roger said.

"What is your first memory of being at the Britannia Royal Naval College in Dartmouth?"

"Being in a fight," Roger replied without hesitation. "An older boy tried to bugger me in my bed, and I gave him a bloody nose. I wasn't bothered again."

"Describe the first meal you ate there."

"I arrived in the late evening, so my first meal was breakfast. I was given kippers, which I did not like but learned to like, a fried egg, and a piece of toast, tinned orange juice, and strong tea."

"Describe your first class at Dartmouth."

"It was an orientation class. We were shown a slide—an aerial photograph of the school—and various places were pointed out on it. We were given a rule book and told to memorize it before the next day, then we were issued uniforms and taught how to wear them properly."

"Who was the first other student you met?"

"Timothy Barnes," Roger said. "We got on immediately."

"Did you have a homosexual relationship with Tim Barnes?"

"No, but I knew he was queer."

"How did you know?"

"Something in his manner toward me. He realized at once that I was not queer, and it never came up again. I knew he had dalliances with some others, though."

"Did you keep a diary or journal?"

"I did for a few days, but we were kept very busy, and I discovered, anyway, that I was not a good journal keeper. I preferred to rely on my memory, which is excellent."

"What did you excel at when you were at Dartmouth?"

"There was no one thing, but I was good at everything they threw at me."

"Were you promoted while a student?"

"Yes, but always just behind Tim. He was a more attractive personality than I, and I knew it, so I felt no resentment. He finished as the student commandant, and I was his executive officer."

....

Alex droned on with his questions, as much to get Roger comfortable with answering him as to glean actual information, since most of it was in Roger's dossier, anyway. He was impressed with the clarity and accuracy of Roger's answers.

He took Roger through his early assignments after graduation, then suddenly asked, "Who was Simon Garr?"

Roger blinked and took a moment to answer. "He was a class ahead of me at Dartmouth and we shared some assignments afterward."

"Did you know Simon to be homosexual?"

"I surmised it. He was the boy whose nose I bloodied my first night at Dartmouth."

"Did you ever report him to a superior as being queer?"

"No, but I let him know that I could, and if I did, he would be cashiered."

"Did you use this knowledge to extract favors from him?"

"Only once, when a promotion was at stake. After that he was very helpful to me without being asked, because he knew I could destroy him, if he crossed me."

"Were there others, like Simon, in this position?"

"Oh, yes. I seemed to have a gift for spotting them, and I always found a way to let them know I knew. They were very helpful throughout my career."

Alex changed course. "Describe the entryway into the offices of MI-6."

"There was a front door, but it was infrequently used by officers. On my first visit there I was told to knock at a rear door in an alley off Shaftesbury Avenue."

"Was there a code pad for entry?"

"No, just a knocker and a small window. The door was opened by a commissionaire—you know what a commissionaire is?"

"Of course. Describe the man."

"Imposing. Six foot three, sixteen stone, florid complexion, gray hair, quite fit for his age."

"What was his name?"

"I never asked, and no one ever told me."

"Describe the route to the director's office from that rear door."

"Elevator to six, right turn, thirty feet down the corridor, double doors to the left."

"And your office?"

"Another thirty feet beyond those doors, facing the corridor."

"What was on the subbasement floors?"

"A canteen and the armory; that was all I ever saw there."

"What weapons were you issued?"

"A Colt Government .380 with a silencer, a switchblade knife, and a holster that held all of it."

"When you left the service were they reclaimed?"

"Yes, on the way out the door."

"But not your diplomatic passport?"

"No."

"Did that surprise you?"

"I gave it no thought until I took it out of my pocket and left it in a desk drawer in my flat. I assumed I'd hear from them about it, but I never did."

"Keep it. It could come in handy," Alex said. "Describe the director's office."

"Big. I should say twenty feet by thirty. A large desk before the windows, with facing armchairs, fireplace at one end, with a seating area; conference table and chairs at the other; naval art on the walls, probably from the National Gallery and the Admiralty; a large, very fine carpet, filled most of the floor; various cupboards and closets behind paneling, probably a lavatory behind a door."

"What are the electronic defenses of the building?"

"They were not in evidence, but probably rather carefully concealed. I should imagine that the latest in surveillance equipment and recording devices are used."

"All speech is recorded?"

"That is my assumption. It was never mentioned to me. Rather like this house, I should think."

The questioning continued until lunch, then resumed and lasted until six o'clock.

But there was more to come.

41

Fife-Simpson was wakened before dawn, told to dress immediately without showering or shaving, and given a one-piece, sleeveless boiler suit to wear. There was no breakfast, not even juice, and Jennifer was nowhere to be seen.

Two large men hustled him to the basement of the building, and he was shut up in a small, brightly lit room containing only a steel table and chair, both bolted to the floor. Two other chairs rested opposite. There was a mirror at one end of the room, which Roger assumed was two-way, with observers on the other side. None of these features engendered confidence, and he was vaguely anxious.

The door opened and slammed, and the two men who had escorted him to the cellar came in with a man Roger had never seen before. They entered the room and slammed the heavy door behind themselves. Bolts could be heard sliding shut on the other side. The two men, one on each side, fastened Roger's wrists under steel brackets and locked them to the table with a key.

The new man was about six feet tall, slender, had a completely bald head, and wore a brown suit and heavy, black-rimmed eyeglasses. "Now," he said. "Alex having failed to extract truth from you, we will employ other means."

"But I *have* told you the truth!" Roger nearly shouted, but the men ignored him. The two men brought chairs to the table and placed them on either side of Roger. One of them produced a medical bag and opened it to reveal a selection of numbered bottles and a box of syringes. One man removed a blood-pressure kit from the bag, fastened it to Roger's arm, and pumped it up. Then he wrote the results on a clipboard. He said something in Russian to the other man, who selected a bottle from the bag, uncapped a syringe, and half-filled it with fluid. He wiped the inside of Roger's elbow with a cotton swab, slapped the vein to bring it up, then slipped the needle into the vein and began pressing the plunger on the syringe.

Roger felt a surge of warmth through his body, so much so that he began to perspire. He slipped into a half-conscious state and felt his heart begin to race.

"State your name," the interrogator said.

"Roger Terrence Fife-Simpson."

"Your age?"

"Forty-nine," Roger mumbled. Someone slapped him smartly across the face. "Speak clearly," the man said. "You are not unconscious."

"Forty-nine," Roger said again, trying to enunciate precisely.

The interrogator began to ask questions about random subjects—his childhood; his first assignment with the Royal Marines; the first, second, and third women he had had sex with; the kind of car he drove; where his suits were made; questions about Station Two and the attendees. They seemed particularly interested in Stone Barrington and would not accept that his presence there was the result of a wager. They demanded every shred of information he had about Barrington and the female doctor he had met at Station Two. They questioned him about the location and style of Barrington's country house and demanded detailed descriptions of the rooms he had entered.

The questioning continued for what seemed the whole day, and Roger was not permitted to eat, stand, or use a toilet. He urinated in his clothing three or four times, and whenever his head seemed to clear a little, more of the drug was administered through the syringe. He was shouted at and slapped repeatedly to keep him on the edge of full consciousness.

Finally, when he felt that everything had been drained from him, a new syringe was inserted into his vein, and a bucket of water was thrown in his face. He snapped to full consciousness, his heart racing.

"Take him," his interrogator said.

The two men unlocked his shackles and marched him back upstairs to his bedroom and into the bath. "Clean yourself up," one of the men said, and he was left alone.

He used the toilet, emptying his bowels, then threw the soiled suit into a laundry hamper, shaved, showered, and flung himself into bed. A half hour passed before his pulse began to return to normal, then he fell asleep.

He came awake with someone kissing him on an ear.

"Wake up, my darling," Jennifer said. She helped him sit up and get into some clothes. By the time he had dressed he was feeling fairly normal again. "It's time for dinner," she said, then walked him downstairs and onto the terrace, where a table had been set again.

Alex was already seated, eating caviar with a spoon and

washing it down with iced vodka. "Sit down, Roger, sit down," he said jovially.

Roger dug into the caviar and blinis, the first food he had eaten all day.

"You did quite well today," Alex said.

"Did I? How?"

"You made them believe you. Either you told them the truth, or MI-6 trained you very well to withstand interrogation."

Roger shook his head. "No."

"No, what?"

"No, they didn't train me for that. I never attended their training school."

"I'm sorry I disappeared today," Alex said, "but your interrogation required that more than one officer question you. Fortunately for you, both of us came to the same conclusion: that you were truthful."

"I don't remember much of what they asked me," Roger said.

"That is the effect of the drugs you were given. A subject can be interrogated, then forget, and, if he is interrogated again, his answers can be compared to the transcript of his earlier session. Good, no?"

"If you say so." Half a roast chicken was set before him, and he tore into it with his fingers, washing it down with wine.

He did not begin to feel full until he ate ice cream for dessert.

"You are tired," Alex said. "You should go to bed now. You and I will meet in the morning, then you will be returned to England."

Roger said good night, then left the table with Jennifer in tow. She got him into bed, serviced him orally, then tucked him in.

....

The following morning, after a hearty breakfast, he sat down with Alex in the library.

"Should I wish to contact you," Alex said, "I will call you on this telephone"—he handed Roger an iPhone—"and ask if this is the laundry. You will say, 'Wrong number' and hang up. Then you will receive a text telling you the time and place of our meeting. You will take a taxi halfway there, walk for a few blocks, go in and out of buildings by different doors, then take another taxi to within a block of the meeting place, then walk the rest of the way, taking great care that you are not followed. Do you understand?"

"Yes," Roger said. Then he was asked to repeat everything he was told.

"One hundred and twenty-five thousand pounds has been placed in a numbered bank account in the Cayman Islands." He pushed a slip of paper across the table. "Memorize this account number now, and the telephone number of the bank."

Roger memorized the numbers and Alex took back the slip of paper and gave him a black credit card with his name on it and the name and branch of his London bank. "You may use this card to pay for purchases or to retrieve money from cash machines anywhere in the world. Twenty-five thousand pounds will be deposited in it on the first day of every month for as long as our relationship lasts. On the second of every January, another one hundred thousand pounds will be deposited, in addition to your regular monthly payments."

"Thank you," Roger said, pocketing the card.

"You will be expected to follow completely every order you are given. Do not ask what will happen if you fail."

Roger nodded.

"Jennifer will move in with you, and you will both move to a better flat. An agent will show you several when you return. Jennifer has her name and number. When you choose a place, Jennifer will pay the monthly rent, so if you are asked how you can afford it you can reply that you have a rich girlfriend. If you, at some point, wish to marry, you may do so. You may travel freely, as long as it does not conflict with your assignments. Jennifer will act as your secretary, pay your monthly bills, make your travel arrangements, et cetera. I hope you two will continue to enjoy each other's company." Finally, he gave Roger a zippered case containing a semiautomatic 9mm pistol, a silencer, and a box of ammunition. "The pistol may be used multiple times in succession leaving a different ballistic imprint each time, so that no connection can be made with another usage, a little trick we learned from our CIA opponents."

Alex escorted them both to the front door, where a driver was putting their luggage into a car. They were driven to an airport and, in a hangar, put aboard an airplane—this one a Citation X, of American manufacture.

They landed at Biggin Hill and were driven to Roger's flat in London. The place had been thoroughly cleaned, he noted.

42

They had breakfast the following morning, then Jennifer said, "We have an appointment at ten o'clock to look at a flat."

"All right," Roger said. He had not yet returned to the full realization that he was a free man in his own home. It was best to just follow her instructions.

They arrived at the address, in Eaton Place, and were met by an estate agent, then took the elevator to the top floor. The apartment was large, occupying the entire floor. There was a large drawing room, a separate dining room, a library with a toilet concealed behind bookcases, an office, two en suite bedrooms, and a garage in the basement with two spaces, with an entrance on the street behind.

"Can we afford this?" he asked Jennifer.

"*I* can afford it," she replied. "Remember, I'm a wealthy woman."

Jennifer signed a lease on the spot, and she wrote a check. "Come," she said, "we must begin packing your things and arrange for removals."

Late in the afternoon of the following day, they occupied the new place, and while Roger unpacked and placed his things in his new dressing room, Jennifer went shopping. The day after that, things she had bought began to arrive: furniture, pictures, sculptures—all of it from antique shops. Within a few days, the place looked as if they had always lived there.

On Saturday morning, Roger's iPhone rang for the first time. "Hello?"

"Is this the laundry?" a female voice asked.

"I'm sorry, you have the wrong number," Roger replied, and she hung up. Shortly, the phone made a chiming noise, and he checked the text messages. The single message gave an address in Hampstead.

"I've had a call," Roger said to Jennifer, who was unpacking kitchen utensils.

"You must go armed," she replied.

Roger consulted his *London A to Z Guide*, then planned his route. He caught a cab in the street, took it as far as Trafalgar Square, then walked several blocks, bought a *Daily Telegraph*, and got another cab. He got out a block short of his destination and walked to a spot on Hampstead Heath, taking care that he was not followed to his destination: an empty park bench. He sat down and opened his paper. Ten minutes passed before a man sat down at the other end of the bench. He didn't look at the man.

"Good morning," said a voice that he recognized as Alex's.

Roger said nothing, but nodded.

"Look up and slightly to your left," Alex said. Roger did so. "You see the little street, with row houses?"

"Yes."

"Simon Garr, your old acquaintance from Dartmouth, lives at number 3. He will leave the house in about twenty minutes for a lunch date elsewhere. You will wait for him on the bench across the street, near the house. When you see him, you will confront him as he looks for a cab and shoot him twice in the head. Do you understand these instructions?"

Roger turned and looked at him.

"Don't look at me!" Alex ordered. "Tell me you understand what you are to do."

Roger thought about it for a moment, then sagged. "I understand."

"A taxi will appear, with its light off. You will get into the taxi, which will drive you to Sloane Square. You will walk to your new apartment from there. Are all of your instructions clear?"

"Yes."

"Before you leave this bench, screw the silencer into the barrel of your pistol." Alex placed a tweed hat and a pair of sunglasses on the bench between them. "Wear these," he said. "Leave them in the taxi when you get out. There will be no need to pay the driver."

"I understand."

Alex got up and left.

Roger pretended to read his paper for another fifteen minutes, then got up, donned the tweed cap and the sunglasses, crossed the street, and walked to the bench near the end of Simon Garr's street. He sat down and tried to work up some of his old hatred for Garr. It wasn't hard; he had harbored it for thirty years. He removed the pistol and silencer from his shoulder holster and screwed them together under the newspaper in his lap, then he waited, not looking at Garr's house.

He heard the door open and close, then get locked, before he allowed his eyes to drift in that direction without turning his head. A moment later, a tall man in a raincoat and hat walked into his field of vision. It was Simon Garr, no mistake.

Roger rose, crossed the street, and walked toward Garr from behind, the pistol concealed in his folded newspaper. Garr stopped and looked both ways for a cab. Roger approached him and at the last moment Garr caught sight of him and turned. "Roger?" he said.

Roger lifted the pistol and fired, striking Garr over his left eyebrow. Garr collapsed, and Roger walked two steps and fired another shot into his head.

He looked up and saw a cab coming, its light out. It stopped, and Roger got inside, saying nothing. He unscrewed the silencer and returned that and his pistol to the shoulder holster. The cab drove away, made a number of turns, apparently to shake any possible follower, then drove across London to Sloane Square, stopping in front of the Peter Jones department store.

Roger placed the cap and the sunglasses on the seat, got out, and walked in a leisurely fashion toward Eaton Place and his flat. He took the elevator upstairs, and used his key. "Jennifer?" he called. There was no reply. He went to the closet and the safe Jennifer had bought, opened it, placed the pistol, silencer, and holster inside, and locked it.

He hung up his coat, then went to the bar and poured himself a large scotch. Then he sat in a comfortable chair in the library and let his mind wander.

....

An hour passed, then Jennifer let herself in and put down her packages and hung up her coat. Then she went looking for Roger. She found him in the library, an empty glass in his hand. She took the glass from him and put her hand on his cheek. "How did it go?" she asked.

"It went as it was supposed to."

"Are you all right?"

"I am, though I could use another scotch. Will you join me?"

She poured them each a drink, then came and sat on his footstool. "I'm glad it went well," she said. "I knew you could do it. Now you can do anything."

Roger didn't reply, just sipped his drink. It occurred to him that Alex had cleverly arranged his debut as an assassin by selecting a victim Roger hated.

43

On Saturday evening, with Holly in residence again after a few days in London, Stone hosted dinner at home. The guests were the same people they'd dined with at the Squadron—the Barneses, the Pinks, the Drummonds, and Felicity, who arrived with the foreign minister, whose wife was away, and a new couple, called Terrence and Dorothy Maldwin, both in their late thirties or early forties.

During cocktails Felicity said to the group at large, "Terry and Dottie are both members of my professional family, and Terry is my new deputy."

Stone had the table set in the small dining room, which could accommodate up to twelve. The chat ran to office anecdotes and gossip, which Stone presumed was proper, since they had all signed the Official Secrets Act.

"What do you hear from Roger Fife-Simpson?" Tim Barnes asked Felicity across the table.

Felicity gave him a little smile. "I think Terry is the person to best answer that question, since keeping track of Roger is one of his first assignments. Terry?"

Terrence Maldwin put down his fork and took a sip of his claret. "Well, let's see," he said. "I believe I can do this without notes. The brigadier got lucky a few nights back, while drinking at his local. He met a charming lady. They had dinner, and nature took its course. The day after that, a large Mercedes sedan arrived outside his flat and Fife-Simpson and another man got in. The curtains were drawn in the car, so we could not see who else was inside. We lost the car in the south London suburbs, so we've no idea where they went.

"Roger and the lady returned to Roger's flat three days later, so we suppose they had a bit of a holiday. Then an odd thing happened: the following morning they left the flat and took a taxi to an address in Eaton Place, where they met a woman who seemed to be an estate agent. Inquiries were made, and we discovered that the couple had taken a flat—a very nice one—on the top floor. Over the next two days, they packed up Roger's place and moved into the new flat, and the lady, whose name is Jennifer Sands, did a great deal of shopping for furnishings. We expect to have photographs in a day or two."

"And who is Jennifer Sands?" Felicity asked.

"She's English, thirty-nine, quite attractive, and has some considerable personal wealth from her father, now deceased. She got a first at Oxford in languages, one of them Russian. She was once a member of the Communist Party in Britain, but left a year ago, resigning over policy differences."

"Sounds like Ms. Sands would be attractive to our Russian friends," Felicity said.

"Yes," Terry replied, "and one might think that Roger, too, would be someone who could hold their interest. Some of you have known the brigadier over the years. Does anyone think that he might be had by the Russians?"

Tim Barnes spoke up. "I think that, given his recent retirement, Roger might be bought by the Russians. By the way, it won't hit the papers until tomorrow, but an old acquaintance of mine and Roger's, Vice-Admiral Simon Garr, retired, was murdered early this afternoon, on Hampstead Heath. Looks like a professional job: two bullets to the head. No one reported hearing the shots."

"That's very interesting," Terry said. "Roger left his new flat at mid-morning today."

"Where did Roger go?" Felicity asked.

"He took a cab to Trafalgar Square, where he bought a newspaper and got into another cab. A traffic foul-up caused our people to lose him. He returned to his flat in the mid-afternoon."

Everyone got quiet.

"I wonder," Terry said, "does anyone think that Roger might have it in him to shoot an old acquaintance in the head?"

Tim Barnes spoke up again. "If the old acquaintance was Simon Garr, I think Roger, at least at one time, might have enjoyed that experience."

"Terry," Felicity said, "I think it might be worth the resources to increase the manpower devoted to surveilling Roger."

"It shall be done," Terry replied.

"And perhaps," Felicity said, "they could stop losing him for hours or days at a time."

....

"You have the most interesting guests at dinner parties," Holly said after they had made love and were resting. "And the most interesting conversations."

"You can thank Dame Felicity for providing both the guests and the topics of conversation," Stone replied.

"Did Roger Fife-Simpson strike you as someone who might be bought by the Russians?"

"Given what happened to his career, he strikes me as someone who might be very angry with his former associates," Stone replied.

44

The following morning Stone received a package from Lance Cabot that contained some personalized CIA stationery, a pair of operations manuals, and a kind of employees' handbook for Agency personnel. He spent a good part of the day reading them and found them enlightening.

That afternoon—early morning in the States—Stone received a phone call from Lance.

"Scramble," Lance said.

"Hang on." It took him a moment to hit the right buttons. "Scrambled," he said.

"Henceforth, all our conversations will be scrambled," Lance said.

"All right."

"Did you get the reading materials I sent you?"

"Yes, and I have already read them."

"Good man," Lance said. "Since you haven't spent three or four months at the Farm, you'll need to fill in a few gaps in your knowledge of how we work."

"It seems to me that my knowledge is *mostly* gaps," Stone replied.

"We can live with that. Occasionally, we recruit someone who has an actual life that can't be interrupted for long periods, so we make do."

"I understand, and I'll try to keep up."

"Stone, I called because there has been a flurry of activity about you on a number of Internet search engines that, normally, would ignore your existence."

"So, word is getting around about our arrangement?"

"We've factored that into our analysis, and we believe that there is more than that going on."

"What do you believe is going on?"

"We've had flurries like this when the Russians have taken an interest in a particular person, especially one connected with us. We keep a watch on the search engines they commonly use. Have you had any recent contact with Russians, or with people you suspect might be associated with their intelligence agencies?"

"No, but at dinner last night with Dame Felicity, her new deputy and his wife—Terrence and Dorothy Maldwin—were there, and the conversation turned to the man Maldwin is replacing."

"I know them both," Lance said, "and Terry is a good choice for her deputy. Why did Fife-Simpson's name arise?"

"Apparently, Terry's principal assignment at the moment is to keep tabs on the brigadier. They've been surveilling him since his, ah, retirement—with mixed results."

"'Mixed' how?"

"They lost him a couple of times—once for three days and once for several hours, which coincided with the killing of a British vice-admiral with whom Fife-Simpson has had a rocky relationship over the years."

"That would be Simon Garr."

"Yes."

"Tell me, does Fife-Simpson have anyone new in his life? A woman, perhaps?"

"Funny you should mention that. Yes."

"How did he meet her?"

"In a pub, and apparently they hit it off immediately. They've taken a new flat together."

"Tell me about her—hang on, I want to record this. Go."

"Jennifer Sands, age thirty-nine, Oxford graduate with a first in languages."

"Russian one of them, perhaps?"

"Right. She's attractive and has considerable personal wealth from her father. Oh, and she was once a member of the Communist Party of Great Britain but resigned about a year ago."

"Clearly, she's dirty," Lance said. "Do they know if she—or Fife-Simpson—has had any contact with anyone at the Russian embassy?"

"That wasn't mentioned last night."

"Where is this new flat where they're shacking up?"

"In Eaton Place."

"Ah, that's revealing," Lance said.

"How so?"

"One of London's finest addresses. That means Fife-Simpson is very important to them. Of course, if Ms. Sands is wealthy, she may be paying. Do you have the exact address?"

"No, but they did say it was a top-floor flat."

"Good."

"Why good?"

"Because it makes surveillance easier for us. We're going to have to take a close look at the woman, then set up our own team on old Roger. We'll have to stand back a bit, since Felicity already has people on him."

"I'd be interested in how you would do that," Stone said.

"We'll rent a nearby flat, far enough away so that our people aren't bumping into Felicity's people, and we'll use electronic and telescopic methods. We'll let them follow Fife-Simpson and the woman when they go out, then we'll follow Felicity's people."

"Felicity was annoyed with the lapses in their surveillance of him and ordered Terry to beef up his team."

"As she would, of course. Those two lapses could account for a multitude of sins, including the murder of Simon Garr. The three-day period sounds like an indoctrination to me. You say they lost contact in south London?"

"Yes."

"There are a couple of airports down there. They could have transported him somewhere. We'll get to work on aircraft registration numbers and flight plans filed. It occurs to me, too, that that period could coincide with the increased activity on researching you. Do you think Fife-Simpson could have brought up your name?"

"I've no idea. He knows my name, of course."

"They would have milked him dry for names. So it wouldn't surprise me that yours would come up, especially since Fife-Simpson knows you to be a friend of Felicity's."

"She brought him to dinner at my house," Stone said.

"Then they certainly would have extracted that event from him, and your name as well."

"Do you want me to do anything at this end?"

"No, you're not trained for this sort of thing. I would like to know if anything unusual happens that you could attribute to Fife-Simpson: if you should bump into him on the street in London or get a phone call from him, for instance. If his name comes up in a conversation with someone outside of Felicity's circle."

"That's a very wide circle," Stone said.

"Granted. You've opened a new channel of investigation for us, Stone, and I'm grateful. This is the sort of thing that made me want to bring you inside."

"Well, I'm just sort of lying here," Stone said, "not exactly doing anything."

"Let me know if someone pokes you in the ribs," Lance said. "Bye-bye." He hung up.

Stone thought his new status at the Agency was already making his life more interesting.

45

oger Fife-Simpson had finished the *Daily Telegraph* and was working on the crossword when the phone on the table beside him rang. He stared at the thing, not sure if he should answer it. Before he could make a decision, Jennifer walked over and picked it up.

"Hello? Ah, yes. Where are you now? We'll be right down." She hung up, grabbed Roger's hand, and pulled him to his feet. "Come with me," she said, leading him out the door and to the elevator.

"Where are we going?" he asked.

"It's a surprise."

Fife-Simpson didn't much like surprises, and he viewed this one with suspicion. They got off the elevator on the ground floor, and she led him to the garage. "I've bought you a surprise," she said. They turned a corner, and a white Mercedes convertible greeted them. "What do you think?" she asked. "Or would you prefer something more reserved?"

Roger grinned. "I would not," he said, opening the car door and climbing in. The interior was red leather.

"It's the S550 version," she said, "the larger one, with the V8 engine." She dropped the key into a cup holder. "It's keyless starting," she said. "Foot on the brake, press that button."

He did so, and the engine leapt to life.

"Press this button," she said, pointing to a row of three on the bottom of the rearview mirror.

He pressed it, and the garage door opened.

"The gear lever is on the steering column," she said. "Press down to go forward, up to reverse, and push it in for parking."

He pressed down and drove out of the garage. It was an unseasonably warm and sunny day.

"Stop," she said.

He stopped, and she opened the center armrest compartment and placed his hand on a switch. He fiddled with it, and the top came down and was tucked away under the rear deck. He grinned and accelerated.

An MI-6 officer on the roof of the building behind the couple's apartment suddenly caught sight of Fife-Simpson driving away. He got on the radio. "The car that was delivered a few minutes ago has left the garage, driven by Myna Bird. Get on it!"

In the next block, on another rooftop, a CIA operative spotted the convertible and its driver and got on the radio. "Scramble," he said. "Canary has driven away from his building in a white S550 Mercedes convertible, top down. Wren is riding shotgun."

....

"Where would you like to go?" Roger asked Jennifer.

"Wherever you like. We could have lunch somewhere."

"Let's go to the south coast."

"I'm all for it."

Roger drove west to the M4 motorway, and after a few minutes, turned off on a country road south, driving fast.

"Don't get us arrested," she said, fastening her seat belt.

They ended up an hour or so later in the village of Beaulieu, then drove south some more and stopped at a country pub. "This looks good," Roger said.

They got out, took an outside table, and read the menu. Roger looked up and saw a couple getting out of a Porsche. "I don't believe it," he said.

"Believe what?" Jennifer asked.

"You recall I was asked by Alex about an American named Stone Barrington?"

"Yes."

"Well, there he is, and the woman with him, if you can believe it, is the American secretary of state."

Stone took Holly's hand and led her toward the front door of the pub, then, dead ahead, he saw Brigadier Roger Fife-Simpson. It was obvious Roger saw him, too, so there was nothing for it, he had to say hello. Stone stopped at the table and extended a hand. "Hello, Roger," he said.

Fife-Simpson stood, shook hands, and introduced Jennifer, then Stone introduced Holly.

"What brings you down my way?" Stone asked.

"Just a joyride. New car, wanted to stretch its legs. Will you join us?"

"Thanks, I think we'll go inside. I'm unaccustomed to so much sunshine." They said goodbye, went inside, and found a table.

"Was that who I think it was?" Holly asked.

"It was, and the woman with him must be Jennifer Sands."

"You should have accepted his invitation to join them," Holly said. "That's what Lance would have had you do."

"Lance doesn't comprehend how boring that man is. It would have ruined our lunch."

"A pro would have jumped at the chance to be bored."

"Then I'm no pro," Stone said. "We would have learned nothing."

"If you say so."

"Why did you ask them to join us?" Jennifer asked.

Roger shrugged. "It was the normal thing to do, in the circumstances. Fortunately, they didn't accept the invitation."

"You must report this to Alex when you next speak to him."

"All right, but it's just a coincidence. Barrington's house is down this road, I think."

"You were there before, weren't you? Aren't you sure where it is?"

"On that occasion we approached the house from the river, on Dame Felicity's boat," he said.

"Believe me, Alex will not see this as a coincidence."

....

Perhaps fifty yards away, on the road, the MI-6 surveillance crew had stopped and were arguing.

"We've got to go on and get an eye and an ear on them," one said.

"Fuck that," the driver said. "We'd be made in a flash. We'll wait for him to finish his lunch, then pick up the car."

Further back, the CIA team had stopped, too. "Let's drive slowly by the pub and get some footage of it," the leader said.

The driver put their van into gear and moved slowly forward, while the cameraman got into position to shoot through a port.

"Faster," the leader said. "Don't attract attention." As they came up to the pub a Porsche parked and a man and a woman got out of it and walked toward the pub.

"Get those two on film!" the leader said.

"Why?"

"Because one of them is our secretary of state! Are you blind?"

"Then who's the guy?" the cameraman asked, adjusting his shot.

"Get the plate number on that Porsche, and we'll find out."

46

oger and Jennifer got back into the convertible and continued down the road toward the sea. They came upon a driveway. "See the sign saying Windward Hall? That's Barrington's place." He slowed so they could look through the gates.

"A handsome house," Jennifer said.

"Handsome inside, too." Shortly they passed a van at the side of the road, and a minute later, it fell in behind them, a quarter-mile back.

Stone and Holly finished their lunch and walked back to their car. Fife-Simpson and his lady had disappeared. They drove back to the house, and as they entered the library, a phone was ringing. It was his Agency iPhone, sitting on the coffee table. Stone picked it up. "Hello?"

"Scramble."

"Scrambled. What is it, Lance?"

"What were you doing at the same pub as Fife-Simpson and his paramour?"

"What a charmingly old-fashioned thing to call her," Stone said.

"Explain, please."

"We went to a local pub for lunch. So did Fife-Simpson, apparently, and they got there first and sat outside. We greeted them, then went inside. That's about it."

"I dislike coincidences," Lance said.

"It doesn't matter if you dislike them," Stone replied, "they happen anyway."

"Nevertheless . . ."

"Lance, how the hell did you know about this? We just came back. Are you having us followed?"

"No, MI-6 is having Fife-Simpson followed, and my people are following MI-6. You know that."

"That's right, I do. Fife-Simpson said he was trying out a new car and drove down here."

"He wasn't lying. We checked it out, and Ms. Sands bought it for him, though it's registered in her name. She must not feel entirely confident of his continuing affection."

"Well, I'm glad you're following MI-6, instead of me."

"Is Holly with you?"

"Yes."

"Did she meet Fife-Simpson?"

"Yes, he invited us to share his table, but we elected to lunch inside."

"Just as well. I wouldn't want you photographed with those people."

"Do you think the Russians are following him, too?"

"No, the woman is, effectively, the Russians. She's living with him, so there's no need for other surveillance on their part."

"Do the Russians rent expensive flats and buy expensive cars for all of their foreign agents?"

"They do not. But Ms. Sands is wealthy and she seems to be in love."

"Go figure."

"I have nothing else for you. Do you have anything for me?" Lance asked.

"Alas, I am bereft of gifts."

"Goodbye." Lance hung up.

"How the hell did Lance know about this so fast?" Holly asked.

Stone explained about the pursuits by MI-6 and the CIA.

"Why do I feel that we're in some sort of spy comedy?"

"Perhaps we are. Who knows? Can I interest you in an after-lunch nap?"

"Yes, as long as there's no sleeping involved."

"There won't be."

Roger and Jennifer got back to their flat in the late afternoon, and the phone was ringing.

"You'd better get that," Roger said.

She did. "Hello? Yes, we just got in. I bought him a car, and we went for a drive down to the south coast. Guess who we ran into? Stone Barrington and the American secretary of state, Holly Barker. It's only a coincidence. It doesn't matter if you hate them, they happen anyway. Dinner when? I suppose so. Is that a good idea? All right, six-thirty for drinks." She hung up.

"Alex?" Roger asked.

"Yes. We're invited to a dinner at the Russian embassy to-morrow evening, black tie."

"Is that a good idea?" Roger asked.

"Alex says it will be just family, which means nobody who isn't Russian. I think he wants to show you off for his boss."

"Who is his boss?"

"The London station chief, Leonid Bronsky, who is on the embassy's rolls as cultural attaché. He's a very slick article."

"I always think of Russians as ham-handed oafs," Roger said.

"Did you find Alex either ham-handed or oafish?"

"Well, no."

"He is typical of these people, as you will learn tomorrow evening. There are no Leninists or Stalinists left—no commissars, either. The ambassador is the most elegant man I've met in London. By the way, you do own a dinner suit, don't you?"

"I do, but it's a bit tatty these days. I'm accustomed to wearing my naval mess kit on formal occasions."

"You'd better get measured for a new suit, then. We may have other such occasions to attend."

"As you wish, my dear."

47

olly had to be back in London for meetings, so Stone took the Cayenne and drove her to the city. "About your suite at the Connaught . . ."

"What about it?"

"If we stay there will we end up as sex entertainment for a bunch of guys at the embassy?"

"We will not. I have ordered it so, and I have a gadget that detects the presence of surveillance equipment. I used it in your bedroom."

"In *my* bedroom?"

"Look, Stone, we are aware that you have attracted the attention of the world's three most important spy agencies, if we leave out the Chinese. Do you think that any one of them would hesitate to wire your home for audio and video, if they felt it served their interests?"

"You have a point," Stone replied. "Thank you for bringing the equipment."

"Your entire house is clean, as far as I can tell."

"Good."

"Is anyone following us?"

"Now? We're on the motorway."

"Do you think those three incapable of tailing you on a superhighway?"

"I suppose I don't," he replied, checking his rearview mirror. "I don't see anything."

"Keep checking," Holly said.

"Why would they want to follow us?"

"If not you, then me."

"Do you care?"

"Of course I care. Suppose you drive carelessly, cause a fender-bender, and it turns into an altercation. Do you want to see that on CNN?"

"I suppose not."

"I'm certain I don't want to see that," she said firmly. "When I get back I'm faced with a national campaign, and I don't want the nation to witness me punching some jerk's lights out."

"So, you're not worried about being the victim of road rage, but the perpetrator?"

"I have a temper, and when you combine that with certain skills . . ."

"I must remember not to annoy you."

"Always a good policy," she said.

"Are you smiling?"

"Not at the moment."

"Just checking." He looked into the rearview mirror again. "There's one of those big Mercedes vans back there."

"A Sprinter?"

"That's the one. It was back there last time I checked, too. It hasn't gained on us."

"Assume it's following us then, and be careful."

The van stayed there all the way to the Connaught, then it parked half a block away. Holly checked in, and they were escorted to her suite. Stone liked it better than the ones he was accustomed to.

"Can I use this when you're not here?"

"Imagine this headline: SECRETARY BARKER'S LOVER STASHED IN STATE DEPARTMENT'S LUXURY LONDON HOTEL SUITE."

"Gotcha. I'll get my own suite."

"Didn't you buy a London house from Felicity a couple of years ago?"

"Yes. It's being redecorated now, which is why I didn't take you there. Next time."

"That reminds me. I have something for you." She went to her suitcase and came back with a State Department envelope, sealed with wax, the old-fashioned way.

"What's this?" Stone asked.

"I asked our ethics review board at State to consider the matter of the house I've been living in for the past two years, the one you gave us. They have determined that the department using such a residence for a secretary while she is fucking the gifter is 'ethically questionable,' as they so delicately put it, so they're giving it back to you. The documents are in the envelope."

Stone scanned them. "These make it seem as though the transaction never took place. Okay. So you're moving out?"

"Certainly not. I'm very comfortable there. Apparently there's no ethical problem if I'm fucking the *owner* of the house I live in."

"I find that baffling."

"The federal bureaucracy at its most discerning. There's a property tax bill in there, too, overdue. The department, in its confusion, never paid them."

"Swell, I'll fax it to Joan for payment."

"The good thing about all this is that I found out how really sweet you are, when you proposed such a thing. You did yourself a lot of good there, buster." She took his face in her hands and kissed him, and one thing led to several others.

Stone called Lance.

"Yes?"

"Scramble."

"Scrambled."

"Holly and I drove up to London earlier today, and we were apparently followed by a white Mercedes Sprinter all the way to the hotel. Do you have an opinion on which of the relevant intelligence groups is behind that?"

"Not us," Lance said. "Could be either of the others—or, perhaps more likely, the State Department."

"They have people who do that?"

"Of course."

"Should I do anything about it?"

"What would you do?"

"I don't know, let the air out of their tires?"

"That would be fun, if it's the Russians, less fun if it's the Brits, and no fun at all if it's State. By the way, are you in State's suite at the Connaught?"

"We are."

"Are you participating in the making of a sex video for their benefit?"

"Holly says all that is switched off, and she has a detector that confirms it. I watched her wave it around."

"Nevertheless, you should be careful about what *you're* waving around," Lance said.

"I shouldn't trust Holly to turn it off?"

"You shouldn't trust those people in the van to turn it off."

"That's if they're from State."

"Behave as if they are, and you won't have to watch the tape on the Internet. Goodbye." Lance hung up.

"Holly?" he said.

"Mmmmfh?" she replied into her pillow.

"Do you trust your people not to record our activities here?"

"Yes."

"Why?"

"Because I saw to it, early on, that they're scared shitless of me."

"Oh, good."

48

The Russian embassy sent a car for Roger and Jennifer. Upon arrival it was driven into an underground garage before the door opened, and they were directed to an elevator.

"A precaution," Jennifer said. "They don't want anyone photographing your arrival."

"Who would care?" Roger asked.

"Your former employers," she said. "Don't be naïve, Roger. You must always be aware of your surroundings and circumstances. The Russians admire such caution."

They were met on the ground floor of the embassy and escorted into what must have once been a ballroom. Roger reflected that the Russians didn't have much use for ballrooms these days. "I was expecting a bigger crowd," he said, "but there are no more than thirty people here."

"I told you, it's all family. All these people work in intelligence in the embassy complex and have high security clearances—as do we, incidentally."

"When did that happen?"

"Right after you were cleared in Crimea."

Alex spotted them from across the room and approached. "Good evening," he said, embracing both. "Roger, I hear you are driving a very elegant new car."

"I am," Roger replied, "and I thank you for anything you might have done to make that possible."

"I only make Jennifer possible," Alex replied. "She does the rest."

"Then thank you for Jennifer."

"Oh," Alex said, reaching inside his jacket. "I have something for you—a little gift."

Roger had thought he would produce a gun, but instead he was handed a Russian diplomatic passport. He looked inside and found his photograph, apparently taken in Crimea, and the name "Sergei Ivanovich Ostrovsky."

"It is a mark of our faith in you, Roger, that you should own this. If you should ever have to disappear from England or from anywhere else, thoroughly destroy all your documents and use this, anywhere in the world. We will also be supplying you with a Russian driving license and other personal papers, including an appropriate birth certificate. Among the other materials is a personal history, which you must immediately memorize, in case you should ever be interrogated by unfriendly entities."

"Thank you again," Roger said.

"I understand from your records that you speak some Russian?"

"Enough to order dinner and vodka, but not to converse fluently."

"Beginning tomorrow, you will undergo an advanced course in our language, and your professor will be Jennifer, who is superbly qualified."

"Why would I need the language?"

"It's like the passport, for use if you should have to run. Also, I should point out that my colleagues tend to view with suspicion operatives who are not conversant in Russian."

"I see."

"Come, now. It's time for you to meet some very important people." In short order, Roger was introduced to the station chief for Russian intelligence, the Russian naval attaché, and the Russian ambassador to the United Kingdom and their wives. At dinner they were all at the same table, being serenaded by a small string orchestra, along with a zither, followed by a pas de deux by ballet dancers from the Kirov company, in St. Petersburg.

Much vodka was consumed, and some of the diners were moved to sing along with the orchestra. Several were inspired by the dancers to engage in athletic Russian choreography, with much clapping from their audience.

It was after midnight before Roger and Jennifer could make their way to their car and return to the flat.

Stone and Holly were returning from dinner at Harry's Bar, when his phone rang. "Hello?"

"Scramble," Lance said.

"Scrambled."

"Have a seat and make yourselves comfortable. I want to show you something."

They did so, and an image appeared on the iPhone screen of a large room with tables and diners and a string orchestra.

"Do you see him?" Lance asked.

"See who?"

"Brigadier Fife-Simpson. Wait, I'll zoom in on his table."

"Got him," Stone said, "and that's his girlfriend, too. Where is this happening?"

"At the Russian embassy in London. All the participants are Russian intelligence, and the brigadier and his lady are at a table with the local station chief, the naval attaché, and the ambassador. This is very significant. It indicates that they place a high value on Roger, probably higher than he understands. Just a minute." Lance backed up the video a few minutes until Roger and Jennifer were speaking to a man who took something from his pocket and handed it to Roger. At the appropriate moment, Lance froze the images and zeroed in on the object. "That," he said, "is a Russian diplomatic passport with Roger's photograph in it and the name 'Sergei Ivanovich Ostrovsky.' The Russians don't hand out those as party favors, so our boy is now, as our Southern friends might say, 'in high cotton.'"

"How on earth did you get these pictures?" Stone asked.

"The embassy underwent some renovations last year, and that gave us the opportunity to install the necessary state-of-the-art equipment. Astonishing quality, isn't it?"

"It certainly is."

"By the way, while you two were dining at Harry's Bar, two men in head-to-toe black duds and hoods visited your suite and discreetly ransacked it. I expect they were traveling in the Sprinter that tailed you to London earlier today. They would probably have installed audio and video equipment, but we dispatched a maid to the room with fresh towels, to rout them, so you may feel secure now."

"Thank you very much, Lance," Holly said. "Now you may

switch off your own surveillance equipment so that we can have some privacy."

"Of course," Lance said. "Consider it done." He hung up.

"Do you think he switched everything off?" Stone asked.

"Probably," Holly said. "Let's make it very dark in here, though."

The two of them went around the bedroom, checking that all the curtains were drawn and shades lowered and night lights extinguished, Holly used her detection device, with negative effect, then they got naked and hopped into bed.

"Isn't darkness wonderful?" Stone asked. "I like feeling my way."

"I like it, too," she said.

49

ance Cabot sat at his desk and looked at stills of the video taken the evening before at the London Russian embassy. His secretary announced Bruce Winn, an Agency analyst on the Russian desk.

"Come and look over my shoulder," Lance said to Winn, who did so. Lance held the magnifier with one hand and pointed with the other. "We know that these three men are the station chief, the naval attaché, and the ambassador, all with their wives."

"Yes, Lance, that's correct."

"But who is this man?" Lance asked, pointing at a middle-aged male at the table, apparently unaccompanied.

"I confess he is unfamiliar to me," Bruce replied.

"I want you to run this through the facial identification software and see if we can make him."

"Right away," Bruce replied, then left the office.

Three hours later, Bruce Winn revisited Lance.

"Did you make him?" Lance asked.

"Yes, but not where we expected to. We ran him against

every employee of Russian intelligence known to us, also through the Russian navy and army, and got nothing, so we had to go random, run him against all known faces in Britain."

"And?"

"We found the face among those attending a convention of rare book dealers in Brighton, two years ago."

"And who is he?"

"His name is Wilfred Thomas. He has a rare-book shop in Burlington Arcade, London, and he is also a bookbinder, very expensive."

"I know Burlington Arcade well, and I think I know the shop, too. What do we know about Mr. Thomas?"

"He is British, sixty-two years old, widowed four years ago, wife died of natural causes. He attended Harrow and Oxford, where he read history and languages."

"Don't tell me," Lance said, "among them Russian."

"Right. Something else interesting: he is the third son of the Duke of Kensington, who is the third-largest property holder in London, after the Duke of Westminster and the Cadogan Estate. His title, which he rarely uses, is the Earl of Chelsea."

"You're right," Lance replied, "that is interesting. Now go back and explore connections between Thomas and Jennifer Sands, the lady with Fife-Simpson."

"Yes, sir." Bruce departed.

Lance got his magnifier and looked again at the faces at the table. He thought that two of the diners bore an odd resemblance to each other.

Bruce Winn came back later in the day, looking pleased with himself.

"Tell me," Lance said.

"Wilfred Thomas and Jennifer Sands's father, Elihu Sands, known as Eli, were lifelong friends and shared rooms at Oxford. They both met their wives at Oxford and Jennifer's mother got pregnant while still a student. That's all perfectly straightforward, but their history contains a rumor."

Lance smiled. "Don't tell me. Thomas fathered his friend's girlfriend's child."

"That is the rumor," Winn said, "but I can't prove it."

Lance handed him the photograph and the magnifiers. "There's your proof," he said. "Look at those two faces, Wilfred Thomas and Jennifer Sands. They have to be closely related."

"I believe you're right," Winn said.

"So, Thomas came to Oxford and got bitten by the Communist bug, probably courtesy of his favorite don, who, I'll bet, taught Russian."

"And Sand's girlfriend got bitten by Wilfred Thomas, with Jennifer as the result. I love it."

"So do I," Lance said, "but I don't know if it means anything for us. Let's just keep it in mind, for the moment."

"Yes, sir. I'll revise the files of the relevant parties."

"Stay with the rumor theory, for the time being. Let's see what else emerges. It would be interesting to know if Jennifer knows who her father is, and if Eli knew."

"I think that would have to be a job for operations," Winn said. "We're unlikely to find that information in a file or a book."

"I believe you are right," Lance said.

When Winn had gone Lance placed a call abroad.

"This is Dame Felicity," she said.

"Good day, Felicity, this is Lance."

"Why, Lance, to what do I owe the pleasure?"

"It would seem that both our services have taken an interest in Brigadier Fife-Simpson."

"Oh?"

"Certainly, and you are well aware of that, so let's not be coy."

"How may I help you, Lance?"

"I believe it might be in our mutual interest to share our findings with each other."

"It might make for a more economical operation, as well."

"Ah, I see we're on the same page. I propose that you meet with our operative, perhaps over the weekend, and that the two of you pour out your hearts to each other."

"Let me guess: The operative in question is Stone Barrington?"

"Convenient, isn't it, since you are close, ah . . . neighbors and you will probably both be in residence at Beaulieu this weekend."

"Quite convenient," Felicity replied.

"May we speak again after you two have had a chat?"

"Indeed. Goodbye, Lance."

Lance called Stone's cell. It was after lunch in London.

"Yes?"

"Scramble."

"Scrambled."

"Good day, Stone."

"Good day, Lance."

"I have an assignment for you—a pleasant one, to be sure."

"I'm all ears."

"I believe Holly is leaving England shortly."

"She is being driven to the airport as we speak."

"First, let me tell you what new information has come our way with regard to our surveillance of the brigadier." Lance ran down for him what had been learned and what was suspected.

"Very interesting," Stone replied.

"It has occurred to me that there is little point in having two intelligence services conducting separate investigations into the same subject, and that it might be better for us both if we combine our assets and information."

"I expect that might be a good idea."

"Felicity is coming down to the Beaulieu River for the weekend. I suggest that the two of you find time for a dinner together, preferably at your house, and share everything I have told you and what she already knows."

"That's an agreeable idea," Stone said. "I'm just getting into the car now for the drive down."

"Perhaps you could give me a ring on Monday and let me know the state of your discussions and what moves the two of you might wish to make."

"I can do that," Stone said.

"Have a lovely weekend." Lance hung up.

Stone had not even gotten the car started before his phone rang again. "Hello?"

"It's Felicity, my darling."

"How good to hear from you."

"Will you have dinner with me tomorrow evening, just the two of us?"

"I would be delighted to give you dinner at the Hall and whatever else your heart desires."

"That will take longer than a dinner, I think."

"Then bring your toothbrush."

"Done." Felicity hung up, and so did Stone.

50

tone met Felicity at his dock and took her lines, then they drove up to his house in the golf cart, chatting about the lovely weather and whatever else crossed their minds.

The table had been set for two in the library, but first, Stone made her a martini and himself a Knob Creek on the rocks. They raised their glasses.

"Collaboration," Felicity suggested as a toast.

Stone raised his glass, too. "Collaboration."

Felicity took a deep draught of her martini. "Tell me what you know about the brigadier's situation," she said.

"Certainly. Let's skip backward to the evening before last," Stone said. "I expect you're up-to-date for the period before that."

"All I know is that a car called for them—he in black tie and she stylishly dressed. Unfortunately, my people lost them again after that, and they did not return until after midnight."

"Our people lost them, too, but they turned up at the Russian embassy, where the Agency, merely by chance, has a very complete and high-definition video and audio system—installed during renovations to the building last year." Stone handed her an envelope of stills taken from the video, and Felicity went carefully through them.

"Well," she said, "it's like the senior dance at the school of espionage, isn't it. I'm quite surprised that our Roger made the guest list—and at the head table, as well."

"That surprised Langley, too," Stone said. "This photo," he said, pointing at one, "shows a gentleman, unidentified currently, handing Roger a Russian diplomatic passport with his photo in it and bearing the name Sergei Ivanovich Ostrovsky, which would seem to mean that they think highly enough of Roger to provide him with a means of escape from Britain or Europe, in the event that he finds himself in deep water."

"Ah, yes," Felicity said. "I've no doubt that they will be providing him with a complete identity package and a legend in due course, if they haven't already." She picked out a shot of the dinner table. "I know all of these people except this gentleman," she said, pointing at Alex. "Anything on him?"

"A great deal, as it happens. He turns out to be an Englishman. You recall that you and I had dinner last year at the London home of the Duke of Kensington?"

"Of course."

"Thomas is the duke's family name, is it not?"

"It is."

"The gentleman to whom you refer is Wilfred Henry Charles Thomas, the duke's third son, who is also Earl of Chelsea."

"I recall that the duke had an heir and a spare, but I thought that number three had been shuffled off into the Royal Army, the Royal Navy, or the Church, which are the usual destinations of third sons."

"Apparently Wilfred exhibited a more independent streak. After studying at Harrow and Oxford, where he read languages, prominently including Russian, he set himself up as a dealer in rare and antique books, and also bookbinding, at a shop in the Burlington Arcade."

"What a nice cover for a newly cultivated spy for the Russians," she said. "I believe I have been into that shop once or twice."

"As has Lance," Stone added. "A little more history: Wilfred and a fellow named Elihu Sands, known as Eli, were friends from childhood and at school and shared rooms at Oxford, where they both found suitable girls to marry. It is rumored that Wilfred also found the time to impregnate Eli's girlfriend, resulting in one Jennifer Sands, the brigadier's new squeeze, who sits at the table next to Wilfred. Perhaps you can detect a family resemblance?"

"It seems quite obvious, now that you point it out. Do we know what the state of knowledge is among this group? Who knows what and who doesn't?"

"I think we should assume that they all know, except Lady Thomas, who expired some four years ago. If he didn't know at Oxford, certainly before his death Eli Sands had observed the resemblance of his friend, Wilfred, to his supposed daughter, Jennifer."

"Very probably," Felicity said. "Now, what does all this mean?"

"Lance and I were hoping it might mean something to you and your people because he doesn't have a clue."

"You overestimate my powers," Felicity said. "It certainly explains the source of Jennifer's net worth, and the new flat and new car. I rather think the girl might be in love."

"Given what I know of the brigadier, I find that surprising.

Perhaps you can give me a female's perspective on the attractiveness of Roger to the opposite sex?"

"Medium, I should think," Felicity replied. "Some women are as attracted to military rank as to money, and I imagine Roger has taken advantage of that over the years."

They were called to dinner. Stone tasted and then poured the wine. "Something else," Stone said. "Roger disappeared from anyone's sight for, what, three days? We wonder where he went."

"I believe I can shed some light on that," Felicity said. "We lost him in the south London suburbs, and we deduced that he might have been headed to one of the airports south of London. We did our due diligence and discovered that a Falcon Jet departed Biggin Hill on that day with three passengers, filed for Copenhagen. Halfway there, however, the pilots changed their destination to Sevastopol International Airport, in Crimea."

"Ah, a holiday in the sun," Stone said.

"We had no track of him on the ground, but he was, no doubt, taken to a house on the sea, of which there are many, dating back to tsarist times. I expect he was made comfortable there while they indoctrinated him to a satisfactory degree."

"Do you think Roger has inclinations toward the Russians?"

"I think Roger has inclinations toward money, and they have plenty of it to throw around, not to mention Jennifer's fortune."

"So, Roger has found both love and money."

"It would seem so," Felicity replied. "I wonder what it's going to cost him."

"Something else we might give some thought to," Stone said.

"What might that be?"

"They've invested so much in Roger in a short time, and taken such pains to give him a new identity."

"They certainly have," Felicity admitted.

"The question arises: Why? What are they readying him for that would require so much effort? And why Roger rather than some clerk?"

"Yes," Felicity said, "we will have to give that some thought."

51

With sunlight streaming through the windows, Stone looked up at Dame Felicity, who was astride him and lacked only a whip in her inventory of inventiveness, for which he was grateful. She was smiling, and then her face became beatific, as she issued the noises of pleasure.

Finally she fell sideways into bed, limp. Stone was limp, too.

"Something we forgot last evening," Felicity said, turning to face him.

"I didn't think we forgot anything," Stone said.

"Forgot to discuss," Felicity said, giving him a light slap across the chops to focus his attention.

"Oh, that."

"Yes, that."

"What?"

"If our suppositions are correct, Roger has already performed a task for his Russian betters."

"I forget," Stone said. "What task?"

"The shooting of Vice-Admiral Simon Garr."

"Oh, yes. He had drifted from my consciousness."

"Well, if Roger was the assassin, why?"

"I believe," Stone said, "having trained with him a bit at Station Two, that Roger had some skills with pistols and knives that might qualify him for such work."

"Yes, but why Simon? He had been retired for two years and, rumor had it, was exhibiting signs of dementia. Why on earth would the Russians want him dead? And, it follows, why Roger to do the job? Lots of people are good with a pistol, and the range was only a few feet?"

"Did Roger have a connection to Garr?" Stone asked.

"They were at the Naval College together, Simon a year ahead of Roger."

"It might be good to read both their dossiers from that time and see if there's something else to consider."

"Well," Felicity said, "it couldn't hurt." She picked up her iPhone and tapped in a message. "There. People will be awake soon, and we'll hear back."

Stone sat up, picked up the room phone, and ordered breakfast, then he lay back. "It occurs to me that we would know none of this new information about Roger, or about his newfound friendship with the Russians, if you had not had him followed after you gave him the boot."

"Probably not," Felicity said.

"Do you have everyone followed who resigns or is fired?"

"Not usually," she replied, "unless the leave-taking is by an employee who is sufficiently disgruntled to wish us ill."

"And Roger was disgruntled, wasn't he?"

"Look at it from his point of view," she said. "First, he was transferred to Station Two, and the Scottish Highlands, in winter, is not a posting most officers of rank would think attractive."

"One reason for disgruntlement."

"Then, somehow or other, he's sent to MI-6, to a posting that he is unqualified for, and he's promoted to brigadier."

"Would the rank come with the posting?"

"Probably. If one is a colonel and receives a promotion, then the rank would follow, or retirement. It's the same in your services, I believe."

"Roger has a history of blackmailing gay superiors to get better assignments, does he not?"

"Yes."

"Who, in this case, would have been his target?"

"The foreign minister, it would seem. He's kept a boyfriend on staff for decades, and the deputy director job was within his gift, though normally he would discuss it with me first."

"And he didn't this time?"

"He did not."

"How long did Roger serve in the post?"

"He claimed it for a couple of weeks, but I don't think he served for a minute. The only task I gave him was to go to the States, to visit your lot and have a chat with them. I had intended to keep him traveling for a year or so, then find an excuse to sack him."

"And why did you do so sooner than planned?"

"The thing with the foreign minister came to light, however dimly, and I did it to show him I would not allow my service to be a dumping ground for the incompetent and, in Roger's case, the disagreeable."

"That's two reasons for Roger to be disgruntled."

"Correct. I ordered him watched because I thought he was angry enough to look for a way to retaliate."

"Quite right," Stone said.

Felicity's phone chimed, and she read a rather long message. "There is a connection between Roger and Simon Garr," she said. "On Roger's first night at Dartmouth, Simon tried to bugger him, and Roger gave him a bloody nose. After that, feelings were tense between them, and there was at least one successful attempt by Roger to blackmail Simon into getting him a promotion."

"So they hated each other?" Stone asked.

"Apparently so."

"And that could be the motive for Roger to shoot Simon in the head? An awful lot of time had passed, had it not?"

"Yes, but they both worked at the Admiralty at one time and would have had contact there, perhaps creating other opportunities for the engendering of ill will between them."

"I believe I'm beginning to get the idea," Stone said.

"What idea? Why would the Russians care if there was ill will between two retired flag officers?"

"Practice," Stone said.

"Practice? What are you talking about?"

"They wanted to see if Roger would assassinate someone, and, for insurance, they chose somebody for whom he already had ill feelings, to give him impetus. It was a practice run, and Roger passed the test."

"I don't understand. Practice for what?"

"Another assassination?" Stone suggested.

"All right," Felicity replied, "that's bizarre, but it makes a kind of sense."

"Also," Stone said, "if Roger is caught and charged with Simon's murder—or, after murdering someone else—he has a motive for the killings that would not seem to involve the Russians. They can just step back and allow him to take the heat."

"Go on."

"I don't know where else to go," Stone said.

"If you're right," Felicity said, "then all we have to do is figure out who the Russians want assassinated next."

"Any thoughts on that subject?" Stone asked.

"Christ, I don't know: the prime minister? The foreign minister?"

"Somebody important," Stone said. "I'm thinking, you."

Felicity blanched. "He wouldn't dare," she said.

"Remember whose car was the target at Station Two?" Stone asked.

52

tone waited until afternoon before phoning Lance.

"Yes, Stone?"

"Scramble."

"Scrambled."

"Felicity and I had dinner and thoroughly explored the why and wherefore of Brigadier Roger Fife-Simpson."

"I'm sure that's not all you explored," Lance said.

Stone ignored that. "Follow this line for a moment," he said. "Roger leaves MI-6 by popular request, and he is disgruntled."

"Got that."

"Previously, he had demonstrated a strong dislike for Vice-Admiral Simon Garr, dating back to their time at Dartmouth."

"Got that, too."

"The Russians recruit Roger in order to use him as an assassin. His first assignment was Simon Garr."

"Why Simon Garr? He's been retired for some time and I hear he was having problems with dementia."

"It was Simon Garr because, as a trial run, they wanted a target that Roger already hated. They wanted a demonstration."

"That would be a smart move on their part, if they were uncertain whether he could or would pull it off."

"He did pull it off, and now they consider him ready for another assassination."

"Of whom?"

"Felicity guesses the foreign minister or perhaps even the prime minister."

"Neither makes any sense," Lance said.

"Why not?"

"Who assassinates a foreign minister?"

"Not an obvious target, I concede. How about the PM?"

"He's a bumbler, and I should think the Russians are happy to have him in office."

"Then that leaves only Felicity herself as the potential target."

"Right. The Russians clearly want her out of the way, and Fife-Simpson hates her guts for sacking him, does he not?"

"Well," Stone said aloud to himself, "I warned her last night." They hung up.

A few minutes later Felicity rang. "After our conversation of last night, I decided to put on more security."

"And change your routine," Stone suggested.

"Do I have a routine?"

"Do you lunch at the same time every day? Go to the same restaurant? Do you have a regular hairdresser's appointment? Nails? You seem to come down to the Beaulieu most weekends."

"All right," she said. "I have a routine."

"You don't have to stop doing those things, just change the

order in which they are done." Stone stopped. "Why am I giving counterintelligence advice to you, of all people, when that's what you do for a living?"

"Nevertheless, your advice is appreciated. It shows you care what happens to me."

"Or rather, what doesn't happen."

"If you were here right now," she said, "I'd fuck you on my conference table."

"God, I hope this is a secure line."

"It is."

"How about the conference table? Will it hold up to a lot of thrashing around by two people?"

"Certainly. Do you think I'd have a weak conference table?"

"Do you often employ it for that purpose?"

"No, but I'm thinking about it. Right now."

"It will have to wait for your next trip south, I'm afraid."

"All right, I'll see you this evening."

"But you just got back to London."

"I left Beaulieu too soon."

"Well, if MI-6 can stand your absence I can certainly stand your presence. Come ahead."

"Will you give me dinner?"

"Among other things."

"I can't talk about this anymore, or I'll do something rash."

"Better not."

"Meet me at your dock at seven." She hung up.

Stone hung up, but ten minutes later his phone rang: blocked caller. "Yes?"

"The PM has just called a national security meeting at six o'clock," Felicity said. "The son of a bitch."

"What's a national security meeting?"

"All the intelligence heads: military, MI-5, MI-6, the signals-and-codes people. All hands on deck."

"Does this mean there is an emergency?"

"Probably not, or he would have summoned everyone immediately, instead of at six. More likely, the PM just wants to bloviate about something."

"Well, I guess you'll have to show. How about tomorrow night? You've got me thinking about it."

"Great minds, et cetera. I can't plan until I know what happens at the meeting. I'll call you."

"I'm not sure how long I can maintain this . . . state of readiness," he said.

"You just relax, and I'll attend to that at the earliest possible opportunity."

"Promise?"

"Swear." She hung up.

53

tone hung up in a state of intense desire, and, if it flagged for a moment, it came back when he thought about their conversation. He and Felicity were not new to each other, but somehow, the flame still burned, and it was burning now.

He was in bed, trying to read a book, when his phone rang: blocked caller. "Yes?"

"All right," she said wearily, "I'm out of the meeting."

"How did that go?"

"I was right. The PM just wanted to bloviate. This always happens when we give him advice, and he ignores it, then everything goes wrong. His refrain is always, 'Why didn't somebody tell me?' when everybody has told him."

"I suppose it's too late to come down here now."

"I have an eight o'clock meeting tomorrow morning in London, and if I came down there, I'd miss it, because I'd wake up at five o'clock tomorrow morning, find you in bed with me, and want to stay all day."

"When, then?"

"The weekend is as soon as I can promise."

"I'll hold you to that."

"I'll aim for Friday, seven PM on your dock."

"Have you ever been fucked on a dock?"

"Probably, but docks have splinters. Your bed is more inviting."

"See you then."

"I'll bring clothes for the weekend."

"You won't need them, but bring them anyway, if we should have a sudden urge to dine at the Squadron."

"Done." She hung up.

On Friday evening at seven, Stone was standing on his dock, waiting, peering into the gloom, when Felicity's boat emerged from the fog. He took her lines, made them fast, and put her suitcase on the golf cart.

They said little until they were upstairs. "Dinner's not until eight-thirty," he said, and they both started shedding clothing and leapt into bed.

"I see I need not have worried about your ability to maintain an operational level of readiness," she said.

"You make it sound like an MI-6 operation."

"Our operations are not this much fun."

"It happens when I clap eyes on you," he said. "Every time."

They conjoined and did it looking into each other's eyes, until Felicity rolled over and on top of him. "This is my favorite position, you know."

"I love the view from down here," Stone said, reaching for her nipples.

"And I love having both your hands on my body."

They stopped before exhaustion set in and dressed for dinner, then went down to the library.

"Osso buco tonight," Stone said. "I remember how you love it."

"Thank you, my dear," she replied.

"Tell me about your week," he said.

"It's just as well I didn't come down here Monday night," she said. "It turned out to be a very busy week."

"Have you heard anything further about Roger?"

"No, but someone brought up his name at the national security meeting."

"In what light?"

"Everyone considers him a threat, now."

"Good. How many people do you have assigned to you right now?"

"Four," she replied, "and armed to the teeth."

"Are they outside now?"

"Yes, and they are rentals. The desire for security among the cognoscenti is such that I have had to turn to your friends at Strategic Services to lend a hand, and no one is complaining about the cost."

"Tell them to get some supper from the kitchen," Stone said.

"They'll appreciate that."

"Lance will be relieved to learn that you're taking the threat seriously."

"Ah, Lance."

"Anything new to report re: Roger?"

"He appears to be wallowing in connubial bliss," she replied.

"'Connubial'?"

"They went to a registry office and got married."

"That says something about how serious the Russians are, that they would allow that."

"I'm sure they encouraged it."

"I wouldn't have thought that connubial bliss would be a requirement for an assassin."

"They clearly want him to be happy," Felicity said. "I'm sure they think it will make him more responsive to their wishes, if he knows that, by refusing an order, he jeopardizes everything."

"Good point. Is anyone doing anything to rattle these people?"

"Apparently not. Someone at the meeting had drawn up a list of Russians to knock off, should they get lucky with one of ours. A rapid response."

"I don't see how that does anything preventative."

"Neither do I," she replied.

"Are your people taking any steps, other than watching my house?"

"All of our people are now bearing upgraded arms," she said. "Everyone now has a sniper scope with night vision capabilities. Everything is silenced, too."

"Well, I'm glad for them not to disturb my neighbors."

"You don't really have any neighbors, Stone, except for the guests in your hotel."

"Especially paying neighbors."

She laughed and polished off her peach tart. "Now," she said, "I'm ready to be bodily carried upstairs."

"I think I can just about bodily drag you to the elevator," he said, "but that's about it."

"Do with me as you will," she said.

He picked her up and slung her over his shoulder. "I fully intend to." He took the elevator.

54

On Saturday, a few hours later and eighty miles or so north, another couple, housed in Eaton Place, were having much the same experience as Stone and Felicity.

"I've never been married before," Roger breathed. "I like it."

"And I only once, and I didn't like it," Jennifer replied. "Now I do. The odd thing is, we're doing the same things to each other that we always do, but it seems to be better because we're married."

"I won't argue with that."

Roger's phone rang. "The hell with it," he said, thrusting.

"You have to answer it," she said. "Otherwise, they'll come looking for us."

"Shit!" he yelled but did not disengage. "Hello?"

"Good morning, Roger," Alex said.

"It is, isn't it."

"I trust the honeymoon is over."

"Don't count on it."

"It's time to talk about a new assignment."

"Does it have to be today?"

"It does. Come to a shop in Burlington Arcade called Literary Antiquities, at eleven AM. Take the usual steps to avoid followers; it's critically important today."

"Got it," Roger said.

"Don't bring Jennifer, but you may employ her in your evasion tactics."

"All right." They both hung up.

"It was Alex, wasn't it?" she asked, still moving with him.

"Of course. And at the most inconvenient time."

"What time does he want you?"

"Eleven AM, in three hours."

She increased her pace and brought him off almost immediately. "There," she said. "Now I'll get us some breakfast. You stay where you are."

Roger followed her instructions and dozed off. He was awakened by the weight of a tray on his lap. She plumped the pillows for him, and he sat up. Eggs, back bacon, buttered toast, freshly squeezed orange juice, and a pot of strong coffee on the bedside table. He tucked into it.

"Is today likely to be another hit?"

"I expect so," Jennifer replied. "They know now how good you are at it."

"After the trial run," he said.

"How did you feel about that?" she asked. "You haven't said anything."

"I knew it would be Garr," he said. "They were smart to choose him."

"They are very smart," she said. "Not just Alex. Everyone you met at the party. They're the smartest people I've ever known."

"Smarter than those at Oxford?"

"Their intelligence is less fuzzy, more directed. There's nothing dreamy about them. Where is your meet? Do you need my help?"

"It's at a shop in the Burlington Arcade."

"Literary Antiquities?"

"That's the one."

"It's Alex's shop," she said. "Or rather, Wilfred's."

"Is that his real name?"

"Yes. Wilfred Thomas."

"Is he English?"

"Very much so—the third son of a duke."

"An aristocrat!"

"Quite so. He's also very likely to be my father. Did you notice a resemblance?"

"No, but now that you mention it . . ."

"He and the man who was supposed to be my father, Eli Sands, were at Oxford together, and they both married there."

"But Alex—excuse me—Wilfred and your mother were having it off?"

"It certainly seems so. He goes out of his way to take care of me in a paternal way. He refers to himself as 'Uncle Wilfred.'"

"Did he recruit you?"

"Yes, but he waited a long time."

"How long have you two been . . . associated?"

"Professionally, a little over four years, since his wife died. I always saw a lot of them, especially after my father died. Wilfred stepped into the breach."

"Did his wife know about you?"

"She'd have been a fool not to. I look a lot more like Wilfred than Eli."

"Is it odd for me to meet him at his shop?"

"It's unusual. I've only been there a few times in the past four years. I think he wants to make you more trusting of him by exposing himself a bit. We will need to be especially careful about being followed."

"That's what he said."

A little after ten they went down to the garage. "I'll drive today," she said, and he got into the passenger seat. "Now, put your head in my lap and keep it there, until I let you out. If we're under surveillance, we want them to think I'm alone and you're back at the flat."

He followed her instructions.

In a van a block from the Eaton Place flat, a voice came over the radio. "The Wren is out of the nest. She's alone. What news from the flat?"

"The TV is on, but I don't hear anyone moving about. Stay on her."

Jennifer drove the car twice around Hyde Park Corner, then turned into Piccadilly, then left into Mayfair. She stopped behind a construction dumpster. "Out, quick," she said.

Roger got out, keeping low, and ducked behind the dumpster. He waited five minutes before walking back to Piccadilly and hailing a taxi. "The Savoy Hotel," he said to the driver.

When the cab pulled into the tunnel that led to the hotel entrance, he got out of the cab and into another, headed in the opposite direction. "Savile Row," he said, "the middle." In Savile

Row he walked slowly up one side and down the other, peering into the tailors' windows, checking reflections, then he made his way slowly to the Burlington Arcade with ten minutes to spare.

He repeated his action of walking up one side and down the other, checking the shop windows. He lingered in front of Literary Antiquities, inspecting the titles in the window, then, after one last look around, went inside, as if he had decided to buy something.

Stone called Rose.

"Dr. McGill," she said into the phone.

"It's Stone."

"How nice to hear your voice."

"And yours, as well. I'd love to see you this coming weekend."

"What a good idea," she said. "I'll take the train down on Friday, if you will have me met."

"I certainly will."

"Will Felicity be there?" she asked.

"Would you like me to ask her?"

"I think I would."

Stone thought he detected a new level of interest in Felicity in Rose's voice.

"Then I will ask her, if you're comfortable with that." He waited to see if the hint had registered.

"I've been thinking about it, and I'm more comfortable with it than I had previously thought," Rose said.

"I'm quite sure Felicity will be comfortable with it, too."

"See you Friday, then," she said, then hung up.

Stone called Felicity's private cell.

"Hello, there," she said, with warmth. "How are you?"

"Very well, thank you. Are you contemplating another weekend at Beaulieu this coming week?"

"I am. I was going to call you."

"Then come to dinner on Friday."

"Shall I bring my toothbrush?"

"Just in case."

"In case?"

"Rose is coming down, too, and she requested your company at dinner."

"Did she really?"

"Really."

"I had thought her rather cool to the idea of . . . me."

"She's given it some thought and now seems more warmly inclined to the idea of . . . you."

"How interesting."

"I thought you would find it so."

"How sweet of you."

"I'll have you met at the dock."

"Oh, by the way," she said, "my houseman, in doing some work in the cellar, came across some very fine and very old clarets. Shall I bring a couple of bottles?"

"That would be wonderful. If you could send them over a day or two before, they can be set upright to allow the lees to settle before I decant them."

"I will do so," she said. "And please tell Rose I'm looking forward to seeing her."

"I will." They both hung up.

....

"May I help you, sir?" a man behind a counter asked.

"I think perhaps you may," Roger replied. "I'm looking for an *Oxford English Dictionary*, second edition, nicely bound in leather."

Alex went to the front door, locked it, and turned over the sign to read: CLOSED. "This way," he said, and started down a spiral staircase.

Roger followed.

55

lex put on a kettle, and it boiled almost immediately. "Tea?" he asked.

"Earl Grey, if you have it."

Alex spooned tea into the pot, poured in the water, and allowed it to steep while he got down cups and saucers from a shelf, and pastries, too.

This was very unlike Alex, Roger thought. Today he was more host than spy.

"Milk or lemon?" he asked.

"Lemon," Roger replied, and Alex supplied it.

"My real name is Wilfred Thomas," he said as he poured the tea. He set the cups on the table next to him, picked one up, and sipped.

"How do you do?"

Wilfred smiled. "Very well, thank you. And so do you."

"I do?"

"Roger, we did not recruit you merely as a matter of opportunism," Wilfred said. "We picked you because you do not fit the profile of the usual asset. That person is a minion—a clerk, a janitor, a secretary—someone unnoticeable. You, on the other hand, are a difficult man—one who is always noticed and often disliked. The main thing noticeable about you is that you bear a grudge against the person who sacked you, and we have kept you well away from her."

Roger nodded. "Your assessment seems correct."

"Your grudge is, as the Americans would say, 'gravy.' As it was with Simon Garr."

"You are correct."

"Our British counterparts at MI-6 would not consider you a threat, because you would be so obvious."

"That's good thinking."

"The other thing that makes you attractive to us is that you see things through. You are relentless, and not easily discouraged."

Roger nodded. "Correct."

"I share that trait," Wilfred said, "but perhaps less noticeably."

"Do you?"

"Yes, and I also have an unshakable faith in the decisions I make. You, for instance: I would not have told you my name if I believed you to be susceptible to betraying me to our fellow countrymen."

"Thank you, Wilfred," Roger replied.

"Nor would I have made you a Russian citizen, under the name in your new passport. That was a very strong signal to my superiors that I have absolute faith in you."

"Thank you again," Roger said.

"MI-5 or MI-6 will tumble to me in due course, because I am a scion of a famous British family name, Thomas. You would know my father as the Duke of Kensington."

"Ah, yes," Roger said, as if he hadn't known.

"I am also," Wilfred said, "your father-in-law."

Roger permitted his eyebrows to rise. "You're Jennifer's father?"

"I am. Her supposed father and I were lifelong friends, until his death four years ago."

"Did he know about Jennifer?"

"I expect so. The resemblance became stronger as she grew. Her mother, of course, knew. The two of us relished our secret."

"Did you tell Jennifer?"

"No, I waited for her to suss it out, and she did. She was very pleased."

"It must be unusual in the Russian service for a father to employ his child as an agent."

"Not at all," Wilfred said. "The bond of family is very strong. After all, who can you trust more?"

"I suppose you're right."

"Not your family, though," Wilfred said. "You disliked your father."

"I certainly did. Nothing I did was ever good enough for him. I was disappointed that he died before I achieved flag rank."

"Yes, it would have given you pleasure for him to know that, wouldn't it?"

"The greatest pleasure," Roger admitted. "I would have loved to see his face when I told him. I dream about that, sometimes."

"Your father knew Dame Felicity Devonshire's father, did he not?"

"Yes, they were at school together and maintained their friendship their whole lives."

"Your next target is Dame Felicity," Wilfred said, then gave that a moment to sink in. "Would you have gotten pleasure from him knowing that you had killed his friend's daughter?"

"I had never thought of that, but yes, very much so."

"Doing so would be a great blow to British intelligence," Wilfred said. "There's really no one to replace her. If she were gone, whoever sat at her desk would, by definition, be inferior, perhaps even inept. The Russians have always taken pleasure in the ineptness of their British opponents. That's why they were so fond of Kim Philby. The British knew for years that he was a mole, but they couldn't prove it. The Russians would shoot such a person and not bother with proof."

"Very efficient, the Russians."

"They, as a race, also enjoy vengeance," Wilfred said. "That is why the assassination of Dame Felicity would be what the Americans call a 'twofer.'"

"And who would be the other half of that?" Roger said.

"Someone else you dislike," Wilfred replied.

Roger smiled a little. "Barrington," he said. "But what is he to Russia?"

"First of all, he has had a number of encounters with their mafia, over the years, and their mafia is, of course, very close to the government at its top. But Barrington has another, perhaps more satisfying qualification."

"And what would that be?"

"He is quite close to Lance Cabot—a favorite, even. Cabot has recently brought him inside the CIA. Whereas before he was a consultant, he is now a personal adviser to Cabot, with the rank of deputy director."

"What qualifications has Barrington for that rank?"

"None, apart from intelligence and wit. The rank is a mark of Cabot's regard for him, to those both inside and outside the Agency. We have learned that this does not set well with others of that rank, and those who hope to achieve it."

"I should think not."

"Taking out Barrington would be a deeply painful blow to Cabot, one likely to affect his judgment. Taking out Dame Felicity would, as I have said, be a serious wound to British intelligence."

"I see," Roger said.

"And taking them out together, simultaneously, would be a more grievous wound than I can characterize," Wilfred said. "Suffice it to say, it would shake the Western services to their core."

56

Wilfred poured them another cup of tea. "This is a sufficiently important operation to employ more than one method," he said. "You should have a choice. At Station Two, we relied on only one method."

"What did you have in mind?"

"I think the most satisfying method would be an apparent murder-suicide. Either one could be made out to be the murderer."

"Felicity," Roger said. "It could be said that the pressures of her position brought this on."

"I agree. I think it would be a very good idea, too, for Felicity to have some competition with regard to Barrington."

"Is Felicity fucking Barrington?" Roger asked, surprised.

"For years," Wilfred replied. "In New York, London, and at his estate, Windward Hall, which you have visited in her company."

"Yes, I have, but I had not cottoned to their affair."

"Felicity is a subtle woman. Still, she has her weaknesses."

"Such as?"

"She likes both men and women in bed—preferably at the same time."

"The woman, Rose," Roger said, nodding. "I admire her taste in women."

"So do I, and Barrington's taste, as well."

"A double murder and a suicide?" Roger asked. "How would we manage that?"

"Careful planning," Wilfred replied. "And *stealth*."

"I can't disagree, but first we would have to get them into bed, all at the same time," Wilfred said. "I have had word from a wiretap that they will all be at Barrington's place next weekend."

"Wilfred," Roger said, "I am grateful for your confidence in me, but I cannot imagine how it would be possible to get three people in bed together and shoot them all."

"Suppose they were all unconscious?"

"Certainly that would make it easier, but how do we induce unconsciousness? If we drugged them, an autopsy with a tox screen would reveal it and point the police to an outside killer."

"Of course," Wilfred said, "but our Russian friends, who are artful in these things, have a substance said to be made from two common household ingredients, which, when mixed, make a poison that works in a few minutes and is chemically un-traceable."

"What are the ingredients?" Roger asked.

"I don't know—and I don't want to know," Wilfred replied. "If they became public knowledge there would be an immedi-ate rash of unexplained domestic deaths in this country and around the world."

"I suppose so," Roger said. "But the Russians have it?"

"They are geniuses at poisoning. Take, for example, the deaths of former GRU agents in Britain."

"Yes, but those don't meet the standard of being untraceable. They were analyzed quite quickly."

"That was the old days, so to speak. With this poison we have entered a new era. In fact, if we were able to introduce it into the food or drink of these three people, it would be the first professional use of the poison—that we know of."

"Ah, yes, 'that we know of.'"

"In order to accomplish our mission as planned," Wilfred said, "they would have to die at a meal or at tea, then be removed to a bedroom, undressed, and suitably posed and shot."

Roger shook his head. "I fail to see how such a mission could be accomplished with my skills alone."

"Perhaps we could have a complimentary dessert delivered to the house from someone they know and trust."

"For instance?"

"Perhaps from the Duke of Kensington."

"Your father?"

"My father once was an officer in MI-6, and his father served in Britain's Special Operations Executive during World War II. The current duke has had Felicity and Barrington to dinner in his London house."

"Rose, too?"

"No, but we have to convince only Felicity and Barrington of the genuineness of the gift."

"But why would the duke, out of the blue, send them pastries?"

"A good point," Wilfred said. "Let's set aside the poisoning for the moment and discuss other methods."

"Good," Roger replied, relieved.

"There are also your skills with the pistol and, particularly, the knife."

"A woman does not kill two lovers with a knife, then commit suicide by the same method."

"I was bypassing the suicide and going straight to murder."

"That would deprive us of besmirching the reputation of Dame Felicity," Roger pointed out.

"Let's call it a last resort," Wilfred said.

"Right. How about wine?"

"How do we induce them to drink it?" Wilfred asked.

"We'd need something really special, like a Château Lafite Rothschild 1929, or 1945."

"And how would we obtain that?"

"At auction," Roger said, "but it would cost many thousands of pounds."

Wilfred shook his head. "Our Russian friends, while generous, do not dispense hard currency with alacrity."

"If we could obtain a bottle, we could fill it with a lesser, more affordable wine, then reseal it."

"But where would one find an empty Lafite '29 bottle?" Wilfred asked.

They both thought about it for a while.

"I'm stumped," Roger said.

They thought some more.

"Let me present you with another alternative," Wilfred said, rising from his seat and going to a bookcase filled with bound volumes. He took down two and put them on his desk."

Roger opened one. The title page read: *The Short Oxford English Dictionary*.

"I bound these myself," Wilfred said. "The two volumes are more manageable than the entire twenty-volume set." He opened one nearer the center, to reveal its contents. "Plastique explosive, a detonator, and a cell phone," he said, pointing to each item. "In both volumes. Perhaps under the bed for setting off at the appropriate moment."

"How would you deliver the package?" Roger asked.

"Our Russian friends have a large variety of skills at their disposal," Wilfred said. "I will engage them and get back to you."

"Thank you," Roger said, relieved. "I'm perfectly willing to kill them all, but I don't want to get caught doing it."

"I understand," Wilfred replied. "Let's discuss time."

"When I had dinner there before, it was called for seven," Roger said. "Felicity and I arrived by boat, at Barrington's dock."

"Where did you dine, and how was the wine handled?"

"We dined in the library, and the wine was already on the table, ready for decanting. I suppose the butler had brought it from the cellar."

"You will have to find a way to have access to the wine for, perhaps, half a minute."

"If dinner is at seven, then at six, Barrington and Rose will be dressing for dinner."

"Then there's your opportunity," Wilfred said.

57

hursday morning, Felicity's boatman delivered two bottles of claret to the kitchen, and Stone inspected them: a Château Palmer 1961 and a Mouton Rothschild 1978. He set them upright in a corner of the kitchen. "I'll decant these at table tomorrow night," he said to the cook. "Please leave them as they are until then."

Lance got into his office on Friday morning at eight, as usual. He was surprised to find the deputy director for operations, his DDO, awaiting him in his reception room, sipping coffee.

"Good morning, Hugh," Lance said. He unlocked his office door with his code. "Come in, please. You're up early."

The two men took seats on the sofa in Lance's office, and he poured himself coffee from a thermos his secretary had left there. "More?"

"Thank you, yes," Hugh English said, pushing his mug over.

Lance poured the coffee. "What brings you to see me?"

Hugh handed him two sheets of paper. "This came in late

yesterday. I'm afraid the transmission was very broken, but what's there is of concern."

Lance read down the two sheets, trying to mentally fill in the gaps. He did not like what he saw. "Where was this recorded?"

"In the basement workshop at a book bindery and antique-book store in London."

"The one in the Burlington Arcade?"

"That's it. Owned and operated by Wilfred Thomas, the Earl of Chelsea."

"Ah, yes, the duke's third. What do you make of it?"

"It sounds very much, in the earlier part of the transcript, as if the earl has intentions where Felicity Devonshire and Stone Barrington are concerned."

Lance read the two pages more carefully. "I see what you mean, but I'm unable to discern when, where, or by what means—not from this."

"Yes, we did better with the early part of the meeting, though we could not identify the second party, and we have been unable to fully read or hear the latter part."

"Can the recording be enhanced?"

"That is the enhanced version," English replied.

"Well, there is nothing here that would allow us to mount a defensive operation."

"That is my opinion, as well."

"All I can do is warn Stone and Felicity to exercise care in their movements. I will make those calls."

"Lance, may I ask: Why is Barrington of interest to you?"

"He has been very useful in the past, and I expect him to be more so in the future."

"To the extent of giving him the deputy director rank?"

"In my judgment, yes. It gives him credibility."

"But you've not made an official announcement."

"Word will get around quickly," Lance said. "I've seen to that."

English slapped his knees and rose. "Well, then," he said, "I suppose I will just have to rely on your judgment."

"That is so," Lance said.

"Good morning, then."

Lance waited for the door to close behind him, then moved to his desk and called Stone on his Agency iPhone. The phone rang six times, then there was a beep.

"Call me," Lance said, then hung up. He could not leave a longer message because Stone was not at the other end to scramble.

Stone asked for the gelding and rode alone around the property and that of the adjoining country hotel, which he looked upon as an extension of his estate. The weather was glorious and promised to be until Saturday evening, when a front would move in. Finally, he turned back toward the house and rode slowly, to cool down the animal.

At noon, Lance, having not heard back from Stone, called him again and again got no answer. He waited for the beep, then said, "Urgent."

A van marked BRITISH GAS pulled up at the rear of the house, and a man in a work uniform got out carrying a canvas bag and went to the kitchen door, which stood open. He stepped inside and found the workspace deserted. He looked carefully around and his eye fell on two bottles of wine on a corner counter.

He slipped on a pair of latex gloves and walked over to the corner. Clearly, they were old and quite dusty. He picked up a bottle and wiped the label with his thumb; it was very old. He set the bottle down, reached into the canvas bag and withdrew a small, zippered leather case, then unzipped it. It held a syringe containing a colorless liquid and a capped needle. This particular needle would not be long enough to penetrate the corks of the bottles, so he replaced it with a longer, thinner needle.

He held the syringe perpendicular to the cork and slowly pushed it through the lead capsule and into the bottle. He pressed the plunger and squirted half the liquid into the bottle, then he began to slowly withdraw the needle. His fingers slipped momentarily, and the needle snapped off, leaving half of it in the cork, its end concealed by the capsule. "Shit!" he said.

He had only the short needle left, and that wouldn't do. He would need another, more accessible, container to use the other half of the liquid. He replaced the kit in the canvas bag and ventured into a long hallway from the kitchen toward the front of the house. He stopped every few feet and listened but heard no sound. He ran up the main staircase, keeping to the inside of the treads to avoid squeaking, and found what was clearly the master bedroom. He set the canvas bag on the bed and carefully removed two leather-bound volumes, then he knelt, placed the dictionary on the floor, and pushed it under the bed as far as he could reach. That done, he retraced his steps to the kitchen, and as he went down the back steps to the garden, a man on horseback came from behind the house, headed for the stables. The man gave him a little wave, and he waved back. Then he got into the van and drove away.

Stone greeted Rose at the front steps, as she was driven in from the station. They embraced, and her luggage was taken upstairs.

"I'd like a nap, if you can do without me for an hour or so," she said.

"Of course. Felicity won't arrive until around seven. I'll come up and change after you wake up."

She went upstairs, and he went back to his book.

Lance was about to call again, when he was interrupted by his secretary. "Senator Bond is here to see you," she said. "He's a little early."

Lance put away his phone. "Send him in."

58

Stone went upstairs to his master suite and, as he entered, caught a glimpse of a half-clothed Rose going into her bathroom. "I'll be another half hour," she said.

"That works for me," he called back. He went into his dressing room, put away his riding clothes and boots, and went into his bath. He shaved, showered, dried his hair, then returned to his dressing room and got into his dinner suit. He returned to the bedroom at the moment Rose emerged in a little black dress that sported deep cleavage, displaying much of her very fine frontage.

Stone kissed her on the cheek, and she felt for his crotch. "I just wanted to see if the dress was having its intended effect," she said. "And it is."

Stone took a couple of deep breaths to calm himself, then they went downstairs to the library, just as Dame Felicity was walking into the house. Geoffrey, the butler, took her overnight bag and coat, revealing a tight dress that was the same red as her lipstick, and there was yet more cleavage to be viewed.

The two women kissed, to Stone's surprise, on the lips, lightly enough not to require makeup repair.

"How gorgeous you look," Felicity said.

"And you," Rose replied. "I love the dress."

Stone interrupted. "May I offer anyone an alcoholic beverage?"

"Yes," they replied, simultaneously. Stone showed them into the library and poured them each an icy vodka gimlet, then one for himself, and served them on a silver cocktail tray. They toasted life, then he went to inspect their dining table. All was in order, and the two bottles of old claret rested on a side table, along with a candlestick, two crystal decanters, and two tasting glasses. All was well, so he returned to the two women, who were occupying the Chesterfield sofa, sitting slightly closer to each other than absolutely necessary, hands touching.

Stone had just sat down when the iPhone on the table next to him rang. He stood and picked it up. "Excuse me, please," he said to the two women, then he stepped out into the hall. "Yes?"

"Scramble."

"Scrambled."

"Why haven't you returned my calls?" Lance asked, irritably.

"I wasn't aware that you called," Stone said. "I was out riding."

"Stone, it's important that you keep that phone on your person at all times."

"I'll try and remember that," Stone said. "What's up?"

"You and Felicity," Lance replied.

Where does he get this stuff, Stone asked himself. "And exactly what does that mean?"

"It means that we recorded a conversation between two men in London who were apparently discussing the demise of at least one of you, perhaps both. The recording quality was very poor, and we only got part of it."

"The important part, I hope."

"I hope, too."

"What do you suggest?" Stone asked.

"It's too late to mount a defense at this point. All I can suggest is that you be bloody careful."

"All right, I'll do that."

"Where are you?"

"At Windward Hall. Felicity is here for dinner, along with another friend."

"Another woman friend?"

"Yes, as it happens."

"My goodness," Lance said.

Stone could hear him smiling. "Who were the two men you recorded?"

"One we couldn't identify, but he was British. The other was Wilfred Thomas, the bookbinder earl, whom we have previously discussed."

"Right. Is there anything else, Lance? I'd like to return to my guests."

"Oh, all right, but arm yourself," Lance said, then hung up.

Stone returned to the library and resumed his seat, but the two women were deep in conversation and ignored him. He hoped it wasn't going to be that kind of evening.

Geoffrey called them do dinner, and they took their seats. "Shall I decant the wines, sir?"

"Yes, please, but only one bottle. They're quite old, and I don't want them to get too much air for too long."

"Of course, sir. Which one shall I uncork first?"

"Oh, the older one, I guess. That's what, the Palmer?"

Geoffrey inspected the bottles. "Yes, sir." He cut away the

capsule and went to work with the corkscrew. He uncorked it very carefully, then lit the candle and decanted it slowly. He poured a little into a tasting glass, sniffed it, then placed it before Stone, along with the cork. "I'm afraid the cork isn't very good, sir."

Stone picked up the cork, squeezed it, then sniffed. "I'm afraid it's corked," he said, squeezing it again. The cork broke in half, but did not separate.

"I thought so, too, sir," Geoffrey said.

Stone looked at the cork, then pulled on it from each end. The two pieces separated, and he found himself staring at what appeared to be a needle, embedded in the bottom half. He beckoned to Geoffrey and handed him the cork. "Preserve this. Take the wine to the kitchen and recork it. Do not taste it, and do not allow anyone else to."

"Yes, sir," Geoffrey said.

"But first, please hand me the Mouton."

Geoffrey did so; Stone inspected the capsule and found it apparently unbreached. "May I see the Palmer capsule? The top only."

Geoffrey handed it to him. There was a pinhole in the top.

"Decant the Mouton," Stone said.

Geoffrey did so, then handed Stone the tasting glass and the cork. Stone inspected the cork and bent it a little, but it did not break.

"Good cork this time," Geoffrey said. "Excellent nose, too."

Stone sniffed the glass several times. "I agree." He tasted the wine and found it full-bodied, complex, and untainted. "Pour this one," he said, "then deal with the other bottle."

The women were talking animatedly and seemed unconcerned with the wines.

....

They finished their dinner and made to take their brandy up-stairs. Stone allowed them to precede him. "I'll be right along," he said. He went to the gun case, removed one of the brace of Purdey shotguns, and picked up a box of double-aught shells, then followed the women. At the last moment, he remembered Lance's caution to keep the Agency iPhone with him at all times, and he slipped it into his jacket pocket.

The women were both in Rose's dressing room, still talking. Stone started to lay the shotgun alongside the bed, and then pushed the gun, barrel first, under the bed. It connected with something and stopped, with the stock still showing. Stone looked underneath, but it was too dark to see anything except what looked like a box. He took a small SureFire flashlight from a bedside drawer and shone it under the bed.

There were two large, leather-bound books stacked there. He read the title, *The Short Oxford English Dictionary*. Then he saw something else at the bottom of the spines: W. THOMAS.

59

As Stone got to his feet, the women were coming out of Rose's dressing room, both naked and holding hands.

"Ladies," Stone said. "Please do as I ask *right now*. Gather your clothes and walk down the hall to the last guest room and get dressed, then stay there until I come for you."

"What on earth . . ." Rose said.

"Do it *now*, please."

Felicity got it. "Rose, let's go." She led Rose back into the dressing room, and they emerged, each carrying her clothes, and left the room.

Stone got out his iPhone and called the local police. "Chief Inspector Holmes," he said.

"I'm sorry, sir," a woman replied, "but the chief inspector has gone for the day."

"This is an extreme emergency," Stone said. "Connect me to him immediately."

"Your name, sir?"

"Barrington."

"One moment."

....

Roger Fife-Simpson stood in a patch of woods a quarter mile from Windward Hall. He stripped the last of the British Gas logo from the van, wadded it up, and struck a match to it. Then he dropped it where the flames wouldn't spread. He took off his cap and uniform, revealing a black sweater and trousers underneath, and added the work clothes to the flames, poking at them with a stick until they were burning readily. He checked the contents of his canvas bag and came up with a silenced pistol given to him by Wilfred, identical to the firearm he had been issued at MI-6, and tucked it into his belt. Then he dug out the throwaway cell phone. He started to dial a number, but decided he wanted to see the effect of his work, so he left the van, crossed the road, and climbed over a stone wall. From where he landed, he had a fine view of the front of the house. He redialed the number.

Stone was waiting impatiently, then finally: "This is Chief Inspector Holmes."

"Chief Inspector, this is Stone Barrington. I've found what appears to be a bomb under my bed, and I need your bomb squad at once."

"Certainly," Holmes replied. "I'll see to it."

"Oh, and please send someone who knows about poisons."

"You're having quite an evening, aren't you?" Holmes asked, then hung up.

Stone suddenly asked himself a question. Why was he standing in his bedroom, four feet from a probable bomb? He grabbed the shotgun and left, closing the door behind him. Then he remembered something someone, perhaps Holly, had told him about the Agency iPhone. He went to the home page and looked at the icons, and then he saw it. *Utilities*, it was called. He touched it and found himself looking at a list. One item read: Create a Dead Zone.

He selected that item and watched as the list disappeared, and the very annoying little circle appeared, spinning. While it spun he reasoned that the bomb would likely not be on a timer, since no one knew what time he would go to bed; more likely, it would be detonated by a cell phone carried by the man who had planted it there.

The circle stopped spinning, and a message appeared:

A dead zone for cellular devices has been created. It will render useless devices within approximately a fifty-foot, obstacle-free radius. Press the Resume button to discontinue and restore cellular service.

Stone looked down the hall at his bedroom door; that was an obstacle. He ran for it.

Roger pressed the Send button and waited, watching the house.

Stone flung open the door and stopped. Nothing was happening. He went to his dressing room and came back with a large furled umbrella, then lay down next to the bed, turned on his flashlight, and reached out with the handle of the umbrella.

After a few attempts, he had pulled the two volumes close enough to reach, and he dragged them from under the bed.

Roger was wondering why nothing had happened, when he heard the sounds of a police car approaching. He vaulted over the wall, dropping the cell phone but continuing to run toward the van. He was in the front seat when a police car and a large van turned into the driveway of Windward Hall. When they had passed, he started his van, turned onto the road, and drove back toward Beaulieu. Then he stopped. Why had the bomb not detonated? He made a U-turn, drove back into his sheltered parking spot, and got out. He would have to find the cell phone he had dropped.

Stone knelt beside the two beautifully bound volumes, then looked hard for any protrusion, even a thread, showing. Nothing there. He lifted the cover of the top volume and found only handsome end papers; then he began, a few pages at a time, looking through the book. A third of the way through, he found himself looking at an inch-deep compartment that had been cut through the pages. Inside it were a block of something that looked like modeling clay and a flip-phone, the display of which was lighted.

Why, he asked himself, had the phone not rung? His dead zone must be effective, but apparently, if he had taken a second or two longer to activate it, the worst might have happened.

There was a detonator plugged into the explosive matter, and he removed that; then he unplugged the cell phone from its connection to the detonator. Stone was no expert on bombs, but he reckoned he had rendered this one harmless. Then he remembered the second volume.

Outside, Roger had found the cell phone. He had a second, backup number to call, and he punched in the number, which he had memorized.

As Stone reached for the second volume, an incredibly bright light blinded him.

"Get out of the way!" a man's voice shouted, and Stone was pushed roughly aside.

"I disconnected volume one," Stone said, blinking rapidly, trying to see something, anything. "I didn't have time to get to volume two." He sat up and he could make out, blurrily, the shape of a uniformed policeman bending over the book.

"Got it," the man said, setting down his large flashlight, then half a second later the display in his hand lighted up. "Jesus God," he muttered to himself. "Why didn't it ring?"

"Because," Stone said, "we're in a dead zone, courtesy of the Central Intelligence Agency." He got out his cell phone, tapped it, and showed it to the policeman.

"I want one of those," the man said.

60

---

hief Inspector Holmes stepped into the room behind Stone and the policemen. "Good evening," he said.

"It is now," Stone replied. "Thank you for coming."

The policeman next to him was inspecting the two bombs. "I reckon," he said, almost to himself, "that if one of these had gone off it would have blown out the windows and destroyed everything in the room, including the paneling."

"And what," Holmes asked, "would the effect have been if they had both gone off?"

"Then, I believe, the resulting blast would have removed this corner of the house, upstairs and down, from the main building and distributed it around the lawns."

"Any idea who might have wished you distributed around the lawns, Stone?" Holmes asked.

Stone picked up one of the volumes and showed him the binder's name on the spine. "This gentleman, I believe. He has a shop in the Burlington Arcade in London called Literary Antiquities, with a bindery in the basement. Beautiful work, isn't it?"

"The binding or the bomb?" Holmes queried.

"Take your pick."

"Odd that he would stamp his name on an instrument of murder," Holmes observed.

"I think he probably bound the books first, then decided to use them to house the bomb. In any case, his name on the spine would not have survived a detonation."

"Was he working alone, do you think?"

"The man is a spy for the Russians, and he's working with half their London embassy," Stone replied.

"And how did you come to know this?" Holmes asked.

Stone reached into a bedside drawer and found one of his new business cards.

Holmes digested the information thereon. "I see," he said, though he clearly didn't.

"I've been a consultant for them for a number of years," Stone said, "but recently I've been sort of promoted."

"And the Russians knew about this?"

"It's public knowledge," Stone said, "though it hasn't been formally announced. I think the Agency thought that those who needed to know would find out in the normal course of events."

Felicity and Rose appeared in the doorway, back in their dinner dresses.

"Also, I think they may have been trying for both of us," Stone said. "Dame Felicity, Chief Inspector Holmes of the Hampshire police. And this is Dr. Rose McGill, of St. George's Hospital, London."

Holmes shook their hands, but said little. It was obvious that the policeman was putting together one plus two and forming an opinion about why the bombs were under the bed.

"Ah, yes," he said. "Stone, I believe you said there was a poisoning afoot. The officer standing behind Dame Felicity is

Sergeant Pepper, no relation, and he is our resident expert on lethal substances."

"Come with me," Stone replied. He led the officers downstairs to the kitchen and found the Château Palmer '61 on a corner counter, beside it a folded towel. He shook the towel, and the cork containing the needle and the top of the capsule fell out.

Sergeant Pepper pulled on latex gloves, picked up the suspect cork, and sniffed it, then he removed the new cork from the bottle, swirled the wine in it, and sniffed again. "As far as I can tell without an actual chemical analysis, the only thing wrong with this wine, apart from being corky, is that someone has injected a substance into it and, in the bargain, broken off his hypodermic needle. I observe that, perhaps, half a glass of wine is missing from the bottle. I sincerely hope that no one drank it."

"It was decanted and the lees thrown away," Stone said.

"It's troubling that I cannot smell any foreign substance in the wine," he said.

"Sergeant Pepper," Holmes said, "is famous for his nose, which can identify hundreds of aromas."

"I've been offered a job in a distillery, blending whiskys," Pepper said with a touch of pride. "As I'm sure you know, blenders do not taste their product, but smell it. Tasting would render the palate incapable of discerning differences in whiskys."

"Ah," Stone said, as if he knew what the man was talking about.

"I will take charge of this bottle and its contents and the damaged cork and needle," Pepper said, "and I will order a proper analysis done."

"How long will that take?" Holmes asked.

"If it's an easy poison to identify, we'll know in a day or two.

Something more exotic could take a week or, perhaps, weeks. That will probably be the case, given that the Russians are involved."

"Well," Holmes said, "I believe we have some arrests to make, so we'd better get started."

"Chief Inspector," Stone said, "you might consult Dame Felicity before you start collaring people. Most, if not all, of the suspects will have diplomatic immunity. Perhaps Mr. Thomas may not, and I should think he would be quite a catch. May I suggest that you have the appropriate officers in London pick him up as soon as possible? His bomber may not have told him yet of his failure here."

"Good suggestion," Holmes said. "I'd better go and find the good lady." He left the kitchen.

Roger Fife-Simpson watched from the woods across the road as other vehicles arrived at the house. He was trapped where he was until all this quieted down and he could escape in the van.

Stone found Chief Inspector Holmes in the library, chatting with Dame Felicity. "May I join you?" he asked, pulling up a chair.

"Of course," Holmes replied. "Do you have any other suggestions for our investigation? You're doing very nicely so far."

"I think it might be a good idea to search the woods on both sides of the road from Beaulieu. The culprit may have hidden there and been trapped by the arriving police."

"Stone," Holmes said, "may I offer you an inspector's commission with the Hampshire police? We could use you."

"Thank you, Chief Inspector," Stone said, "but I am otherwise engaged."

"Of course. Tell me, have you seen any strangers about the house today?"

Stone thought about it. "Yes," he replied. "A man from British Gas was here—to read the meter, I suppose."

Holmes frowned. "I don't think gas has reached this far south, yet."

Stone's face fell. "Oh, God, I forgot. We have two large propane tanks out back that are periodically filled by a local supplier. You're right, we don't have a gas meter."

"I think my people should have a look around the neighborhood then," the chief inspector said. He excused himself and left the room.

Gradually, the police drifted from the house, and Stone was once again alone with Felicity and Rose.

He gave them each a kiss. "Where were we?" he asked.

61

oger Fife-Simpson could hear people on foot nearby now. He abandoned the van and melted into the woods. Then it occurred to him that the safest place for him might be near the house, since the police had, apparently, completed their search there.

Stone had reached the second floor, right behind Felicity and Rose, who had begun to unzip things, when his phone rang. "Yes?"

"Stone, it's Holmes."

"Yes, Chief Inspector?"

"My people have found a van in the woods across the road from your house, which shows signs of having had something stuck to it. There's also been a small fire, where something cotton was burned. It occurs to me that our man may still be around and that you should be on your guard."

"Thank you, I'll have a look around," Stone said. He fetched his shotgun. "If you'll excuse me," he said to Felicity and Rose. "I have to take a walk around the house."

"It's all right, darling," Felicity said, "we'll still be here when you get back. May we start without you?"

"Of course," Stone said with a sigh. He got out of his dinner jacket and black tie and into a barn coat. Then he dropped a flashlight into a pocket and held the shotgun crooked in his arm as he trotted down the stairs and down the hall to the kitchen—the door of which was still open—then out into the garden. Some fruit trees stood in rows on one side of the vegetable garden, providing cover for an intruder. He checked the shotgun, found it still loaded, and began walking toward the little orchard. He could hear the voices of policemen and the barks of dogs from across the road.

He walked to the end of each row of trees and looked down the furrows, finding nothing, then he turned back to check the other side of the garden. Someone could hide by lying on the ground between rows of plants. Nothing.

He walked over to the stables; the grooms were long in their beds, but the horses snuffled as they became aware of his arrival. There was a loud noise from down the row of stalls, as if someone had knocked something over. He checked each stall carefully, playing his flashlight around the corners, as he moved down the row.

He checked the tack room and found everything neat and undisturbed, then he started back toward the main stable door, moving past some stacked bales of hay and straw. He heard something like a foot scraping the concrete floor and turned to look behind him. As he did, a pitchfork flew past him and impaled itself in a bale of hay. Before he could move, the shotgun was knocked from his hands.

"Now," a voice to one side of him said. He turned again to

find a man dressed in black and wearing a black mask, standing in something like a combat position. Why hasn't he shot me? Stone asked himself. Then he saw that the man had other plans: he was holding something in his hand. Then Stone heard the release and snap of a switchblade opening.

There was something familiar about the figure. "Hello, Roger," he said.

"Good evening," Roger replied, ripping off his mask and casting it aside. "I've longed for this moment." He lunged at Stone's ribs.

Stone sidestepped, took hold of the pitchfork handle, and wrenched it from the bale of hay. He liked his chances better now, but as he turned, something sharp raked across his back, bringing a short cry of pain.

"First blood," Roger said. "More to come."

Stone stabbed at him with the pitchfork but came up short. Roger grabbed a tine and yanked the tool from his hand.

Stone backed away, looking for another weapon or a place to hide, and the blade swished past his head, the tip slicing his cheek. Now he was bleeding on both sides of his body. He tried to remember what he had been told about defense from a knife at the police academy all those years ago. Step into the swing of the blade, not away from it. He tried that, holding up his left arm in defense, and felt a hot cut as the blade went through his canvas jacket and caught his forearm. He was losing this fight.

He remembered something else from some forgotten weapons instruction. He snatched the SureFire flashlight from his pocket, held it in his fist, and pointed it at Fife-Simpson, pressing the On switch with his thumb.

Roger's eyes were open when the incredibly bright beam hit him, and he staggered backward, momentarily blinded.

Stone went for the pitchfork on the floor between them and got a grip on it with his weakened left hand. He wasn't giving up the flashlight, though; he slipped it back into his jacket pocket and got both hands on the pitchfork's handle. He thrust at the man's chest, but the tines didn't have the desired effect. Roger was wearing some sort of ballistic garment, Stone decided. Stone's thrust had knocked him to one knee, though, and the next thrust was at his face.

Roger jerked his head aside in time, but a tine caught his ear, causing him to scream and back away. He came to a stop against a bale of hay, blood streaming down his neck.

Stone thought he had one more good thrust left in him before he bled out, and he drew back with his right, prepared to throw the thing at the man's head.

"No!" Roger shouted, then threw away the knife.

Stone heard it clatter across the concrete floor.

"No more!"

Stone's foot kicked something, and he knew what it was. Keeping the pitchfork aimed at its target, he bent down and scooped up his shotgun. He dropped the pitchfork, pointed the shotgun upward, and pulled the trigger. The blast nearly deafened him, and Roger slipped down the side of a bale of hay onto the floor.

"One more round left," Stone said, pointing it at him.

"You can't," Roger said. "That would be murder."

"I suppose it would be," Stone said, aiming at his head.

Then a light hit him, and a voice yelled, "Drop the shotgun! Hands up!"

Stone froze, then slowly bent and laid the fine weapon on the floor. "I'm Barrington!" he yelled. "And I'm fucking bleeding to death!" He sank onto the floor and leaned against a hay bale.

"It's Barrington!" someone shouted. "Don't fire! Medic, medic!"

Then Stone passed out.

He woke on a stretcher in an ambulance van, half naked, held in position on his side by a policeman, while an EMT attended to his back.

"He's conscious," someone said.

"I'm a surgeon," a female voice said. "I'll deal with this."

Then Stone passed out again.

62

Stone slowly came awake in a sun-filled room. A beeping noise from his left side told him he was in a hospital room and that he was hooked up to machinery. He moved his arm and found that he had an IV running, too. The room was devoid of other people.

Then, as if on cue, Rose entered the room, wearing surgical scrubs, followed by Felicity, similarly clad. Apparently, dinner dresses were not de rigueur on this ward, and they had changed into whatever was available. "You're alive!" Rose said, kissing him on the forehead.

"Have I had a close call?" Stone asked, and found his mouth dry.

"Not for a minute," she replied. "You were lucky enough to encounter a qualified surgeon in the ambulance that brought you here—that was me—and both Felicity and I have the same blood type as you, so we insisted on contributing. We thought blood with a little fine wine and brandy in it would be best."

Felicity came over, too. She kissed him on the ear and let her tongue flick inside for a moment. "Don't worry, my dear," she said, "no injury below the navel."

Rose gave him a cup of water with a glass straw, and he sucked some of the water down.

"Where are we?" Stone asked.

"Salisbury, the nearest hospital to your house with a trauma center," Rose replied.

"And it is, by your reckoning," Felicity said, "the day after tomorrow, or rather, the day after yesterday."

"I've been out for that long?"

"Yes," Rose replied. "We thought it best that you became accustomed to having blood in your veins again while resting."

"When do I get out?"

"Oh, come on, you don't *feel* like getting out, do you?"

"No, I guess I don't," he replied.

"Perhaps tomorrow, if you're more confident."

"What was the result of the events last night? I mean, the other night."

"There are those here who can better explain that than we can," she said. "We'll leave you to their company." She and Felicity left the room and were immediately replaced by Chief Inspector Holmes.

"How are you feeling, old boy?" the policeman asked.

"Drained," Stone replied. "Is Fife-Simpson in custody?"

"All in good time," Holmes said. "I wanted to tell you about the results of the testing of your very fine Château Palmer '61."

"It was poisoned, wasn't it?"

"No . . . well, yes. That is to say that the initial testing revealed nothing but wine in the bottle."

"But the broken needle in the cork?"

"I said they detected nothing in the initial test, but then, just when someone at the morgue had produced glasses, for drinking it, someone else had the idea of giving a drop or two to a lab rat."

"And?"

"He pronounced it a fine, full-bodied claret with an excellent nose and a clean finish. Then he rolled over and died."

"Of what?"

"Of poisoning, but we still have no idea what poison. The Soviets—pardon, the Russians—have skills in that department that, momentarily anyway, exceed our ability to detect them."

"You didn't answer my question about Fife-Simpson; is he in custody?"

Holmes frowned. "Not exactly. He was taken to our local shop and when his pockets were emptied, one of them produced a Russian diplomatic passport with his photograph affixed, and the name Sergei Ivanovich Ostrovsky on it. After consultation with Foreign Office officials, two Russian gentlemen appeared and walked him out of the building, not to be seen again, so far. We believe him to be at the Russian embassy, up to his arse in Beluga and Stoli."

"That's very disappointing."

"Oh, I expect that MI-5 will be watching the place like hawks. If he leaves they will scoop him up."

"What about Wilfred Thomas?"

"You have another visitor who can tell you more about that. I'll see you when I have other news." He patted Stone on the knee and left the room.

Lance Cabot quickly replaced Holmes. He dragged a chair up to Stone's bed and sat down. "Congratulations on still being alive," he said, "though not for want of the Russians trying to kill you."

"I hear Roger skated because of the diplomatic passport we saw on your video of the party at the Russian embassy."

"Not just Roger, but also his wife, Jennifer Sands, but I think you may regard their escape as temporary."

"What about Wilfred Thomas, whose dictionaries are so nicely bound?"

"Vanished," Lance replied. "Minutes, perhaps seconds, before our people reached his shop. They did find a treasure trove of bomb-making equipment, along with a fountain pen and an umbrella that shoot poison, and an unlabeled bottle of clear liquid that we suspect might be what was in the wine. It's being tested as we speak, and the search is on for the earl. His diplomatic passport might work with the police, but not with MI-5."

"Isn't he at the embassy with his colleagues?"

"Oddly, no. At least, we haven't detected his image or voice at the embassy with our equipment, which is still operating. Apparently, from what we've gleaned from their conversations, they are waiting for the earl, known in spy circles as Alex, to accomplish some deed or other, then shelter with them until transport out of the country has been arranged."

"What sort of deed?"

"I'm afraid we have no clue, though we're not ruling out another go at your person. Not to worry, measures have been taken."

"When did you arrive in England?"

"Yesterday. They told me you were still alive, but I wanted to see for myself."

"I promise not to die without telling you first," Stone said.

"You're still looking a bit peaked," Lance said, "so I'll leave you to a nap or two. As soon as you're out we'll have a good lunch somewhere and chat about some things."

"Thanks, Lance, I'll see you then." Stone closed his eyes and let sleep take him.

63

Stone awoke the following day feeling much more himself, which condition, he felt, was mostly due to the ministrations of Rose and Felicity late in the previous evening.

A nurse came in with a breakfast tray of scrambled eggs, toast, and sage sausages, which he wolfed down. She came back for the tray.

"Looks like you're getting the boot this morning," she said. "One of the ladies brought you some clothes, and I've hung them in your closet. The doctor will be in shortly to approve your discharge, and someone from administration will have your release documents to sign, then you're out of here."

"I'll miss you," Stone said.

"I doubt that," she said, "given the attentions you got from others overnight."

"You're a Peeping Tom," he said.

"No, there just happens to be a camera over there," she said, pointing to a high corner of the room. "Dame Felicity had someone in this morning to erase the tape."

"Oh, I would have liked to see it," Stone said sadly.

"Why? You weren't doing anything but lying there." She left the room.

There was a knock on the door, and a man carrying a clipboard entered and closed the door behind him. He was dressed in a necktie and shirtsleeves and wore a pocket protector that sported an array of writing instruments. "Good morning," he said. "I'm Assistant Administrator Willis. I have some forms for you to sign, so that we can discharge you." He had an owlish look because of his heavy black spectacles, and he also sported a Vandyke—mustache and goatee—as if to make up for his receding hairline. "I hope you're feeling up to it."

"I'm feeling very well, thank you," Stone said. "Where do I sign?"

Willis walked over and set his clipboard on Stone's rolling hospital tray. "There are four," he said, extracting a fat Mont Blanc fountain pen from his shirt pocket and handing it to Stone.

"This is the first actual fountain pen I've seen for years," Stone said. "Very handsome."

"I'm a bit old-fashioned," Willis said. "I like the old ways."

Stone unscrewed the cap and pushed it onto the other end of the pen. Then he thought of something Lance had said. They had found a fountain pen in Wilfred Thomas's workshop, one that administered a poison, much like one the CIA has developed. It also occurred to him that there was something, he wasn't sure what, familiar about Mr. Willis. "Oops!" he said, allowing the pen to slip from his fingers and bounce off his tray table to the floor. "I'm sorry, that was clumsy of me."

"Not to worry," Willis said, taking some tissues from Stone's bedside and walking around to the other side of the bed to retrieve the pen.

Then Stone remembered something he had forgotten: he had seen Wilfred Thomas in the video that Lance's people had made of the party at the Russian embassy, and without the glasses and the Vandyke, Willis could be Thomas. It was the hairline that pegged it for him. Stone slipped out of bed and stood facing the man. "Your mustache is slipping," he lied.

The man reflexively raised a hand to stick it back on.

"Only joking, Mr. Thomas," Stone said, looking about him for a weapon. "By the way, my compliments on the handsome bindings on *The Short OED.*" The only weapons Stone could use were the rolling tray table and a visitor's chair, and he wasn't sure he could lift the table, since one arm was out of action. "I'm glad your bomb-making talent doesn't match your binding skills."

Thomas picked up the pen, holding it between two fingers with tissues.

Was he going to shoot poison at him? Bullets? Would it explode? Stone looked for the button to call the nurse, but it was on Thomas's side of the bed.

"I don't know what you mean," Thomas said, seemingly uncertain of his next move.

Stone got hold of his visitor's chair at the end of the bed and was pleased that it weighed much less than the table. He placed it on the bed, between him and Thomas, and held it, lion-tamer style. "I think your best bet is to make a run for it," Stone said, hoping the man would take his advice.

Instead, Thomas got a grip on the end of the pen and held it before him, as if it were a knife.

There was a knock on the door. "Come in!" Stone yelled.

The door opened, and Felicity stood there, wearing a business suit with her handbag over her left arm.

"How good to see you, Felicity," Stone said. "May I introduce

you to the Earl of Chelsea, aka Wilfred Thomas? I believe you
are armed. Would you shoot him, please?"

Felicity began digging into her handbag, and Stone picked up
the chair and threw it at Thomas's head, which connected,
knocking him to the floor, sending his glasses flying, and putting his mustache genuinely askew.

"What's taking you so long?" Stone asked Felicity. "The man
has a poisoned pen!"

Felicity finally came up with a small, semiautomatic pistol
and pointed it at Thomas. "Kindly stay where you are and do
not move, Mr. Thomas," she said. "And let go of the pen, or I'll
kill you where you stand. Or sit, as it were."

Thomas looked carefully at her, then tossed the pen on the
floor between them. It rolled a couple of times, leaving behind a
thin trail of clear liquid.

Felicity reached into her bag again with the other hand and
did something, Stone couldn't see what. There were running
footsteps from the hallway, and she stepped aside to let two large
young men into the room. "Mind the pen," she said, "it's danger-
ous. But please take charge of the gentleman on the floor. Hand-
cuff him and search him for other weapons, including pens."

The two young men went to work and got Thomas out of the
room, denuded of pens.

Felicity walked over to the Mont Blanc pen on the floor and
looked down at it. "My word," she said.

Stone and Lance sat in the Rose & Crown, near the gates of Windward Hall, consuming a lunch of sausages and Cornish pasties.

Lance washed down his food with a draught from his pint of

Guinness. "Well, Stone," he said, "I'm sorry you have had to go through two attempts on your life—no, three, isn't it?"

"I've lost count," Stone replied, sipping his pint of bitter.

"How are your wounds?" Lance asked.

"I can't see my back, but it hurts. My arm, too. But Rose has found me a physiotherapist, who is moving into the house this afternoon, so I won't have to go to the hospital for rehab."

"Excellent," Lance said. "By the way, this episode has had the salutary effect of silencing comment at the Agency on your appointment."

"I'm not surprised there was comment," Stone said. "Frankly, I thought it might blow up in your face."

"Stone," Lance replied reprovingly, "I'm too careful for that to happen."

"I suppose you are."

"Oh, I almost forgot." He reached down, took a gift-wrapped package from a shopping bag and set it on the table. "This is for you, by way of my thanks."

Stone regarded the package with suspicion. "Will *this* blow up in my face?"

"Not this time," Lance said. "The earl is safely housed in one of MI-5's secret places, where he is being interrogated. His diplomatic passport seems to have been misplaced."

"I'm glad to hear it." Stone pulled the bow on the ribbon and tore open the package, revealing volumes one and two of *The Short Oxford English Dictionary*, beautifully bound by Wilfred Thomas. "I trust the bombs have been removed?"

"They have, but the spaces where they once lived remain. Who knows, you might one day wish to hide something in plain sight."

"All the time," Stone said.

AUTHOR'S NOTE

I am happy to hear from readers, but you should know that if you write to me in care of my publisher, three to six months will pass before I receive your letter, and when it finally arrives it will be one among many, and I will not be able to reply.

However, if you have access to the Internet, you may visit my website at www.stuartwoods.com, where there is a button for sending me an e-mail. So far, I have been able to reply to all of my e-mail, and I will continue to try to do so.

If you send me an e-mail and do not receive a reply, it is probably because you are among an alarming number of people who have entered their e-mail address incorrectly in their mail software. I have many of my replies returned as undeliverable.

Remember: e-mail, reply; snail mail, no reply.

When you e-mail, please do not send attachments, as I never open these. They can take twenty minutes to download, and they often contain viruses.

Please do not place me on your mailing lists for funny stories, prayers, political causes, charitable fund-raising, petitions, or sentimental claptrap. I get enough of that from people I already know. Generally speaking, when I get e-mail addressed to a large number of people, I immediately delete it without reading it.

Please do not send me your ideas for a book, as I have a policy of writing only what I myself invent. If you send me story ideas, I will immediately delete them without reading them. If you have a good idea for a book, write it yourself, but I will not be able to advise you on how to get it published. Buy a copy of *Writer's Market* at any bookstore; that will tell you how.

Anyone with a request concerning events or appearances may e-mail it to me or send it to: Publicity Department, Penguin Random House LLC, 1745 Broadway, New York, NY 10019.

Those ambitious folk who wish to buy film, dramatic, or television rights to my books should contact Matthew Snyder, Creative Artists Agency, 2000 Avenue of the Stars, Los Angeles, CA 90067.

Those who wish to make offers for rights of a literary nature should contact Anne Sibbald, Janklow & Nesbit, 285 Madison Avenue, New York, NY 10017. (Note: This is not an invitation for you to send her your manuscript or to solicit her to be your agent.)

If you want to know if I will be signing books in your city, please visit my website, www.stuartwoods.com, where the tour schedule will be published a month or so in advance. If you wish me to do a book signing in your locality, ask your favorite bookseller to contact his Penguin representative or the Penguin publicity department with the request.

If you find typographical or editorial errors in my book and feel an irresistible urge to tell someone, please write to Sara Minnich at Penguin's address above. Do not e-mail your discoveries to me, as I will already have learned about them from others.

A list of my published works appears in the front of this book and on my website. All the novels are still in print in paperback and can be found at or ordered from any bookstore. If you wish to obtain hardcover copies of earlier novels or of the two nonfiction books, a good used-book store or one of the online bookstores can help you find them. Otherwise, you will have to go to a great many garage sales.